Layers of Life

By Spilt Ink Writers

ISBN 9798541733365
Binding type : Paperback
1st Edition: Feb 2021
2nd Edition: Aug 2021
Book cover designed by Betibup

Contents

Religion and Spirits

Jennifer's Prayers	Marion McNally	11
Losing the Plot	Stephanie Thornton	23
The Light in the World	C.I. Ripples	29
The Last Pomegranate Seed	Stephanie Thornton	37
Foresight	Sacha Quinn	43

Work and Retirement

Summer Job	Renata Kelly	53
The Bobbin Doffer	Stephanie Thornton	66
First Day	Sacha Quinn	75
Thorny Package?	Marion McNally	81
When Work Becomes Leisure	C.I. Ripples	88
Getting on	Stephanie Thornton	96
Play On!	Sacha Quinn	102
Retiring Down the Track	C.I. Ripples	107
The Wasp	Stephanie Thornton	120

Travel

The Journey for New Life	C.I. Ripples	131
Sekhmet's Nose	Renata Kelly	145
Shoestring Luxury	Sacha Quinn	153
The Sun Shines Brightest on Shallow Ripples	C.I. Ripples	161
The Traveler	Stephanie Thornton	166

Children and Learning

A Curious Encounter   Stephanie Thornton   175
Finding the Light   Marion McNally   183
Finding Henry Moore   Stephanie Thornton   196
Rockets on
    the Playground   C.I. Ripples   201
Kieran's Colours   Sacha Quinn   206
Georgiana Does Paint   Stephanie Thornton   215

Relationships

Odd Folk   Stephanie Thornton   225
Agent Nineteen   C.I. Ripples   232
One Summer's Day   Stephanie Thornton   240
Toxic Relationships   Sacha Quinn   246
The Nosy Parker   Stephanie Thornton   250

Political Correctness

A Matter of Minds   Stephanie Thornton   261
PC on the Beach   C.I. Ripples   270
Double Standards   Stephanie Thornton   280

Money

Money, Cats
    and Charlie   Stephanie Thornton   293
Beyond Price   Sacha Quinn   300
True Value Lies
  Only in Survival   C.I. Ripples   308
Uncle Willy   Stephanie Thornton   319

Author Biographies

327

Foreword

Global Writers group 'Spilt Ink' present an anthology of stories reflecting on the Layers of Life. The authors have written tales which inspired them from a list of seven categories, spanning religion and relationships, to children and learning as well as a mostly humorous take on Political Correctness in all its absurdity, not forgetting some of the funnier aspects of ageing and retirement. Work and money feature in creative ways too with much inspiration for all the stories drawn from the people and situations the writers have encountered.

Enjoy the layers in all their glory from past, present and future: funny, sad, poignant or absurd, each tale entertaining and giving pause to ponder. From tears to laughter emotions are stirred taking the reader into the all too real world of believable characters as many facets of our own lives are exposed. As complex as modern art yet delightful as a box of chocolates there is a flavour to suit everyone.

'Layers of Life' is the first book in the series 'Looking at Layers'

New books are already being worked on. Look out for 'Colours' coming next where categories of colour inspire the Spilt Ink Writers to flex their imaginations once again to put pen to paper or fingers to keyboard to entertain you.

Readers who have aspirations to write short stories or have ideas for stories they would like to see written are encouraged to contact the authors at the e-mail addresses in the author biographies. We look forward to hearing from you.

Layers of Life

The purpose of our lives is to be happy
- Dalai Lama

Life is what happens when you are busy
making other plans
- Allen Saunders

Life is really simple, but man insists on
making it complicated
- Confucius

In order to write about life, you must first live it
- Ernest Hemmingway

Be where you are, otherwise you will miss your life
- Buddha

Religion and Spirits

Have a little Faith
                    - Mitch Albom

Toleration is the best religion.
                    - Victor Hugo

My religion is very simple. My religion is kindness.
                    - Dalai Lama XIV

Science without religion is lame,
        religion without science is blind.
                    - Albert Einstein

I do not feel obliged to believe that the same God
    who has endowed us with sense, reason, and
    intellect has intended us to forgo their use.
                    - Galileo Galilei

Jennifer's Prayers

By

Marion McNally

Jennifer was in the worst of moods. A lousy week at work, a lousy month with her mother in hospital and a lousy feeling in the pit of her stomach every time she thought about Martin.

The taxi driver took a fast turn right on to the High Street. It was rush hour so the roads were busy.

"Slow down, for God's sake," Jennifer called from the back seat.

Her mobile fell to the floor as the driver came to an abrupt halt behind a double decker. Off in the distance she heard a siren. Jennifer picked up her phone and clicked on her WhatsApp messages for the third time in ten minutes. She needed to hear from him.

The siren grew louder and louder. Within seconds, it seemed, a fire engine followed by an ambulance and a police car, raced ahead of the traffic as buses, cars and lorries moved to the pavement, on the left side of the street, to allow the vehicles through.

"What's goin' on here then?" mumbled the driver.

Before Jennifer had time to answer, a WhatsApp message popped on to the screen of her mobile,

"Remember to pick up flowers for mum! Have you heard from Martin yet? What about the wedding?"

It was a message from Jo, her younger sister. Exasperated, Jennifer thought of everything on her 'to do' list for the night - she didn't have time to get home, change, cook, feed and walk the dog, pick up flowers and *then* go to the hospital to visit her mum. *Life stinks sometimes,* she thought. Martin's cousin's wedding, she'd been hoping that he would cave and call her to talk about that...

Salisbury Road, as they approached it, seemed unusually busy. A policeman was standing outside number 2 and the rest of the street was cordoned off. An ambulance suddenly appeared out of nowhere. Just then Jennifer noticed that the fire engine they'd seen earlier was parked along the way – just outside number 15! She grabbed her briefcase from the seat and raked around inside for her wallet.

"Just take this," she shouted at the driver as she threw a ten-pound note into the front seat.

Emerging from the taxi she was alarmed to see plumes of thick, dark smoke and fierce yellow flames reaching up into the early evening air - just where the family detached house stood.

"Oh my God," she screamed.

As she dashed towards the opening the police had made to allow foot traffic through, she spotted her beloved West Highland Terrier, Brandy, chasing around her neighbour's garden. Mrs. Doolan was kneeling on the grass desperately trying to calm the dog down.

Jennifer could see that the fire engine had already attached its massive hose to the back of the truck and a senior fireman was yelling orders to the others to get a move on and target the flames that were now engulfing the living room of the house.

"Please let me through," Jennifer said to the officer who was securing the entrance to the street.

"That's my house, I need to get my dog; he's in the garden with my neighbour."

"You can't go through love – not yet. They need to get this under control. You'll have to stay here for now."

Mrs. Doolan and her daughter Nell approached the opening. Nell was carrying a traumatised Brandy in her arms. The little black dog leapt out of her arms. Jennifer grabbed him and held the trembling terrier tight to her body. She sobbed – big heaving sobs.

Mrs. Doolan, dishevelled and in shock, placed her arm around Jennifer and the dog.

"With your dad not long gone, and your mum in hospital – and now this – I don't know what to say Jennifer."

Nell, Jennifer and Mrs Doolan huddled together holding on to each other tightly. Brandy, considerably calmer now, sat at Jennifer's feet. They moved silently together to sit in the back of an ambulance where a young nurse waited to attend to any casualties. Brandy settled himself between Mrs Doolan and Jennifer. No – one spoke. All eyes were on Number 15 and the firemen who seemed to be finding it difficult to control the fire.

It was almost eight o'clock when they eventually managed to quell the flames. The chief fire officer approached the back of the ambulance to speak to Jennifer. She braced.

"Are you the owner of number of 15?"

"The house belongs to my family, yes."

"You'd better make plans to stay elsewhere for the time being. You won't be able to get in for a week or so. Do you have somewhere to go?"

Taking a tissue from her briefcase she wiped the tears from her eyes.

"I can stay with my sister for now," she sighed.

"We'll get the house boarded up tonight and let you know when it's safe to go take a look," the fire officer said. "I honestly think it's not as bad as it seems. Only the living room seems to be affected. Mrs. Doolan was right to call 999 as soon as she smelt smoke."

Jennifer hugged Mrs. Doolan tightly and thanked her.

"I'll take Brandy for a few days," she said, "You need to think about your mum and Jo for now."

Jennifer hadn't thought about her mother at all in the chaos of the last couple of hours. Realising that she'd missed the hospital visiting time she called Jo and told her what had happened.

"I can't believe this. What else could possibly go wrong in our family," said Jo. "What do you think happened? How did the fire start?"

Jennifer had no idea, and what's more, she didn't have a single shred of energy left to begin thinking about it. Jo explained that she was stuck in horrible traffic on the M1 and wouldn't be home until after 9.00.

"I'll call the hospital and tell them to let mum know I won't be there tonight; I hope the nurses can think of a good excuse so that we don't worry her."

With an hour or so to pass before she planned to call the hospital, Jennifer decided to walk to the nearby cemetery to visit her father's grave. Maybe he would be able to give her a little comfort, she thought.

As she approached St. Mary's Church her stomach heaved with feelings, the depths of which she had never known before in her twenty-seven-year old life. Martin, her boyfriend of four years, the man who'd wanted to marry her and be the father of her children, hadn't been in touch in almost a month. Those dreadful photographs, why had she been so stupid and why had her even more stupid friend put them on Facebook for the whole world to see? Of course, Martin was sure to have seen them.

She passed her old primary school and walked towards the cemetery and St. Mary's church. Strangely, the lights of the church were on; even with the enormity of what had happened in the events leading up to this appalling night, she could feel a separate but easily identifiable rage at what had happened with Jo seven years earlier – the young parish priest had taken advantage of and had almost seduced her fifteen-year-old sister. She'd sworn then that she'd never set foot inside another church – and she hadn't. Tears streaming down her mascara covered face she reached into her briefcase and grabbed another bundle of tissues. She thought about

Martin who had always been a believer, a Sunday mass attender, a stalwart of the church choir.

Just then something deep inside her body stirred - a long forgotten feeling, maybe from when she'd been at primary school, when she loved this 'entity' called God and truly believed everything the nuns had told her about His (God could only be a he, according to the nuns) never ending forgiveness, his unconditional love, his deep affection for children. She had been such a believer all of her life - until the night she'd walked in on Jo and Father Burgess… The hatred and resentment she'd felt about 'The Church' had overflown into her feelings about God himself – she'd stopped praying. Martin had said that it 'was just a phase' – she'd come out of it in time.

She rubbed her eyes with the tissues and, stopped before the entrance to the cemetery. She thought about what she'd say to her dad. Suddenly, with no real understanding why, she decided to turn left and headed towards the church. Entering through the back-porch door, she was vaguely aware of organ music playing softly upstairs in the choir. She stopped at the last pew and sat in a darkened space at the back of the church. Her body heaved. Uncontrolled thoughts of her father's recent death, her mother's heart attack, Martin - and now the fire, caused an otherworldly cry to escape her lips. Her head bent and her body rocking she prayed for the first time in seven years.

"God, if you really do exist *prove it*. Make mum well. She's suffered enough already. And what about *me* God? My heart is being torn apart and I have no idea what to do now."

Muffled voices from above distracted her from her desperate pleas.

"From the beginning then, last time."

Suddenly, the organ began to play the first chords of the hymn she had loved most - Ave Maria.

A voice, a deep mellow voice she knew only too well, started to sing… Ave Maria….

Her brain and body went into lockdown. She froze in her seat. It was Martin. What the hell was he doing in the church at this time on a Thursday night?

Sobs of despair ripped through her as she slumped onto the seat and curled up into a ball. The hymn was too evocative, too poignant, too wrong. She and Martin had talked about it – this would be the hymn that would be the highlight of their wedding service.

"Think we've got it Martin! That was wonderful. I'm sure it will be a huge hit at your cousin's wedding."

In the panic of the evening Jennifer had totally forgotten that Deirdre, Martin's only cousin, was to be married the following week.

She heard the lid of the massive organ closing.

"I'll put the lights out and lock up. See you on Tuesday."

It was John Doolan, her neighbour's son who was the organist in St. Mary's church. Soon she heard footsteps coming down the stairs. Jennifer covered her face and shifted slightly to the right of the pew, where it was darker.

"Oh my God," thought Jennifer.

Suddenly, her mobile rang out! Jo was calling.

"Is somebody there?" called Martin, as he was about to follow John into the vestry to switch off the lights.

"Sorry, we didn't realize anyone else was in the church. We need to lock up now," said Martin.

He could see the outline of a figure, now seated, holding a mobile phone in her left hand. It was young woman who was slumped at the end of the pew in the darkness. Her phone was ringing but she stared ahead at the altar, unable, or unwilling to pick up or switch off.

"Are you okay? Can I help you?" he asked.

He drew closer and stared at the small crumpled figure. The long tousled dark hair was half in and half out of a silver hair band. At first, he wasn't sure, but it took no more than a few seconds to realize that this sorry sight was Jen, his Jen.

"My God. What's the matter? You look awful. What are you doing here Jen?"

He moved into the seat and sat next to her

"I'll lock up John," he shouted to his friend. "There's someone here I want to talk to."

Jennifer switched her mobile off and stared at the altar in front of her.

For a while they both sat staring up at the crucifix at the front of the altar.

Then Martin broke their silence.

"Why did you do that Jen? Why were you kissing your ex-boyfriend at that party? From what I heard from the girls you two got quite re-acquainted again."

He took his tie off, unbuttoned his shirt then stuffed the tie inside his briefcase.

"Martin before I explain anything, I need to tell you that mum's house caught fire tonight."

"Are you being serious? What happened?"

"For now, I have no idea. The firemen told me that I couldn't go back until later in the week. Mum doesn't know yet – I don't know what I'm going to tell her."

Martin fiddled with the keys to the church.

"Jen, I'm so sorry to hear this. What can I do to help?"

You can take me back, thought Jen, you can cuddle me and tell me that you love me…

"Jen, you're shaking. Let's get out of here and get a drink."

Jennifer picked up her briefcase and walked out of the pew behind Martin.

After ordering two gin and tonics they sat together in silence. Jennifer started to speak.

"I … I … I don't know what to say about those pictures on Facebook Martin. I'm ashamed for a start. We had far too much to drink. I know that's a stupid excuse, the whole thing was stupid. Nothing happened Martin. It was just some drunken pictures of people who weren't quite in control of what they were doing. I left the party not long after they were taken. I had no idea Irene had put them onto Facebook that night. I couldn't understand why you weren't answering my calls."

Jennifer took a large gulp of gin and tonic.

"I'm ashamed - and I am so, so sorry, Martin. I don't know what else to say."

Martin's eyes, Jennifer knew, said that this was a situation that was far from resolved. He held his gaze on the gantry and absentmindedly flipped a bar mat. Jennifer had no doubt whatsoever what had happened had been a dealbreaker – she knew too that if things had been the other way round, she would feel exactly the same way.

"Why did you come to the church tonight Jen? Thought you swore you'd never step foot inside one again?'

"I didn't mean to end up at the church – I was on my way to speak to Dad – in the cemetery. I was waiting for Jo to get home before I went to her place – she's stuck on the M1 and won't be back until after 9.00."

Martin didn't respond.

"I had the weirdest feelings going back into the church after all this time. It was as if my childhood self was reaching out to me, it was maybe even Dad – I had a peculiar feeling that he was walking behind me, doing his bit... Who knows? The only thing I know is that I've never prayed so hard in all of my life. It's mum...I don't know how she's going to cope when she hears about the house."

She looked at her watch. "I'd better order a taxi – Jo should be home now."

She took out her mobile and started to call an Uber

"Stop," Martin said," I'll take you back. Wait here and I'll get the car from the car park."

During the fifteen-minute drive to Jo's apartment Martin didn't say a word. Jennifer, meanwhile, offered up every prayer she had ever known. She spoke to every saint, as well as to Jesus, Mary and Joseph. All to no avail...When they arrived, he turned off the engine. He turned to Jennifer and took her hand in his.

"Look," he said. "I'll pop into the hospital and see your mum this week – I promise. It's going to be such a shock for her. You take care and tell Jo I'm asking after her. You'd better have another drink before you go to bed."

He took his hand out of hers and turned on the engine.

Jennifer grabbed her briefcase from the back seat and opened the car door.

"Thanks for the lift. See you." She got out of the car and pressed the entry button to Jo's apartment. As she turned around, she saw the black Mini take off down the road.

Over the next week Jennifer and Jo spent the days either with their mum in hospital or with insurers and firemen. Both had taken two weeks off work to sort out the problems related to the fire. Bizarrely, Jennifer's mother had taken the news better than they could have ever imagined.

"The house is not the same now without your dad there," she'd said, as if she herself didn't need a home anymore!

Jennifer was desolate and heartbroken. Martin hadn't shown up at the hospital and there had been no texts or calls. What a fool she had been to think that he'd forgive her.

One night, a week after the fire, when Jo and Jennifer were in the apartment working on insurer's claims, Jennifer's phone pinged. She'd stopped jumping up every time it rang, too many workmen and neighbours who meant well, had been calling throughout the week. Both she and Jo had decided not to answer calls after 6.30, so that they could have a drink and eat dinner in peace and get on with the paperwork that had to be done.

That night Jennifer crawled into bed. Her body was drained and her chest was tight. Her head was aching – she thought she might be going down with something, what with lack of sleep, her mother, the fire - and the stress of losing the love of her life.

Before putting out the light she decided to take a peep at her mobile. There was a message from Martin! She sat up in bed.

"Jen, I've been an idiot."

That was all. She scrolled down. He'd added a link. Hurriedly she clicked on it. 'Ave Maria Gratia Plena,' rang out the voice of Andrea Bocelli. Jennifer sobbed and sobbed and sobbed, well into the wee hours of the morning. She played and replayed the hymn until her eyes were red and blurry.

Just as she thought she couldn't cry anymore another text came in from Martin "Speak tomorrow, Jen?"

Maybe her dad had helped, maybe it had been the endless prayers that she'd said since the night of the fire. She'd never know for sure. One thing she did know in the depths of her soul was that someone or something had been listening when she begged unreservedly for Martin to forgive her.

Losing the Plot

By

Stephanie Thornton

Prologue:

Enter: The vicar. Christine – newly Reverended. Waddly and rotund, flowing with robes and regalia. Underneath the vicarliness, she has one fatal flaw. She is not tolerant of sins and frowns when told this is not very Christian.

Exit: The body. Elizabeth – very military and full of British Legion zeal, of the much medaled and flag waving type. Underneath the military-ness, she has also suffered from the same flaw.

The Setting:

Her funeral in an ancient country church. Where everyone gathers in black and huddling on pews for four. For some reason, several groups of six decide to sit together. They are squashed – like sardines – and are muttering and most uncomfortable.

The Sexton arrives fresh from his grave digging and is exhausted. He collapses on a pew at the back covered in soil. He has had two graves to dig that day

– left for health and safety reasons to the last minute. Burials are rare these days and two together even rarer. No wonder he is tired.

We are told there has been a delay. But not told why. Fifteen minutes pass whilst we listen to a bevy of organ music, when eventually, this changes to Vera Lynn singing "White Cliffs of Dover", to accompany the coffin with its roof of flowers wobbling like a jelly down the aisle.

The Service:

The Very Reverend starts the service in a very soothing Preacher's voice and leads into a hymn.

We stand, we sit. We stand, we sit.

We are told we are now going to be told about Elizabeth's life in a tribute given by her family.

Silence. The eyebrows raise. Christine dissembles quickly telling us the bad news. No, the family are not going to do this, the good news is that she is to. But this is a surprise to her.

What can she say about Elizabeth? The anticipation mounts. You can see that she is pondering on it. Then follows more bad news, no one has told her anything at all about Elizabeth. In asphyxiating panic, the Vicar states 'she was sister to us all' – and that will have to do. We'll have to skip that bit. The silence in church deepens.

So, we sit and then stand again.

Good news; Christine is to read Ecclesiastes 3 to us from the Good Book. She starts turning pages. Then more pages. Quickly. Bad news, it's not in her bible. She announces it's in a different bible. One of the Ushers runs to the back to the Presbytery to try find another bible. But will it be the right one? More bad news, it seems this church doesn't have many bibles. They have probably been sent to Africa? But after loud scrabbling and sounds of searching, we are all saved.

The Congregation breaths again.

One has been found and we hear of 'a time to live, a time to die' etc. I wait for the bit that says 'a time to be lost, and a time to be found' but it appears that Ecclesiastes missed that bit out. But it does say 'there is a time to search…and a time to give up'. Very appropriate and what a relief, all is not lost (or is it?)

Back to the service and another hymn. This time the Organist, who has probably been having a stiff gin and tonic round the back after all that introduction, waxes lyrical. They can play and they are showing us they can by introducing twiddly bits to the music. As it's already quite complex, the congregation valiantly try to keep up – somehow it doesn't sound quite right. Several people are singing off-key. In the distant churchyard, a dog is howling.

Soon we are all saved.

Good news - Christine is going to read a poem. It's called 'A letter from Heaven.' Exciting stuff as none of us have ever read this letter. More bad news follows - she hasn't got this either – and this time, it isn't found. It would have been possible to find it on our mobiles but God has said (on tablets?) 'Thou shalt turn them off' before the service starts. And in any event, no one even thinks of this until well after the service has ended.

So, Christine states we'll have to miss that bit out. We decide to blame it on the Royal Mail. They would have charged such a high postage from Heaven and having done so it probably wouldn't have fitted through those silly slot things they produce at the post office which they used to demonstrate 'what will fit through and what won't' (maybe that should be in Ecclesiastes too?)

Exit the service:

Everyone is too quiet. Are we all so traumatised with what we have seen or just trying not to laugh? Would Elizabeth have liked it or would she be shocked it failing all her military aspirations?

The coffin exits to strains of Vera singing 'We'll meet again' – I hope the Vicar gets the date right for this if we do in fact meet Elizabeth sometime in the future.
The coffin proceeds up the footpath past those long gone and is interred into the first hole and covered over.

Everyone can now leave down the winding path to ham sandwiches at the village hall trying not to mention the unmentionable – the service which also missed out most things mentionable. We can do what all we English do in times of crisis, drink tea and think of better times. This time, lots of tea is drunk whilst we think, and say, a great deal.

Prologue:

Some days later, the headstone arrives and the Sexton studies his plan of the Church yard and the names on the stone which has been re inscribed with Elizabeth's name under that of husband John. Good news, this can now be put in place. Bad news. A mistake! John is in the grave next door and on top of him is Betty who was buried yesterday.

The surviving son finds humour in this and laughs – he states John would like to be next to Betty. He'd always found her most attractive and he always did have wanderlust. He would have felt that Elizabeth was too much of a martinet to spend eternity with and thus he had been spared. Maybe both Christine and Elizabeth would now discover the charity of forgiveness in what had turned out to be a very unusual funeral.

The Good Lord had worked in his usual mysterious ways. And an arrow on the headstone now indicates Elizabeth is 'next door'.

Postscript:

Churchill said 'Now this is not the end. It is not even the beginning of the end. But it is, perhaps, the end of the beginning' which is why this story has two prologues rather than an epilogue to conclude the tale and in line with the style of the rest.

The Light in the World

By

C. I. Ripples

The old man was making his way up the hill to the square in the Albaicin, his small rucksack with his water bottle weighing heavily on his back. He could feel his heart pulsating in his chest as he struggled along in the sunlight of the uneven cobblestoned streets trying to place his walking stick.

His granddaughter was ahead, turning every so often, outwardly patiently waiting for him to catch up, whilst her young pup of a son ran up and down, covering the distance he made at least four times over.

He would have preferred to stay in the silent charm of the garden of their casa de huéspedes and nod off in one of the lounge chairs, especially after a whole morning sightseeing at the Alhambra. He would have preferred a cold glass of cerveza, and to ponder upon his dream. But she had insisted this was 'a must see', the place to see the sunset, to see the Alhambra disappear out of the light against the backdrop of the Sierra Nevada.

As always, her youth, energy and enthusiasm had infected him and he had taken his hazel wood walking stick and fedora straw hat and with a gentle sigh followed. If only the young could feel the challenges of the old.

He had dreamt of his wife again last night, an eon of consciousness and light traversing the universe.

She had passed away many, many years ago now, but he still missed her as if it were yesterday. Yet, every time he feared he might lose himself in his boundless grief, she came to him, stroking his soul with her whispers, consoling and advising him, although she never truly spoke. Last night he had heard her more clearly than ever. It was as if her words seeped into his neural pathways, telling him something about death, something about a transition into the light.

He was sure there had been more, but he lost her again when a ray of early morning sunlight had fallen with a thud upon his face, awakening him in a moment of absolute clarity.

He knew now. He knew what had taken him a lifetime to believe, what had been obvious all the time and it filled him with a purity of faith, the certainty of which he had not felt since his very young self, if ever.

"Opa," the boy shouted, shaking him out of his contemplations, when he finally came upon the square on the edge of the Moorish quarter.

He was a little short of breath, somewhat bewildered by the crowds, the nuns, rabbis, imams, and faithful, the black widows, the Roma women selling sprigs of rosemary, the tourists jostling for position on the square in good time for the sunset. The boy shook his sleeve and pointed:

"Look Opa, it's Mohammed following Jesus!"

Two young men, treading in each other's footsteps were crossing the square, stopping in front of Iglesia de San Nicolas, Christianity built on Islam. Both looked remarkably similar and the old man wondered if they were twins. Both were olive skinned, had short beards, and were of similar height. But where Jesus wore an undyed mantle, Mohammed wore a turban, the end of which hung between his shoulder blades. Where Jesus wore a basic thin woollen tunic and was barefoot, Mohammed wore a white Jubbah and leather sandals on his feet. They were the epitome of what one would have expected, thought the old man, comforted by the fact that the order of things was in accordance with the Bible.

He wondered, however, what it all meant.

The boy pulled him towards a small crowd of the faithful of all persuasions that was beginning to surround the prophets, making a path so that the old man could make his way to the fore. Silence fell as the men raised their hands and began to speak with one voice:

"We are the Messengers of God as one soul and one body, as one light and one spirit. We are the same luminaries and our outward condition is of the same light, part of one being, united in our words, united in our multiverse".

There it was again, thought the old man, this mention of light and he wondered if they knew what he now knew, whether they too were enlightened in the truest sense. It all made sense.

He understood immediately that they were talking about photons.

He had read about these tiny packages of light recently in the National Geographic. It was his only magazine subscription and he had had it most of his long life. He had learned that all living creatures emit light, because they all contain photons holding atoms together like a glue. And, as all matter, including he himself, is made of light, when Jesus said he was the light of the world, he was no different to the old man himself. We are all, thought the old man, the light! "A measurement of one photon," he heard the united voice say, "can instantly affect another, far-away photon with no physical connection."

Yes, thought the old man. That is why he can still communicate with her in his dreams. She can affect his photons from the other side of the universe.

There were murmurs of scepticism around him and some, who refused to see what they had decided not to, turned away. Others with a lesser fear of knowledge, moved a little closer.

The old man didn't move, letting the spoken word wash over him. He didn't need to hear. The truth was already inside him, the rest of his dream now flooding back.

He had been in the solar system, floating past its numerous moons, asteroids, comet material, rocks, and dust, with her beside him, part of him, showing him the union of souls all around them to which she now belonged.

"Death is not death," she had told him, "all that is light is around you in the world, the galaxies and universe and forever."

And that meant he too was immortal. They all were. In fact, he now realised this had already been scientifically proven.

From his National Geographic he knew that photons lasted at least one quintillion years, could travel forever in a vacuum as long as they didn't meet matter or another photon. And even if they did, he remembered, they were merely absorbed by the particles in question. At least according to a scientist called Heeck, who suggested that if photons do break down, the result would be even lighter particles, called neutrinos, which would travel even faster than photons and rarely interact with matter, rushing through everyone and everything all the time. Assuming of course that photons have mass. Most scientists agree that they do, although if he recalled it correctly, the current upper limit was less than two-billionths of a billionth of a billionth of a billionth of a billionth of a kilogram.

"But you have all been living in the darkness of an unproven one-sided belief," the voices now continued more forcefully, commandingly, "and it is time the light dawned. It is time you came out of your closed mindedness, left behind your non acceptance of the truth, of each other. It is time you discarded your ignorance."

A shocked roar went up amongst what remained of the faithful crowd, which seemed to surge forward, hissing and heckling, almost throwing the old man, who was leaning heavily on his walking stick, off balance.

"How dare you doubt the very existence of Allah; praise be upon him," a Muslim faithful beside him called out.

"You guys need to be put in a lunatic asylum," a black widow screeched from the other side.

"Get out of here. You're taking the Lord's name in vain," a priest yelled, waving his fist.

The old man was reminded of the shock caused when his parents back in 1924 had been told that the serpent might not have literally spoken to Eve. The doubt and war of words this had caused. That, thought the old man, was the essential question for everyone of faith: the extent to which one could doubt the word of God, the Tanakh, the Bible, the Koran, without being blown and tossed by the wind. If only they could understand that what these young prophets were teaching was certainty, not doubt. If only they could understand that it was all irrelevant, that they were all the same.

He looked around for the boy, but the young one must have lost interest, and the old man couldn't see over the heads of the fervent faithful, to locate him or his granddaughter, as those around him made their way to deal with the two young men. He could no longer see them, but he imagined they stood fearless, smiling, almost as if indulging their children.

For himself he felt a rising concern, fearing he would soon be wedged in by an increasingly agitated mob. And he was tired, of standing, of the noise around him. He yearned for a bench, longed for peace and tried to shuffle his way to the back when the small crowd almost as an answer to his prayer fell silent once more.

"When we speak of darkness," the voice spoke pleadingly, "we mean the dark forces, a portal into the dark world. We are referring to dark photons, as the dark side of light."

This too resonated with him. Darkness, too had featured in his dream.

"There are many other soulful unions in the multiverse, with whom we have no contact, but it's dangerous to leave the union of souls within our own universe," she had told him.

"It's dangerous to venture too far, to the edge of our universe which is like a wave of black mass without photons or light, hiding what is real, giving power to what we cannot see. We know this from the old souls, some at least two hundred thousand years old, who tried to reach other universes and have been to the point of no return. Some went beyond and did not return, but those that did, warned us not to come too close to the dark holes, for fear of falling in, for fear of our light souls be trapped forever in their dark energy."

"There you are, Grootvader," his granddaughter tugged at his sleeve, shaking him back down to earth. "What are you doing here? You've missed the sunset!"

The crowd had dispersed, he knew not how, and only the two young men remained, standing in light where darkness had fallen. As he went to follow his granddaughter back down the hill, the love of his life beside him in the light of the stars above, he turned back for one last look. The men were watching him and he lifted his hat in recognition of each other. As their eyes met across the square, light filled him and he could finally express clearly what he had known since his awakening: religion is nothing more than physics undiscovered.

The Last Pomegranate Seed

By

Stephanie Thornton

King Zedikiah liked to walk along the beach. A moment of sanity away from palace life.

The body guards followed at a distance keeping careful vigilance. The king had lots of enemies.

There was something very calming about the waves and the feel of sand upon his toes. He needed this quiet space, as he was a man prone to terrible tempers, and the walk on the beach was a very good solution.

He was beset with problems. The most urgent one of all concerned his beautiful daughter Teila-Tephi, who had yet to find a husband. He had been looking for a suitable man for many years now and soon she would be over twenty years of age. Time was running out. There was no son who could rule if he were to die. He paced up and down the beach lost in thought. There seemed no solution to it.

One windy, stormy day, whilst the azure seas swirled and eddied round his feet, he felt a hard object come between his toes. It was a bottle of the most curious green colour and he picked it up to have a closer look. It had strange ridges round the sides and the top was corked and sealed with the heaviest of wax. There was some parchment held inside and he could see there were some words upon it.

Once back at the palace, the bottle was uncorked, but only after great difficulty. Whatever lay within it, was in no hurry to get out.

Several days went by until finally, the cork came out in a desperately dying rush, accompanied by a tiny puff of pale grey mist which drifted to the ceiling where it hung until it slowly disappeared. The tiny strip of parchment was pulled out with the thinnest wooden stick. Upon it were some hieroglyphs.

The king summoned wise councillors from the palace staff to look at this most curious slip of reed. No one knew what the writing said. It was in a language none of them had seen before. The parchment appeared to be much older than the Tower of Babel which had separated all the languages. If they had known this, they would have left it well enough alone as the message spelt out danger; 'Do not open'.

The message had been written at the time the world was born, by the greatest spirit of all that came to be known as God. God had prepared the bottle as a test to see if the sins of Adam and Eve could be undone and to give the world a second chance.

It was of course too late. Within the bottle, had been trapped a spirit, who was both good and bad. The spirt-genie was God's servant-messenger and trapped within the bottle until his time had come to serve his purpose. Whoever found and opened up the bottle would condemn the genie to weave his fate however wise, or foolish, good or bad, for all eternity to come.

The spirit knew all things and all the history of man since the dawn of time. He looked around the place where he had just been freed and with great presence saw within his soul what sort of place it was. He knew in an instant the kingdom the king ruled over and he also knew inside the daughter's mind cloaked within the beautiful body she had been given.

That same night, God told him he was to plant an idea in the mind of the king. He had selected one born of wisdom and of insight. The spirit cloaked himself in velvet and drifted through the darkening sky, through vivid hues of violet and purple against the setting sun, until he hovered over the king's bed and thus could whisper in the king's ear. The velvet brushed against the king's cheek and he dreamed a vivid dream.

It was soon to be the festival of Rosh Hashana and the king had been told, in his dream, to give his daughter's hand to any man who could find 614 seeds in a pomegranate knowing this would only happen to a man of great virtue. This the spirit had revealed to him.

The pomegranate was long regarded as a luxury. It excited passions and created legends. The king thought it most appropriate to choose this most special fruit in the search for his daughter's hand in marriage. He would read the 'Songs of Solomon' with their erotic descriptions of the precious fruit and marvelled at the wisdom of the test.

Thousands of suitors appeared and bought the exotic fruit which was measured out in silver buckets from a row of market stalls all along the palace walls.

The traders soon ran out and the vast lands of the Babylonian empire were combed until all the pomegranates had been harvested.

But some of the would-be suitors were cunning men full of avarice and greed. They thought to add an extra seed to make up the correct number. But when they did this, all their seeds decayed. So, the palace steps were now covered by millions of the blackened and discarded seeds. The dead seeds lay in vast heaps, rotting in the sun, and the city permeated with a smell of rotting fruit. The entire crop of pomegranates was diminished and in rage, the king put to death all the suitors that had failed the test and cheated.

The spirit watched the happenings below as he floated through the skies above the kingdom. He saw the seeds, the corruption of the men and the ruthless king. He had carried out God's orders and created all that happened in the world below. It was a most interesting experiment.

On these same palace steps sat a blind beggar in ragged clothes. He had lost his sight when he was twelve years old in a fall from a horse. He earnt a living now by playing on a whistle reed pipe. There was no chance he could win the prize.

One dark night, he felt the fabric of a velvet cloak fall across his face and a soft voice said to him, "this is the last pomegranate in the land. If you find what you want in it, you can choose. It can either restore your sight by placing the seed between your brows or win the hand of the princess. Choose wisely."

The beggar wished the voice, 'Shana Tova' (Happy New Year) and felt a hard and wizened fruit placed in his hand. It had been left behind as no one else had thought it worthy. He opened it and counted out the seeds. Indeed, the magic fruit contained the extra one. He did not hesitate. He placed the seed in the centre of his forehead and he could see again. It was an excellent decision.

By morning, the passing crowd stopped to marvel at the ragged man sat on the steps. The seed had turned into a golden bhindi which shone in the sun. It had given him the gift of second sight. He thus made his fortune by telling others what their future held. And the king offered him his daughter's hand in marriage which he refused.

And so, it came to pass that the princess married a man called Heremon, but winning her was false treasure which the blind man had observed beforehand and which the spirit had revealed to him.

The daughter was not at all what she seemed to be. Beautiful on the outside, but inside, spoilt and full of avarice and spite. She matched all the blackened pomegranate seeds in the hardness of her heart.

Zedikiah, the last king of Judah, lost his kingdom and with it the Babylonian Empire ended. And his granddaughter, Irial, was exiled to a land which came to be named after her – Ireland. God had thus decreed that this land would be ruled by descendants of the king, the Irish, and they would inherit his fiery temper and his love of fighting.

The spirit dwelt above the earth creating equal measures of both joy and misery in all the coming

Ages. And the pomegranate remained much vaunted and valued as a precious fruit.

(Author's note: some of this is historical fact and the fruit is supposed to contain 613 seeds which are used to celebrate the Jewish New Year in September)

Foresight

By

Sacha Quinn

Mrs. Walsh was sitting in her office looking over her notes, checking to make sure she had caught the most salient points from the day's clients and whether they needed anything further.

Julie, her first client of the day, popped in early before work at the nursery school next door. She seemed in a bit of a different flux from usual. Her usual insecurities were not immediately apparent today, which Mrs. Walsh thought a good thing. It appeared she was simply wanting to know whether she should take the offer as a nanny on a cruise liner. Mrs. Walsh thought it was an excellent idea for all sorts of reasons, glad that the girl was at last starting to think for herself in even contemplating it, concluding that her nursery would still be there when she got back.

Next, young Andrew, a nervous young man, taking time out from his study leave to visit her practice, wanted to know if he would be in a fit state to pass his exams, what with all the home-led stress he was suffering. In reality, it wasn't so much home stress as just his concerned parents wanting him to pass. They just weren't going about it in the right way to persuade him to knuckle down.

"Of course, Andrew, there is no reason you shouldn't pass. You are a very intelligent young man," she told him. "Thing is, you need to channel that and use it to your own advantage. It's no good fighting your parents against their beliefs. If they think you need to go and pray to a God you don't believe in, for an hour once a week to help you pass your exams, it is a small price to pay to keep the peace. Use the time to revise the periodic table, or imagine labelling a diagram of an eye, or just use it to have some kind of nice, peaceful thoughts. A time-out from the studying if you like."

He went away agreeing, that was indeed an option.

Mrs. Murphy came next. A Catholic mother of five young children. Always, tired and run-ragged with a house full of screaming kids and their noisy pets, always tear-stained, unkempt and desperate not to have a sixth child. Mrs. Walsh, ever practical, suggested she have a word with her parish priest, because surely, she had now done her duty to God in this already well-populated world. If he couldn't help by forgiving her in the name of the Father, the Son and the Holy Spirit, and indeed give absolution via a few Hail Mary's to any confession regarding the use of contraception, then the family planning clinic would, she'd suggested. She finished by saying gently that sometimes, people had to make their own decisions, and that God often helped those who helped themselves, as she pulled a tissue from the box on her desk, offering it to the tearful woman.

A run of the mill day. She sighed contentedly as she glanced at her watch and packed up, ready to start her evening, pondering her clients. Mostly, they simply did not know how to solve problems, believing she had some magical gift of foresight that in reality steered them in a different way.

The village summer fete meeting was on item three of the agenda, when Mrs. Walsh entered the church hall. She noted that The Rev Michael Jephcot was absent-mindedly scratching a patch of eczema behind his ear in that nervous way he often did when he was in a dilemma. Mrs. Walsh wondered what it was this time as the meeting came to a temporary stop whilst she took a seat.

"Ah, Mrs. Walsh good you er, arrived at this point. We, ahem are just onto the topic of erm Madam Zara and were wondering…er?"

"Evening Vicar… And everyone," Mrs. Walsh said, continuing, as she took her seat and pre-empted the vicar's question, "Ah right, and yes of course I'll be Madam Zara again. The fortune telling booth, I assume will still be in as much demand as ever."

"Ah er. but erm," stuttered the vicar, before Miss Frobisher interrupted.

"Well that's just it. It isn't right."

'What isn't?' questioned Mrs. Walsh puzzled.

"Madam Zara… and fortune telling isn't."

"Why not? I've been Madam Zara for years. She is very popular."

45

"It's not Madam Zara, per se," continued Miss Frobisher, "It's the fortune telling that's the problem. You see, it's against Christian values. And forbidden by the church."

Really?

Mrs. Walsh wanted to laugh at the absurdity, but managed to control herself instead saying,

"You cannot be serious. What do you think, Vicar?"

"Hmm well, er, ..." He scratched at another patch of eczema on his left hand this time, looking up at the cross decorating the wall at the far end of the room, seeking some spiritual guidance. He knew there was going to be a problem this year when Miss Frobisher had mentioned it after the Morning Service last week. He'd been worrying about it ever since.

Miss Frobisher was looking smug as she picked up her bible and turned to a marked page spouting what Mrs. Walsh could only describe as 'Christian dogma', which, generally interpreted, the vicar thought was correct. His eyes went upwards as a drop of water landed on his meeting agenda. It was raining again. The church roof still needed fixing. The money from Madam Zara's booth would be most appreciated. He was torn.

Seeing the Reverend Michael thus torn, Mrs. Walsh stood up and held up her hand, saying,

"OK. I think that is enough Miss Frobisher. What you are talking about is clairvoyance, which actually means to 'see clearly'. And whilst people who were thought to see clearly were regarded as clairvoyants in the past, you are mixing the old meaning with what we have come to know in modern times. Use of the five senses to interpret what is before us and what might shape our future as a result is not against God's will. As far as I can see it is in no way against any Christian religion and therefore there are no broken rules. What I do is a bit of fun. I see what is in front of me, I make use of the knowledge I have, and sometimes I astound people with information about them that is clear for all to see if they only were that bit more observant. It is nothing to do with religion, nor is it any predicting of the future. But if it makes them happy to think I did that, then who am I to complain?"

The vote to retain Madam Zara was carried. Whether this was as a result of Mrs. Walsh's speech, or the fact that even more rain was dripping, due to some divine intervention wanting the roof fixing, wasn't entirely clear in the vicar's mind, but he wasn't going to dwell on the gift bestowed upon him to boost church funds.

On the day of the fete, after a busy morning, Madam Zara was just about to go for lunch when she recognised a young woman approaching her booth. Stella had sought her opinion only a month ago, but maybe hadn't yet decided which man to choose if she was seeking her fortune to be told. The look on Stella's face was quite the picture of incredulity as Madam Zara told her exactly the same as Mrs. Walsh, psychologist and life coach, had told her recently. In her heart Stella had to admit that yes, Peter was exciting, but he was a waster, unreliable and selfish, so much so that even his mother had thrown him out. Paul on the on the hand was good and steady and would take care of her. Who knows, maybe that could be exciting too. They could make their own excitement.

A few days later Mrs. Walsh received a letter:

Dear Mrs. Walsh,

Thank you so much for your advice. I have finally made a decision about which boyfriend is the one for me. Paul is the one. Peter left home. I did hear his mother had thrown him out, which I think also helped me in making my decision. I mean, if he was so bad that even his mother didn't want to live with him, I don't think it boded well for a long and happy marriage, do you? I'm thinking an autumn wedding would be nice.

However, I think I may have another problem. This time with an interfering mother-in-law. I'll call your secretary and make an appointment in case you can help again.

Yours faithfully,
Stella.

Still holding the letter in one hand and her mobile in the other, Mrs. Walsh heard the call connect.

"Hello, Reverend Michael Jephcot, here how can I help?"

"Reverend, It's Edna. Edna Walsh. My son, Paul, is getting married. Three bridesmaids I think would be nice, don't you? Dressed in pink, oh, and a big fancy cake, with some matching pink icing. Alas, Peter won't be best man, he doesn't live here anymore. I know you'll be busy with Easter and all, but can you check for free dates in April. I think a spring wedding is far nicer than an autumn one, don't you?"

Work and Retirement

Life is not what we live;
it is what we imagine we are living.
- Pascal Mercier, Night Train to Lisbon

It is never too late or too soon.
It is when it is supposed to be.
- Mitch Albom, The Time Keeper

Find a job you enjoy doing, and you will never have
to work a day in your life.
- Mark Twain

Autumn leaves don't fall; they fly. They take their
time and wander on this, their only chance to soar.
- Delia Owens, Where the Crawdads Sing

Your work is going to fill a large part of your life,
and the only way to be truly satisfied is to do what
you believe is great work. And the only way to do
great work is to love what you do. If you haven't
found it yet, keep looking. Don't settle. As with all
matters of the heart, you'll know when you find it.
- Steve Jobs

Summer Job

By

Renata Kelly

It was perhaps a bit strange that parents, who in their youth never had to work during school vacations, would be so anxious for their daughter to have a summer job as soon as she entered High School. Granted, the said 'job' was in another country from theirs, and that country being the United States it was a rite of passage, generally accepted with enthusiasm by the hapless teenager, eager to prove his or her maturity and reliability, whilst earning money and whiling away the long summer school-break.

At that point in life, I did not question my parents' decision to enrol me in the phalanx of American child-labourers. My friends had jobs and three months was a long time to spend reading books or even swimming and sun-bathing on the sandy beaches of Montecito, California, which is where we lived at that time, the Pacific in close proximity from home. Another aspect of the location of our home, on a lemon ranch in an area of other large properties, was that the type of 'job' which I could secure at that time was mainly baby-sitting and moreover generally for the children of people we knew. Possibly that figured in my parents' calculations.

However, in the summer following my final year of High School and just before launching myself into the adult world of university education, I was encouraged to try some 'real' work. Hence, reluctantly, I applied for a job at Thrifty's Drug Store on State Street in the neighbouring town of Santa Barbara. I didn't have to be a pharmacist to work in a Drug Store, since drugs played only a minor role in the Thrifty's establishment. More a supermarket than a pharmacy, Thrifty's stocked many food items besides soaps and toothpastes; it had an ice-cream bar and a soda-fountain, a marble-topped counter where you could sit and order milk-shakes and ice-cream sodas.

As a fresh recruit, my first task was restocking shelves and sticking price labels onto new items, a task which I found excruciatingly boring. However, within a week I was promoted to the ice-cream bar where the novelty of doling out scoops of various flavours soon lost its lustre. Looking around me, I noticed that many of my fellow workers were mature individuals, more the age of my parents and even, in some cases, grandparents, than of myself. All of a sudden, the need for an education, for amassing knowledge and expertise in something other than ice-cream flavours, became a revelation that both thrilled and frightened me. What if I failed? Even a further promotion to the check-out stations, where I learned to manage a cash register and give correct change, which necessitated a modicum of attention and mathematical skill, did not help to alleviate my sense of dissatisfaction.

I must have communicated my frustrations and boredom to my parents for after only a month at Thrifty's, an offer of an alternative summer job came my way – needless to say, from a family friend. Thus, I happily gave in my notice and spent the rest of my summer mornings tutoring seven-year old Johnny and his sweet nine-year old sister, Sally, in rudimentary maths and reading. Then at noon, I was tasked with driving my two charges in their family station-wagon to the Coral Casino Beach Club, where we all ate lunch and spent the afternoon swimming and playing. Since the children often met up with their little friends at the Club, this would leave me time to lounge by the pool and read a book. Somehow this labour, which necessitated dutiful glances at the pool to check that Johnny and Sally were still above water, neither frightened nor filled me with foreboding. In fact, I thoroughly enjoyed myself.

But it was in the summer after my first year at university that I landed, in retrospect, a job that exceeded all expectations. Once again, the right connections (that network of friends and acquaintances that can act as the good fairy with a magic wand that sprinkles stars over cribs) played a role in the scenario of myself, on a fresh Californian June morning, driving through the gates of one of Montecito's grand estates. I was on my way to meet with an esteemed and legendary gentleman, Charles Edmund Magnus, who had made his fortune on Wall Street in the early decades of the 20th century, but had devoted most of his life to the active study of archaeology and anthropology, especially examining how his own and other archaeologists' findings might shed light on the earliest inhabitants of the American continent.

However, as my Volkswagen "Beetle" made its way up the long driveway flanked by manicured lawns, tall palm trees and enclaves of flowering bushes, I had no idea what my future job would entail. Finally, I drew up to the Magnus mansion, sprawling with grace at the crest of a small incline which facilitated a stunning view of the Pacific Ocean seen beyond the tree-tops of the countryside below. With a sudden feeling of trepidation (what did I know about archaeology?) I approached the front door and rang the bell; the door was opened nearly immediately by a rotund and smiling little lady in uniform.

"I've come to see Mr. Magnus," I said returning the lady's smile. "I'm Maja, spelled with a 'j' but pronounced like a 'y'," I added automatically, having honed that addendum to thwart any mispronunciation of my written name. I extended my hand. With a look of puzzled surprise, the lady extended hers.

"I Rosa," she said shaking my hand, "I from Mexico. Mr. Charles waiting you," she added, leading the way through the large entrance hall to a door further on the right.

As I entered the Magnus study, the gentleman himself rose from his desk and walked towards me. He smiled, "Ah, Maja," he said, pronouncing my name correctly, "so good of you to come!"

Mr. Magnus was meticulously dressed; he had gray hair and a small moustache, kind eyes and an equally encouraging smile. He reminded me of my grandfather, as much as I could remember of that kindly presence from my early childhood.

I smiled nervously, "Mr. Magnus," I stammered, "I know very little about anthropology and archaeology, but have always been fascinated by ancient civilizations and the emergence of the human species. It sort of compliments philosophy, which I am considering as my major …" I came to a halt, noticing a slight amused twitch of my employer's mouth.

"My dear," Mr. Magnus gallantly pointed to a chair in front of his desk, "do sit down. Your reputation has preceded you. I am writing a book on, exactly, the emergence of the human species. I want someone who is not an expert in anthropology, a lay person so to speak, to read through my manuscript, ask questions, query my assumptions. Would that be of interest to you?"

"Of course it would!" I nearly jumped up from the chair where I had just sat down. "You can't imagine how that would interest me! Learning about a subject which I always wanted to study and ... I can't thank you enough ..."

"Well, then, it's a deal!" Mr. Magnus held out his hand across the desk and I proffered mine. We shook hands.

So, started not only my best and most interesting summer job, but one that would continue for the four summers of my undergraduate studies. Mr. Magnus became my friend, my mentor, in many ways my inspiration to pursue knowledge. How much I contributed to his grand project on the human species is questionable. I tried my best; read through the chapters, written by hand in his small neat script, and stored in leather-bound, three-hole binders. I wrote out questions about points that were difficult to understand, occasionally queried the construction of a sentence and the sequencing of ideas. But mostly I enjoyed my weekly visits to the mansion on the hill, to the book-lined study where Mr. Magnus presided, to our conversations and debates on Pithecanthropus Erectus and his various slouching relatives, to the coffee and cookies unfailingly proffered during our sessions by the smiling Rosa.

On the first day of my employment, as Rosa led me, clutching my first leather binder, out of the front door, she introduced me to her husband, who was conveniently trimming a hedge near my parked car.

"This is Hesus, my husband. He chief gardener for Mr. Charles" she said beaming, and then added, sheepishly, "name spell with 'J' but say with 'H'."

"Oh, he's Jesus! That is 'Hesus'", I corrected myself. "Happy to meet you, Hesus. I'm Maja, spelled with a 'j' but pronounced like a 'y'." We all laughed. And so, through this small peculiarity of Spanish and Slavic pronunciation, we felt a bond; we became friends.

As I returned home for the long summer break after my second, third and final fourth year at university, I relished the thought of resuming my amazing 'summer job' at the Magnus mansion, of seeing Mr. Charles and reading the chapters that he had written, and equally of refreshing my friendship with Rosa and Jesus, who lived on the estate in a small but picturesque ivy-covered gate-house. It was there, as I stopped at the gate after a heady session of tracking the evolution of the human species, that I was often invited for a quick bite of home-made tamales or enchiladas, or given a package of Mexican delicacies to take home to my parents.

At the beginning of the final summer of my coveted 'summer job', with a Bachelor of Arts in English Literature, not Philosophy after all, and a secured scholarship to continue my graduate studies at Oxford, in England, I drove through the gates of the Magnus Estate with a welter of feelings: sadness, tinged with excitement and happy anticipation of my reunion not only with my beloved employer and grandfather-surrogate, Mr. Magnus, but with Rosa and Jesus as well.

The familiar driveway climbed gently through the palms and lawns of the park to the rotunda in front of the mansion. I parked my car and bounded to the door.

As I rang the bell, I fully expected Rosa to open the door and was prepared to give her a big hug, so as the door opened, I moved forward with a smile. To my surprise, the person opening the door stepped back. This was no Rosa, but a tallish lady neatly dressed in an elegant beige dress, with an expensive-looking leather belt cinching a somewhat non-existent waist. I knew immediately that the apparition was not the fabled Mrs. Matilda Magnus, whom I had never met nor seen in all the years of my frequent visits to the Magnus establishment. I had been told by Mr. Magnus himself that his wife was in poor health and rarely left the house. Rosa, when asked, had only sighed and murmured something to the effect of 'Mrs. Charles, very nice lady, not strong, not eat much'. So, this was definitely not Mrs. Magnus; she could have been a daughter, she appeared to be about the age of my own parents, but I knew the Magnus's had no children.

The lady looked at me questioningly.

"I ... I've come to see Mr. Magnus," I stammered. "I'm Maja, spelled with a 'j' but pronounced like a 'y'," I added automatically.

The lady raised one eyebrow. Now this was something I had often practiced but failed to do. It annoyed me as it seemed to be a gesture not just of enquiry but of superiority. Nonetheless, the lady stepped back and allowed me to enter.

"Please follow me," she said. As if I needed to. I could have found my way to Mr. Magnus's study with my eyes closed. However, I followed obediently. Then, as we crossed the large entrance hall, I saw a door open on the far side and a familiar small figure emerge into the hallway.

"Rosa!" I quickly ran across the hall and gave Rosa a kiss and a hug.

"You're back," she said. "So good!" She looked at me with tears in her eyes. I gave her another hug.

"So good to see you too! We'll talk later. I must go to Mr. Charles now," I said, glancing across the hall to where the lady in beige stood waiting. I scurried back and the lady knocked then opened the study door.

"Charles," she said, smiling for the first time, "here's your little friend, Maja, spelled with a 'j' but pronounced like a 'y'," she giggled. It was my turn to raise one eyebrow, but as usual I failed, raising both eyebrows instead.

Luckily no one noticed, because Mr. Magnus got up from his desk and came across to me. "Maja," he said, embracing me, "here you finally are! And congratulations to you on your graduation and scholarship! Your parents told me all about it. But at least you're here to help me this summer," he took both my hands.

"Of course I am! I was so looking forward to seeing you and can't wait to get to work!"

I suddenly became aware that the lady in beige was still standing behind me. Mr. Magnus, who was facing her, moved a little to one side and gestured in her direction.

"Maja, I see you've already met Priscilla?" a conjecture on his part that did not quite square with reality, the lady never having introduced herself. I smiled weakly.

"Priscilla is a dear family friend. She's come all the way from Boston to help, well, to keep poor Matilda company this summer. And me too, of course," he added with a nod towards Priscilla.

The lady in question, her face a picture of sympathy and helpfulness, sighed.

"Ah, yes, it's a pleasure to offer what little I can to make Matilda's life more comfortable."

She glanced at me, then added, "I must leave the two of you to get on with your grand project!"

With that, she left the room, with a smiling glance towards Mr. Magnus.

Soon Rosa arrived with a pot of coffee and her special oat chocolate-chip cookies. She hovered discreetly near Mr. Magnus's desk.

"Mr. Charles, sir," she started, "Miss Priscilla like to know if you go to Country Club today for lunch?"

With a hint of annoyance, Mr. Magnus replied to the negative: "No, we'll have lunch as usual in the conservatory, with Mrs. Magnus, if she's able to join us."

Rosa nodded and with a grin in my direction left the room.

As the summer days unfolded and my departure for the next chapter of my life approached, I began to experience everything around me with, it seemed to me, enhanced clarity: the lingering morning mists that inevitably melted away to reveal cloudless blue skies, the smell of lemon blossoms, the rhythmic thudding of waves breaking on long stretches of sandy beach, the excitement of diving through those towering glossy breakers before they got hold of you and tumbled you towards the shore.

My weekly visits to the Magnus mansion became likewise a revelation: had I never noticed the blooming hibiscus bushes along the driveway, or counted the different species of palms that dotted the sloping lawns? I mentioned this to Jesus one day, and he proudly escorted me to the other side of the mansion, which looked out across the Pacific. He showed me the rose garden, the fuscia bushes and fragrant jasmine and behind a trimmed hedge the long, sparkling pool, where –splashing somewhere in the middle – I saw Priscilla, her hair neatly packed into a blue swimming cap with pink flowers. I think she was wearing a dark blue bathing suit, which contrasted with the whiteness of her flailing arms. I stood uncertainly on the edge of the pool and waved, then retreated quickly. The lady in question might not have noticed me, because she did not return my wave.

It was Rosa again who now opened the door of the mansion for me when I rang the bell and saw me out after my mornings with Mr. Magnus.

I did not see much of Priscilla, though she did once burst through the door to the study with a winning smile and asked, almost breathlessly, "Charlie, Matilda would like to know whether you'll be taking me to the San Ysidro for dinner tonight?"

We had been engrossed in a deep deliberation about the putative 'soul' of early humanoids, so Mr. Magnus looked up and answered a bit curtly, "Let's discuss that later, Priscilla, if you don't mind!"

She looked down at me for the first time and raised one eyebrow, "Sorry," she said, "forgot your little friend was here today."

That episode prompted me to ask Rosa the next time I saw her, "How is poor Mrs. Charles? Any stronger? Is she happy to have Priscilla taking care of her?"

"Mrs. Charles not so good," said Rosa sadly, "and Miss Priscilla very bussy!"

"Bussy?" I enquired, "do you mean bossy or fussy?"

Rosa looked up at me with a conspiratorial smile, "Both!" she said, "bussy and fussy!" We laughed.

"I think she want to make this summer job into winter job too," Rosa added more gloomily.

And so, the final summer of all my 'summer jobs' drew to a close. Mr. Magnus came to our house for a farewell dinner in my honour. He handed me my final check, which I soon discovered multiplied my already generous remuneration manifold!

"To help you with your new ventures," he said, kissing me on the head.

I was about to enter a new life, on a different continent; a life that would give me the knowledge and degrees to seek a proper 'job', to start a career, to travel, to enjoy new friendships and flirtations, and finally to meet the young man who would later become my husband. I wrote dutifully to my parents and received much awaited reports from their life in distant California.

Probably over a year into my studies at Oxford, my parents communicated to me the sad news that Mrs. Magnus had passed away. More surprisingly, two months later, a clip from the local newspaper accompanied my parents' letter: it announced the marriage of Charles Edmund Magnus to Miss Priscilla Edith Adams. Was I surprised? Certainly, a little, as I think were my parents and others in the community. More likely I felt a churning discomfort and a sadness at the upheaval of a blissful vision: the beautiful driveway with its palms and flowers, Rosa opening the door with a smile, Mr. Magnus in his book-lined study with windows that looked over sloping lawns and tree-tops to the distant Pacific.

But by the time that my new husband and I returned to Santa Barbara, Mr. Magnus had sold his gorgeous estate in Montecito and moved to Carmel, likewise a prestigious coastal community a few hundred miles to the north. As he told my parents before he left for his new home, it seemed that the cooler climate of Carmel "suited Mrs. Magnus better."

As my witty husband summed it all up: "It seems that your friend Priscilla managed to transform her summer job into a lifelong career, and with a Magnificent pension to boot!"

The Bobbin Doffer

by

Stephanie Thornton

Five of them slept in the big wooden bed with its straw mattress and the cover of thick ticking. Ma tried to keep the bed bugs away with regular brushings and a clean but sharing was the only way to keep warm in the ancient tiny farm house. And besides that, there were only two bedrooms. The two girls slept with Ma and Pa in theirs. They were lucky to have the rooms. Most of the terrace houses* in the nearby town had only one, built to house the workers in the last few years when factories and wool production had increased to gobble up great swaths of land. So, the tiny farm was a little different.

Drafty windows and slate floors froze in the icy winds that swept across in Pennine* winters. Today, sleet drifted across the moors and the washing water froze over in the pale. Time to get up in the darkness.

By five o'clock everyone was dressed. Even Ma with the bad back and half way to baby number eight. The fire had long gone out in the black lead grate* in the kitchen and wouldn't be lit again 'til home time so all the small cottage was cold. The sort of cold which sank into the bones and chilled the blood.

A hunk of bread and some weak porridge shared amongst them all then off to the Mill.

It gloomed ahead in the darkness of the morning. It's vast shape and blackened stones rising to six floors in height on the valley floor. It was placed that way, as at one side, the canal, partially frozen over and edged with snow, waited for the barges* to arrive to take the precious cargoes away to lands unknown. At the other, the raging river, responsible for the quality of water needed for the fine production of worsted and woollen cloths. The best in all the world. It was this geography that made Yorkshire so important and the hills behind which was home to massive flocks of sheep grazing on the hills and moors*.

But at the time, no one knew that the position of such mills in deep damp valleys would result in the worst of all lung conditions, due to smoke caught there between the hills. The endless smog and fog and mist to trap the unsuspecting residents. As a result of this, Frank Thornton, the third of Henry's sons, would suffer from chest conditions all his life and regretfully, two more generations from the same complaints before conditions changed for the better.

It was a treat to wear clogs* even though the wood wore through and slipped on the cobbles. In the summer, he would be barefoot. Frank's brother Luke held his hand to stop him slipping on the icy streets. Luke put both their hands in his pocket to try to keep them warm. Frank needed warm hands for the work ahead.

He had been at work since his tenth birthday. It was at least warm in the mill. In fact, it could be really hot when all the machinery was running. And it was a proud moment when he got his first wage –

seven shillings and six pence * for the week as Bobbin Doffer. At least he was skinny enough. It was what the "Throstle Jobber" needed of him – a skinny lad, as lithe as a whippet that could change the bobbins of wool or cotton yarn once full, spinning on the spindles and put new ones in their place, when it was time for the throstler to do his job and whistle time to change them. Fancy, thought Frank, to be called after a bird because of the sound you make at work and he thought this rather wonderful.

All the mill stopped when the bobbins were changed as the ten little boys ran around nimbly changing full for empty ones as fast as greased lightening. And there were as much as 10,000 bobbins spinning round. The boys were called 'the devil's own' and 'luck' would be added to the name if they were quick enough. It could mean an extra penny in his tin. But he hoped his back would last. He had seen it. The sight of Jo Atkins from down the road who had got curvature of the spine from changing bobbins. It was the curse of the design of the machines and the need to crawl in tight spaces that had caused it to cave in. Or the newer machines, so tall you had to climb high up to reach. That and the lack sunlight and of cheese and milk. Frank's Mum Lydia used Jo as a threat and told Frank to stand up straight.

'So, you'll not end up like that,' she would lecture and hug him close. And they kept a cow in the old barn behind the farm so milk would never be a problem.

The bobbins doffed and at once the chattering looms started up again. The roar was so deafening, the only way to talk was by reading lips chapped and parched with cold from the long trudge to work, but at least the little boys could play. In summer, it would be in the sun outside but in winter by running around the factory floor keeping out of the way of women hard at work. They worked a shift of twelve to fourteen hours, six days of the week and church on Sunday for a two to three-hour service. So, there was little time for anything else.

The fibres from the threads made everyone cough and a pale misty haze of lint hung in the air in a sort of oily sheen. It was the sort of sheen that filtered light, giving it a ghostly yellow hue as it shone through the iron framed windows all along the factory walls that ran with moisture from the workers' breaths. Spectres of dust motes rose into the air like tiny floating fairies.

All the family were now at work including pregnant Ma. Only little Annie was left with a neighbour as she was only two. The three 'between kids' went to school and would eventually start work when they reached the age of 10. The eldest Luke was a worsted oiler. It was better paid than most. The fibres running through machines must be kept in ever ready moistened state – if dry, ruination would follow. Luke intended to escape it all. It would be a prelude to his work in engineering.

Second son Willy, had already escaped the Factory life that beckoned, to work on making bricks. If it was by the furnace baking them, he would be warm, but otherwise outside in freezing cold. It played havoc with his hands. In later years, he would smile at thoughts of India where they made bricks sometimes hardened in the baking sun, but at present, his schooling was too minimal for him ever to have known this. And besides, who had ever heard of such heat in the grey and sombre Yorkshire valleys.

Da had no work at present, he was a stone dresser and the Yorkshire Mill stone grit* did not take kindly to being prepared in frost and snow. If you tried to break it up when cold, it would produce strange unusable shapes no good for anything at all. He would construct the dry-stone walls* when the weather improved which gave the Yorkshire landscape it's boundary walls so unique in character.

The seriousness of responsibility was already beginning to weigh heavily on Frank's young shoulders as he made the daily trudge to work. He could be young and run around having fun, but the ethic of work hung like a spectre in the shadows, waiting to claim him, together with all the rest of them. It was like the cowl of a new born baby. It clung and was insidious, covering his body and his mind. But this was no more, no less than he expected, together with everyone else. This seriousness of mind would be added to as the years passed, getting heavier and heavier. He would become a business man in the end although wounded in the war and something of a success, but the grind and the weight of it all would remain with him forever.

And it was expected that everyone would work in wool or cotton. There was no other life thought of or dreamt of beyond the factory walls. The walls were there to claim everyone who lived in the valleys like a living tomb reaching out to keep them at the daily grind. It was thought of as a prize. To work in among the looms and grow in wealth and stature feeding the world with cloth. What privilege! Wool was everything to the Yorkshire valleys. It lived in the architecture and the villages like a living thing there to claim whole families into its embrace.

It was unthinkable that the whole family would not work. It was expected and looked upon as necessary. It was years before The National Health Service or Benefits of any kind as a form of Public welfare. You worked or you starved. And furthermore, your neighbours looked down on those that stayed at home. Mothers would 'donkey stone' their outside steps as a form of pride, designing the edges with chalk in either brown or the more classy and expensive white in a sort of pavement art. They cleaned their windows that were often decorated in intricate patterns of leaded lighting * with great vigour. Those neighbours that were scruffy and with overgrown gardens were talked about and avoided. Respect and work made good companions of the daily task of living.

So, it was really not so strange that these early endeavours would produce a sense of both spirit and survival in young Frank. And his family influenced him too. With positive thinking and encouragement.

If he had but known it, he would need these if he was to survive what was to come. But at that time, it was the only chance to really have fun and get up to mischief. Those early factory years.

By the age of 23, Frank had become an Overlooker, watching over all the rest and on a good wage before three years passed and the First World War came and took away all the men and all the laughter with it. They couldn't wait to leave. Leaving the looms was an adventure. A chance to escape. They had no idea what was waiting there over in the land called France. And if they had known, they would still have gone as what they would have shrugged off as 'tall tales' would not have been convincing enough for what they were about to experience. Impossible, don't tell us such silly things!

Four years! And they had said it would only last a few short months. His brother Edgar had lied about his age and gone to war only to die soon after. So, for Frank who remained alive, but only just, memories of the past when he was a boy, were all that remained of the carefree but skinny boy he had been. The skinniness remained but the smile behind the eyes was dimmed and dull.

He really never laughed again. Not even at his little Granddaughter whom he dearly loved. He had long ago lost the ability to laugh. It was lost somewhere, in the mud and blood of the trenches of the Somme.

But his very history, the legacy of his working life, gave those that followed him a gift of priceless treasure. The inspiration of a work ethic as sturdy as a giant oak, that would continue to inspire and motivate and bring success for the generations yet to come.

To my Grandfather, Frank Thornton with love
Frank Thornton 1888-1973 of Elland and Brighouse,
West Yorkshire, UK

* Author's Notes:

Yorkshire: the 'West riding' ('The Ridings' – a name of Viking origin – Yorkshire was made up of three areas, North riding, East riding and West riding) The west included towns of Halifax, Huddersfield and Bradford. Main centres of the woollen industry. In 1974 the name Ridings was changed and replaced with that of Yorkshire – West Yorkshire etc.

The Pennines: the main row of sombre hills and moorland dividing the counties of Lancashire and Yorkshire - responsible for much of the rain falling on the western edge of Yorkshire within their shadow, due to prevailing winds from the Irish sea driving Eastwards and resulting clouds.

Terrace houses: typical to parts of Britain and especially in Northern England when they proliferated due to the Industrial revolution in the 1800 and 1900s. Built in lines with communal walls to reduce building costs often with twenty or more to a row and with a row behind them joined on and known as 'back to backs' with communal walls on all three sides except the front. If the row was single and windows were at the back but without a back door, these were known as 'through by light'. No one had a bathroom – toilets were in communal blocks half way down the street (n.b.: These houses are now renovated and full of charm and character far different from their previous existence). Later on, around the 1930s, there would an introduction of houses split in half (again to reduce costs) and these were called 'semi-detached' and were very fashionable.

Black lead grate: The living room would have a fire place set into the wall with an oven adjoined at the side of it, hooks above to keep things warm and a trivet (a revolving shelf of the same material) to stand pans on which could be swung above the fire to cook. The whole thing made of leaded metal which had to be cleaned with black paste and a scrubbing brush. It was the only heating in the house.

Barges: A special type of flat bottom boat to fit into a canal to carry goods usually with a tarpaulin (a waterproof cloth) to cover them. Originally pulled by horses down a bridal path at

73

the side of the canal and later by engines which ran on firstly steam combustion, then diesel.

Moorland; treeless areas of scrubland due to soil conditions where heather grows and course grass but little else.

Clogs: A shoe carved from one solid piece of wood.

Yorkshire mill stone grit: A special stone peculiar to the West Riding being of grey colour with a slightly mottled surface. A type of hard durable sandstone especially useful for water mills and grinding - hence its name.
Drystone walling: made by skill without any sort of holding cements. Used to separate land without any fencing or need for wood and typically northern England in design. Made from mill stone grit or limestone dependent on the area.

Leaded lighting: where strips of lead were attached to the glass panes to give intricate patterns and sometimes with stained glass colours in between.

At the time of writing (2019) seven shillings and six (pre-decimal) English pence would be worth forty-three GBP in today's money per week.

First Day

By

Sacha Quinn

"Are you sure you don't want me to come in with you?"

"We've already been through this. Of course I'm sure."

Angela started to open the car door then, turning back towards her mother gave her a perfunctory kiss on her cheek adding, "I'm a big girl now and this is the seventies. One does not take one's mother to work."

She heard her mother sigh and ignored it, wishing she'd let Sophie drive her instead.

The pavement was icy following a hard, early morning frost. She picked her way carefully to avoid slipping, stopping momentarily to lift her face to feel the warmth of the winter sun on her face. She reckoned the ice would be gone by lunchtime, making life and walking easier for everyone.

Mrs. Brown, her new boss had explained that outside of normal banking hours there was a door the staff used. She found the door bell, pressed it and waited.

"Do you have any I.D.?" came a man's voice from the door.

"Er, no sorry, it's my first day."

"Angela Daniels?" the man questioned.

"Yes. I'm Angela Daniels."

She heard a bolt being driven back and a lock being turned, before a door on creaky hinged opened.

"Do you know where you are going?"

"I'm working in the typing pool, I think. But I'm not sure how to get there."

"Righty-o. Down the corridor, turn left at the end and carry on passed the lifts and the staff room, up the stairs...." Then realising he'd already lost her he tentatively suggested he should take her. He noted the look of relief on her face.

Mrs. Brown looked out of her office window at her latest employee, headphone covering her ears, fingers flying over the keyboard. Marking the speed tests following the preliminary interview she had looked at Angela's results and invited her for a second interview. There was no doubt about her ability and audio typists were in short supply, but she was unsure whether or not Angela would fit in. Seeing the disappointment and resignation on the young girl's face, Mrs. Brown felt a rush of compassion, deciding to take the risk.

Now she wasn't so sure. Starting a new job was always difficult and though she had introduced Angela to everyone it had been awkward and stilted. Her staff just didn't know how to respond.

Doing a walk about the office Mrs. Brown took in the scene stopping at Angela's desk.

"Hello Angela. Just thought I'd stop by and see how you are getting on."

"Fine Mrs. Brown. Thank you."

Mrs. Brown looked around. Sitting amongst a group of girls roughly the same age, Angela still seemed out of place. She'd declined to offer an opinion on whether Blondie looked better as a blonde or should try brunette for a change, was indifferent about fashions, the new autumn colours, make-up and hairstyles. And when she spilt a cup of coffee, Mrs. Brown was sure she would feel clumsy and helpless, while a couple of girls rushed to help mop it up.

When Mrs. Brown went reluctantly to her Monday morning meeting, leaving her staff to cope, the atmosphere lightened almost immediately.

"Hey Sandra, what did you get up to over the weekend?" asked a girl sitting near to Angela. Angela determined it was Tracy. A bit of giveaway really since she'd detected her accent was clearly from Liverpool.

"Och wouldna you like ter know? Especially since yous all know Jimmy's parents, are on holiday on the Costa Brava this week," Sandra from Scotland replied, with a humour in her voice that set some of the other girls giggling.

"Yes of course we would. That's why we're asking, but maybe just the summary. Spare us the gory details," a posher but local accent chipped in.

"Oh no, we want the details," a local girl added in her Lancashire twang, resulting in more laughter.

Angela was loving listening to the banter as they discussed shopping trips, and boyfriends, going around the town and to the discos, the latest music charts, the groups they liked; Queen, Abba, Boney M and then the heavier stuff of Deep Purple, Black Sabbath and Led Zepplin. She loved them all too. She wanted to join in desperately but she sensed their embarrassment at her presence. Not wanting their pity, she wanted to put them at their ease. After all she had been born this way. To them it was new. She knew no different. She felt it was probably harder for them than it was for her as she finally plucked up courage to speak, wanting to put them at their ease. The questions came quickly after that.

"Who does your make-up?"

"How do you manage to shop for clothes?"

"Who does your hair?"

"Well as you can see," she started, lifting her hands and pointing with the forefinger of each hand to her hair, "I was blessed with straggly curls. I think I'm right in saying perms and curly hair are the in thing now. So, hair wise I don't need to do anything except wash and go. It goes its own way. God help me if straight page boy styles come back."

She laughed.

They laughed with her.

Mrs. Brown came back from her meeting not in particularly good spirits since a number of the management team seemed to be faulting her for her choice in Angela. But she'd held her ground. She'd picked a person for the skills they had to benefit the organisation. Seeing her team crowded around Angela, she no longer felt vilified noting her new recruit seemed perfectly happy holding court. She decided for once, the word-counts and targets could take a hike in a good cause. She was feeling rather good actually. Maybe her instincts had perhaps been right after all. She left her office door open a tad, so she could eavesdrop, just a little bit, and was surprised at what she heard.

"Hey Angie. Oh, hope it's ok to call you that?" Tracy from Liverpool asked.

"Yeah Sure. Actually, I prefer Angie."

"Would you like to come shopping at lunchtime?" Sandra from Scotland asked, continuing with, "I dunnae think yer mammy has much idea o fashion fer these days hen."

Then she quickly added, "no tha there's anything amiss. You looks neat 'n tidy anyways, but ye know?"

The question was left open ended but Angie understood the sentiment assuring them that she wasn't offended.

This was one of the reasons she wanted an office job. She wanted to know how most normal, ordinary girls lived, do the things they did, go to the places they went to, wanting to experience a bit more of life and people and have some fashionable clothes and a boyfriend would definitely be a bonus. She'd need one of those if she was to marry and have children. She wondered many a time about that.

Mrs. Brown also wondered about things, mainly how Angela's first day had gone, keeping her crossed fingers under the desk as she asked.

'Wonderful,' Angie replied.

Detecting Mrs. Brown's puzzlement, she went on, "Spilling a cup of coffee is no great tragedy. It happens all the time. Of course, I'll have to ask for it to be put in one particular place and not move it so I know where it is. But I'm sure they and I will soon learn. Most people are only too willing to help once they know how. I guess that's up to me to tell them. And do you know? They are going to take me shopping. For new clothes. How on earth will I know whether the stuff is ok?"

She paused, then continued, "I won't. But I trust they will want to make me look good and not bad. I have no idea but I'm no threat to them. I like to think positive and yes, why would they want me to look anything else but good? I think I'm going to like it here."

With that she picked up her white stick and held out her arm to Mrs. Brown.

"If you like, you can help me learn the layout of the building. I'll soon be able to manage on my own."

"I'm sure you will," replied Mrs. Brown taking hold of the pro-offered arm, "I'm sure you will."

Thorny Package?

By

Marion McNally

I glanced at the computer: rotating images of adorable kittens flashed across the screen at three – second intervals. The new boss, who was sitting directly across from me with her back to the kittens, was explaining what my role would be with regards to literacy in the school. I was listening of course, but I couldn't help but notice the large mahogany desk where the computer sat was empty, apart from a solid silver mouse that sat off to the right-hand side of the old Mac. There wasn't a post-it note, or a book, or a piece of paper - not even a photograph. *How odd*, I was thinking. I'd never seen a principal's desk look so devoid of evidence of 'busyness'.

The new boss, was now in full flow explaining the 'extra' roles I would have in the school.

"Did I tell you that you would be in charge of buildings as well?"

I thought at first that this may have been some sort of joke but no, there was no evidence of humour as she continued to talk.

Alarm bells rang out in my brain – what on earth did I know about buildings? I had been employed to be one of the two Assistant Principals in the school with responsibility for Literacy and the Upper School– where did *buildings* come into it?

Unable to concentrate further on the mumbo jumbo coming out of the tight-lipped little mouth, I stared above the boss's head at the shelves of precisely placed box files, each and every one labelled in the neatest of fonts. On one shelf there were neat rows of oddly coloured files. It wasn't easy from where I sat to read those perfectly placed labels but I did see a few referring to 'Buildings', 'Lifts' and 'New Classrooms' – I felt another lurch in the gut.

"It's going to be good having you with us," declared my new principal. "I'll take you to your office now to meet Chris, who is in charge of the lower school. I'll explain some of the procedures we have in place."

At this point she unscrewed a small silver pen that dangled around her neck on a fine silver chain. She jotted a few notes in her diary then stood up. Her rigid upper body, squashed into a fitted jacket, seemed to move of its own accord as her ample hips, tightly ensconced in a matching pin stripe skirt, swivelled out of the chair.

"Bring your things with you," she said as she teetered out the office on pointed toed shoes, which were attached to high, thin heels that reminded me of chopsticks.

We arrived at a very small office, more of a cubicle I remember thinking, where I met my new colleague, Chris. She smiled. Her eyes told me that we would talk later. I realised that this would be someone with whom I would bond and share. I had met Chris a few times before, at meetings and inter school gatherings and I had taken an instant liking to her – so I was very much looking forward to working alongside her in my new role.

"I've left some notes on the desk for you," said the boss. "We use a colour coded system for sharing information: pink for staff, blue for parents, green for students and yellow for buildings related information."

What's the point in having computers and modern-day technology and then not using it? were the thoughts going through my head.

On top of my new workspace, perfectly placed, were rows of colour coded handwritten notes- at least fifteen. A quick glance at Chris' desk showed that a similar array of coloured papers sat on hers. The boss was about to start talking again when she noticed my cardboard boxes and files sitting under the table.

"I see you've brought your old files with you; we like all of *our* school files to be the same colour – lilac.

Ah! The school colour, of course it all made sense now, the files in her study, all lilac.

"Ask the resources co-ordinator to give you some," she continued, pointing to a space above my desk implying that this would be where my files would go. "Ask for some printed labels while you're at it," she said.

Hmmm…Now I was really beginning to panic. Since when did principals care about the colour of teachers' files? Of course, I'd heard the gossip:

She cares more about cats than kids;

She knows nothing about modern teaching methods so she concentrates on presentation and organisation;

She doesn't know how to talk to teachers, parents or kids;

She can't use a computer;

She just plays with the mouse;

and, the scariest one of all, she's a bully.

I had been excited about my new job - taking charge of a large department and exploring new ways of teaching reading and writing to primary school students. However, it was slowly becoming clear to me that organizational skills and 'buildings' knowledge was highly prized in this particular school and the education, which hadn't been mentioned at all at this point, seemed to be of secondary importance.

My new colleague grimaced. "It's just her being her," she said, once the clickety clack of heels was out of range. "Wait until the applications for jobs come in next week," she smiled, "then you'll see how many trees we kill …"

We shared a giggle and discussed reading and writing policies. At last I felt that I was on more familiar ground - talking about things that mattered!

After a blurry first week of meetings, introductions, classroom visits, staffroom chats, playground duties, endless chats with students … oh, and two episodes of the lift breaking down, which under 'buildings' was my responsibility of course, the final date for applications for six available teaching posts arrived.

The following Monday morning I arrived at school to find an industrial size trolley sitting outside the main office, containing a mountain of paper. The caretaker stood next to it, apparently waiting for instructions as to where it should go.

I had no time to ponder further on the paper as an Upper School staff meeting had been scheduled for 7.45 a.m. that morning. I raced off to the third floor to the meeting room. After my first department meeting, where one member of staff sat with her legs outstretched on a stool as she marked kids' work whilst chewing gum for forty-five minutes, AND two of the six teachers refused to respond to my questions or to participate in any group discussions, I found the staff toilet and stayed there for a while, ruminating on what I'd done.

Feeling overwhelmed, my brain started to predict all sorts of calamities and unwanted outcomes. Slowly, stifling the worst of these thoughts, I began to think about the wonderful teaching team I had been part of in my old school. Meetings there had been lively and invigorating. Invariably when they were over, I returned to my classroom feeling motivated to move forward on some aspect of the curriculum or to investigate ideas and outcomes further. Now, I felt depleted, judged, despondent and, worst of all, regretful about my decision to move.

I headed back to my office and almost tripped over the trolley I'd seen earlier – but now it was empty. I rounded the corner. A quick glance inside my cubicle confirmed what I had felt in my gut earlier that morning. I couldn't see my work space for paper…multiple bundles, a foot high at least, sat in neat rows covering the whole of the surface of the table, apart from my laptop, which had been moved to a corner making space to accommodate the paper.

Chris was organizing similar bundles on her desk when I arrived.

"What on earth is this?" I asked, not quite believing what I saw in front of me.

"Application forms," said Chris.

"We only have six jobs – how can there be so much paper?"

"There have been hundreds of applications," replied Chris," they've all been printed out so that senior management can sift through them this week."

My brain couldn't compute.

It truly beggared belief that every single application had been printed out five times over, with approximately eight pages per application, and without any sort of initial vetting process. A quick glance at the top three immediately confirmed it, my worst fears:

'I'm a pilot in Canada at the moment but I'd like to be a teacher. Please consider me for the Year 6 post.'

'I have done some home tutoring but would now like to work in a primary school.'

'I have a degree in law but have decided to become a primary school teacher.'

I was speechless!

Whilst my befuddled brain was attempting to comprehend what was going on here, the boss popped her head in the door.

"You should cancel anything you have on this week and keep your weekend clear too. It's going to take at least ten days to go through the application forms."

I went into a tail-spin: I had visitors arriving the following weekend, several events and outings were already in the diary.

I stared at Chris. "Is she being serious?"

"Totally."

Bloody hell!

It took some time for me to get up to speed with this new set up. Fortunately, apart from the new boss, the other members of the Management Team were professional and supportive – and somehow, after spending a few late nights at school and hours of our own time at the weekend, we managed to get through the application forms

During the process of sifting through the piles of paper I began to get to know the other team members - slowly it became clear that I would fit in. These folks welcomed me unreservedly. Through the weeks and months that followed I not only became friends with them I often found myself gasping in awe at their skills and talents as well as their dedication to the important work we were doing.

In the end, even though this had been the toughest move I'd ever made - and I often found myself walking on egg shells over minor issues with the bitter, fickle boss - the team more than made up for it and my passion for education continued to expand. Change is inevitable – what I discovered however is that growth and expansion are magnified tenfold when they come wrapped up in a thorny package.

When Work Becomes Leisure

By

C. I. Ripples

Jack was born a quarter of a century after a World Economic Forum report predicted that sixty-five per cent of jobs for primary school children hadn't yet been invented, but that there was nothing to fear. Even if seventy per cent of jobs would disappear due to automation, robots would create many, many more.

At the time, unions took a positive stance, arguing that if and because automation could produce goods faster and more efficiently, the workforce could happily, comfortably change to a four-day working week.

This was the same decade that the World Health Organisation described the world population's lack of physical activity as a global health problem, a soon to become pandemic. In Post Brexit Britain, or PBB, as it was now known, not unlike many other industrialised countries, two thirds of adults were overweight or obese. Like them, PBB had tried to tackle the problem by introducing a sugar tax and like them had found it had little impact. The Slim Agreement ensued, setting global targets for weight reduction. It too failed, as increased automation reduced the working week to three, resulting in more time spent on computers, gaming and watching Netflix, all the while eating robot produced processed food. By 2030, almost seventy per cent of fourth industrial revolutionised countries were overweight or obese.

By 2040, over eighty-five per cent of jobs were automated or done by robots – even in the police force, army, teaching, healthcare and hospitality. New jobs had not been created. People were bored for lack of 'work' and increasingly depressed as they saw robots, who became known as Robosapiens or 'RSs', gain rights. You see, with improvements in AI, RSs behaved like humans but were much better looking and without the latter's flaws.

It seemed that, after all, Homosapiens (HSs) had much to fear.

All this led to the World Health and Happiness Forum in 2041 where RS Psycherob delivered hiser (a combination of his and her as RSs are asexual) famous speech. That HS society's happiness depended on work, or rather the need to get up and do something structured, with regular hours and appropriate pay. That what HSs see as 'work' is what they are told to do, following instructions, meeting the spec and being managed. This was why the Finnish universal income experiment had failed – HSs no longer saw any purpose to their life. And, as most of what had been HS work, was now done overwhelmingly by the superior RSs, more efficiently and more reliably, what was needed was an overhaul of the whole concept of 'work'.

A select committee of both HS and RS members was set up to come up with something akin to work. It concluded that people needed to believe that what henceforth would be labelled as work, was not only valued, but essential in order to live a healthy and happy life. That the 'something' needed to be physical with a corresponding wage, preferably dressed in overalls or a likewise appropriate uniform, with promotion based on ability, so that people could equate activity with achievement - the ultimate achievement being sustained physical health. This would save a fortune on health care. Only with sustained physical health would reproduction be allowed as long as the prospective parents were below the age of thirty. After all, there was no need to increase the HS population beyond current levels. A gradual reduction would be immensely more preferable.

Basically, the committee concluded that what used to be seen as 'work' now needed to be re-characterised as leisure and vice versa. And this meant that the 'something' needed a rewiring of the HS brain and thus a completely new educational system.

So here we are - the year 2068.

It's 7 a.m. on a Monday morning. The screen opposite Jack's bed switches on, delivering a tiny electrical shock to his big toe, awakening him instantly.

"Good morning Jack," a female voice beams from the bright blue screen. "This week you've been allocated to the wheeling department. On your days off you may continue to participate in computer programming on Tuesday, road-building on Wednesday between the hours of 2 and 5 p.m. and bartending on Saturday between the hours of 7 and 10 p.m. Please report to the Activdale Centre by 9 a.m. today for your physical and further details."

Jack groans, swings his slightly podgy frame off the bed and drags himself into the shower. At least he hadn't been forced into the Water Department. He has a horror of cold water. Nonetheless, he wishes now that he'd made more effort at Hikedale. He'd enjoyed the countryside, although he'd admittedly never really put his back into the job. Its better wage had meant he'd been able to buy luxury items such as croissants and even the occasional bottle of wine. After the first year, he'd gained seven pounds and failed the physical. For sure, he'd received a warning, but he'd been bored and hadn't altered his lifestyle. Then his mum came to visit at Christmas (for a whole month!) and, to show off his relative career success, he'd splashed out. By then he'd gained a stone, failed the second test and was demoted.

True, he had been forewarned and it was undoubtedly his own fault, but the wheeling department again?

He thought of his now retired uncle, who was lucky enough to not only have excelled academically at school, but to also have been very athletic, gaining tennis coaching certificates whilst still a teenager. This combination of skills meant he had run the Tendale Centre, where he'd not only coached, but also controlled the RS tennis coaches.

Jack was envious of anyone who had made their work their leisure. Like the few HSs who had skills RSs considered necessary for the mental wellbeing of the HS working population, such as psychologists, recreational counsellors, and massage therapists. Or those very few who had talents RSs could not compete with, such as composers and fine artists. Or the even fewer who had the brains to outsmart RSs and were required for continued AI and biochemical improvements.

The rest of HSs had to make do with the work allocated and promotions based on physical health.

At the bottom of the pay scale were jobs such as running and lifting. These were the jobs for those who had not had the privilege of a university education in physical health such as golf, tennis, skiing, horse riding and the like. The very elite could apply for degrees involving life threatening skills such as arching, fencing, shooting, bungee jumping or sky diving. To get onto any of these you required at least AAA at A' level from a good gram school. Which was impossible unless you'd been selected after the 11+ exam to enter a Gramsci school where RSs taught non-physical subjects as well, such as physics, chemistry and math, or a Gramart school where HSs taught creative and fine art. But that was only about five per cent of students. Another physically talented ten per cent were selected to attend Gramphys schools and the rest went to the local Phys school, as had Jack.

Hence, he'd started his career in the running and weights department as soon as he left school at sixteen – and he'd hated it. Six hours a day of running and lifting with two half hour breaks and one hour for lunch.

If only he was more like his sister. A caring Gramphys student, she'd been selected to study childcare at the vocational college and was now a nursery worker. RSs struggled with the unpredictability of young HS children. But he'd sucked it up, saved from his meagre wage and after a year been able to buy a new computer and applied to be allowed computer programming for leisure on one of his days off. Not for him the hairdressing or client relations hobby his sister enjoyed. And he would never qualify for medicine and didn't think he had the caring qualities for nursing.

After two years in running and weights, he'd applied to Bootcampdale, which required all rounded fitness, failed the physical and been rejected. He was accepted by the wheeling department at Activdale instead. Six hours of wheel turning wasn't much better, but at least they had occasional days on moveable bikes and were allowed into the countryside. He became quite skilled at skateboarding and roller skating as well. In fact, so good had he been at his job that he was promoted after only one year to mentor and then group level 1 leader. His job was to lead lesser wheelers around the circuit or outside in accordance with the GPS coordinates provided.

After three years, however, he was sick and tired of this work and had applied to Tendale. He would have preferred football, but knew it was extremely competitive and cutthroat, assuming he could even get in. And anyway, he was lucky to have been taken by the tennis camp and suspected his uncle had a hand in it. The work was certainly more physically and mentally challenging, requiring strategic problem-solving skills, allowing him to improve his concentration, balance and hand-eye coordination. The pay was better too. And he'd met Felicity.

Unfortunately, after eighteen months it was decided that he would never progress at Tendale – his supervisor told him he just didn't have the stamina and drive, both physically and mentally to succeed.

The result had been Hikedale, where the pay was higher, even if status was lower and the pace slow, where his physical health deteriorated by four points – enough to be sent back to wheeling.

He could forget any future for his relationship now, as it was unlikely that twenty-five-year-old Felicity, who was very ambitious and wanted to reproduce, would wait for him to work his way back up the ladder.

Perhaps he lacked ambition, but even if he didn't, he knew that the highest he could probably attain in any of the Dales was a level 5 group leader. Management and task allocation were almost exclusively in the hands of RSs, who could ensure non-discrimination and well managed work days.

What he really aspired to was the Landscapdale. There, at least, work seemed to have a purpose higher than mere physical health. There he would learn about the natural world, about plants, trees and shrubs. There he could use creative skills to imitate nature for pleasure. But he had a long way to go and would be lucky if he could even make it to Builddale, where the work was sufficiently varied for RSs to hand it to HSs, retaining supervisory functions of course, because HSs couldn't be fully trusted when it came to health and safety.

This was a world where physical health was the currency to success, reproduction, holiday and leisure. Where even leisure activities were controlled. And where any activities such as computer programming, plumbing, and especially truck driving were coveted. At least Jack hadn't lost his computer programming activity with the demotion, although … he wouldn't have minded a stint in plumbing, electricity or even camping skills and he couldn't wait for the holidays, which he would spend at the beekeeping centre.

As Jack waited for his smartbus, he contemplated whether life had been any better fifty years ago, when leisure was work and work was leisure.

Getting on

by

Stephanie Thornton

If I am retired, I suppose this means I must be 'getting on'? Just what does 'getting on' mean? It's weird! Do I get on with my angry next-door neighbour over the garden wall? Do I get on in this modern world? Do I get on the bus?

If so, is it a hippopotamus type of bus with little sticky out ears that looks a bit like me these days when I look in the mirror? And maybe has the name 'Mortuary' on the front. In my case, 'getting on' is supposed to mean 'in years'. But I think I'll change it to 'life' instead. So, I AM going to get on with it.

I intend to go kicking and screaming to the grave and enjoying every moment. If I feel I need a toy boy I will get one. I have already started to look at younger men and even ones with tattoos which I always thought not cool, as interesting. And my builder – twenty years younger than me – has an ear ring. And I find that interesting too. I'm also so much more risqué than I used to be. I flirt more and don't notice the flowers of death on my hands: my mother's name for those liver spots now decorating them.

In fact, I want to swing from the chandelier – and if I feel like it, run away to India to live in that Hotel*.

I should consider first that getting up to the chandelier will be easy but getting down from it, will not. And if 'Health and Safety' hear of what I intend to do, they will put barbed wire round the lights and a sign saying 'do not try this at home'.

It's the same with chairs. Those high seat things that catapult you into the air when you want to get up and the getting up from down when you have had to sit on the floor. If I turn to the Bible for solace, I find Ecclesiastes 3 doesn't fit the bill. It doesn't say 'a time to get on' and 'a time to get off'. Just lots of things about finding and losing which I do often now.

Perhaps I should have a tattoo as well. They say it's painful but at least I'll know I'm not dead. They liken it to childbirth and that was OK. I could go all out and have 'I love Jason Statham' carved in ink there. Trouble is, if they exhume my body in another 50 years, no one will have heard of Jason and have to look him up on the Hologram. I suppose I could have a nipple stud and have my hair dyed bright red with green and purple stripes. My husband seems to quite like this – on other women!

My children will then have me committed to some lunatic asylum then think they'll get to spend all my money without realising there isn't any left. They already have Power of Attorney, so all they will need is a friendly doctor who will declare I am loopy and that my getting on has truly made it so. Then, I can get one of those funeral plans and choose a velvet coffin in purple with silver handles just like Dracula.

I took my usual hair spray back to Tesco and told them it was making my hair turn grey. The Manager gave me a pitying look so I went home and looked at my hair again – I realise I should have gone to Spec Savers first?

One thing I can't do now is wear six-inch Sillitoe heels I used to wear when shopping. This has resulted in bunions and corns. It serves me right. Whoops - I've just put Sillitoe when I know I mean stiletto. Hey ho, so I'll wear carpet slippers and ask for a chair once I reach the checkout. I may even reminisce with the check-out girl. She won't understand a word I'm saying as all my experiences are too old for her. If I say I walk like Max Wall in tights, she'll look at me and think of other things: the night time date when she will go out with Jo and have sex with him or her, if Jo is a woman.

I do remember sex and write about it often. Those rainbow days when I walked in fields of gold. My American friend calls this 'getting it on' and I had to ask her for a translation. I also consider that if I do go ahead and get a toy boy, my limbs will probably not go in the same directions he should choose and I'll have to teach him new tricks instead. At the thought of this, I go giddy with excitement and have to sit down to catch my breath.

I can tell the checkout girl I like her three-inch nails. I don't, but at my age I can lie and won't be cast into the fiery pit. She has them sharpened into elongated points and they are painted a putrid shade of green which she uses to try to type the numbers of the bar code into the machine – and fails. I would like to tell her to get them cut but this would upset her Human Rights and we can't do that can we?

I'm not sure what we can do any more. But I'm hanging on trying to fit into this strange modern world. I can just about tiptoe in my carpet slippers to be in line with Political Correctness which seems to brainwash all the young. I'm forgetting I am getting on. Now I have time to cogitate, my brain can ruminate like a cow chewing cud and I ask myself impossible questions no one has the answers to. This includes 'who did give birth to Political Correctness and was it a difficult birth' – the sort when you want to give your children away afterwards. In these PC days, we are stuck with what we have created. But seeing as I am getting on and the promised fiery pit is waiting in any event, I often say what I think. It feels GOOD.

I will have tea and cakes with a friend. We'll try not to talk about our health. We'll also not mention the dreaded 'D' word. 'D' for diet. No, not 'D' for death or D-Day. If we forget we are trying not to, we may end up comparing notes in a sort of one-upmanship usually reserved for rounds of golf. I'll relate this to my husband and hope he can hear me with his new hearing aid. At least his eye sight spares him seeing my vivid hair style and I doubt he will spot my flowers of death. I have become a piece of furniture designed by Ikea – useful and functional. I decide to choose to be a sofa – comfortable and roomy with lots of curves and billows. The sort where cats like to sit and grandchildren come to endless text on mobiles.

They say there is a chance of getting burgled. The Police will ask me who it was, it may be some drug fuelled local, or it may even be a black man. I would describe him as a negro and they will say it's racist and give me a colour chart so I can choose a shade. Like choosing paint.

I know I'm not a racist but prefer to see the burkha in more exotic countries. I can never understand why a crowd of women will stand in front of The Tower of London all heavily veiled and take a picture. Do they go home and draw a cloud above themselves with an arrow saying 'this is me'? But no one wants to take a picture in Bradford do they, unless it's in Undercliffe cemetery.

Now I am over three score years and ten, I liken my body to a rental car. I have to return it to the rental company devoid of fuel, so for now, I'm running on the reserve tank until only fumes are left. I believe in being thrifty.

I'm now officially, a grumpy old woman. I shall design a new dance suitable for my age and call it 'The Grump'. It should get a million hits on YouTube and compete with that mouse that chases a cat. And I'll file this piece of craziness in my "Drop Box". That's a very appropriate name for someone getting on and I like its name. It is after all just a bit of purple prose – to match my hair. What fun!

Post Script: I did in fact get on with it. To such an extent that I did swing on the chandelier as I've never liked other people telling me what to do. Of course, I ended up dead and am pleased to report that I didn't go in the aforementioned fiery pit. It's super here. All you have to do is think hair colour and it changes in an instant into any colour you want – and a second later into another. No sitting around with those metal things on your head. The toy boys are great too and so is the food. We can eat as much as we like of things such as 'Angel Delight' and

'Ambrosia'. No one is bothered about what they look like any more, they're much too interested in what you did in your life on earth. No one's bothered about age or face lifts or celebrities or spending money or Hello Magazine. Just about having a good laugh at how silly we all have been.

So, send me a postcard when you can and I'll send you one back in the form of a little white feather.

*reference to The Best Exotic Marigold Hotel – 2011 film about a hotel for retirees.

Play On!

By

Sacha Quinn

'If music be the food of love, play on;
Give me excess of it, that surfeiting,
The appetite may sicken, and so die.
That strain again! – it had a dying fall:
O, it came o'er my ear like the sweet sound
That breathes upon a bank of violets,
Stealing and giving odour! - Enough; no more:'

Alan read the words one more time before picking up his pint of bitter and taking a long draft, then raised his eyes towards the ceiling. He noticed the party taking place upstairs on the mezzanine floor. According to the balloons and banners it was a sixtieth birthday. The resident DJ had swapped his usual noise, that passed as music, by the young crowd who usually occupied the space on Friday and Saturday nights. It had been tempered, to be more fitting, for the older audience being served tonight. It might have been his imagination but the volume had also been turned down too. He understood that, coming from that same generation. Loud music now meant you couldn't hear what the person next to you was saying.

Eyes now locked on the ceiling, Alan recalled the words he'd just read, pleased when he found himself reciting them to himself with little effort. Maybe his memory wasn't failing him yet. It was a different story for his eyes and ears. They seemed to be succumbing to an ever nearer old age, far too quickly now for his liking and certainly seemed more so since he'd retired. Or he mused did it only seem so. Had he spent the last few years at work kidding himself? Fooling others? A make-believe of just as sprightly, just as competent, just as flexible as today's work ethics seemed to demand. Then again maybe he had just slowed his pace in readiness for a more relaxed lifestyle.

He took another swig of beer on a sight that said he didn't have an answer.

God knows how he'd been talked into joining the cast of Twelfth Night. He was a spectator more than a performer these days and had never really taken to drama. And certainly not Shakespeare. When his long-time friend pleaded with him for a third time however, explaining the original Duke was still lying in a hospital bed, with a broken leg, which was just not healing, he finally agreed. He decided he was becoming a soft touch in his dotage.

He recited the words again, then gave some thought to those opening lines. They could mean so many things.

So many songs, so many lyrics that held meaning. Of course, in his youth he'd gravitated to the heavy rock school of music, with the likes of Deep Purple, Black Sabbath and Led Zepplin: who all had their own individual voice to speak for the youth of the day. Much to the disgust of his parents, he'd grown his hair, wearing it in the same straggly style as his musical heroes. He'd adopted their 1970's fashion too, strutting around in faded denim jeans, which sported fake patches, teaming them with sloganed tees. They were called Tee-shirts in those days though. Looking around at the youngsters crowding the bar he decided nothing much had changed, fashion wise at least. Still the faded jeans, only now they were ripped too, just to add a bit of a design feature and some kind of uniqueness.

Food of love, he mused. Yes, he recalled the lyrical love songs that he'd smooched to with many a girlfriend at the youth club discos. Leaving teenage years behind he'd frequented night clubs instead. The girls always seemed to like it when you could sing the latest chart hits to them. With no Googling in those days, he had to listen to them over and over again after recording them on to cassette tapes and write the words down longhand. Then he'd try to pick the tunes out on his guitar.

Inviting the girls to his bedroom to listen to him practice was, he supposed, another version of 'come up and see my etchings'. He was rarely disappointed. Looking back now, he mused as to whether those girls might have been just a tad disappointed, when they didn't quite capture his heart. But yes, music had been the food of love for him. Being in a local boy band probably had its pull too.

A surfeit of it? That the appetite may sicken and so die? Yes, any number of songs depicting unrequited love sprang to mind. Songs of futile love. Unavailable love. Desperate love. One particular record would play over and over in his mind. One that had been released all those years ago in his

104

teenage years, by the Bay City Rollers, if his memory served him right. The teen boy band with their tartan scarves round their wrists which the girls up and down the country mimicked. It wasn't his thing. Their brand of pop music had by-passed him until in his mid-thirties he finally fell head over heels in love with HER.

The One.

Only she, he thought, never even knew he existed. At least not on that level. And she never knew, or so he thought until the night of her leaving party. The one where they'd been the last to leave and they had locked eyes. In that moment he knew she felt the same. The irony of the record playing on the juke box singing,

'Bye bye baby, baby good bye, Bye bye baby don't make me cry'

Then HER changing the words from 'There's one girl in town I'd marry', to 'There's one guy in town I'd marry, marry you now if I was free.'

If only she had been free. But she wasn't.

He'd walked her out to the taxi and she had hugged him and kissed him that one and only time, then looking into his eyes whispered sincerely, "It's not our time. Another time another place who knows what might have been. What might, might be."

With a final wave, mouthing, "bye bye, baby," she was gone. Yes, he remembered that song all too well. A surfeit of it sickened that love appetite until it finally died and she was no more than a distant memory as the years rolled on by.

Of course, life didn't stop just because SHE wasn't available. Because it wasn't their time. He thought with tenderness of the beautiful woman he eventually married and had now been with him for so many years. She should be here now he thought helping me learn these lines.

Alan snapped out of his reverie to the strains of 'Bye bye baby' now fading from the music system.

The DJ's voice was now cutting in, "And that was dedicated to Alan with the message from the birthday girl to say, 'There's one guy in town I married, married when I became free, I wished it to be' Oh and she adds, 'I'll be down to help you learn your lines soon'. Whatever that means?"

'If music be the food of love play on. Give me surfeit of it!' Alan recited again. But he decided it had never really withered and died. It just hibernated until the time was indeed theirs.

Alan looked up at the mezzanine floor. SHE was looking down at him blowing him a kiss and he felt that familiar swell of his heart knowing that now she was sixty and had decided to retire, they could indulge in this retirement lark together. It was still their time! They would play on!

Retiring Down the Track

By

C. I. Ripples

He held the treasured little Bible that had shaped so much of his life, testament to the fact that in the layers of life God sometimes does reach out, close to his heart as he made his final descent from Shell Mex House. He wouldn't miss this place one little bit: his sad, lightless little office in the hull of the building; the petty politics, even if they did have lunchtime music in the canteen. Well, perhaps he would miss his walk to and from Waterloo station, on a beautiful sunny early summer day like today.

As Joe made his way along the Strand, he inhaled the particular smells of summer in London, perhaps for the last time paying extra attention to its familiar cacophony, scents which he'd never completely been able to place his finger, or rather his nose on. To him it smelt of salt, brine and oil, but also of flowers in a damp steaming basement, mixed with cigarettes and strong coffee.

He recalled, as he rounded the corner towards Waterloo Bridge, that when he'd first arrived here, they hadn't even really known what coffee was – or they had, but it was a sad thin, light brown liquid, a bit like the colour of the tea he used to drink in his home country. In contrast, the tea was strong, dark and bitter like espresso, with no more than a dash of milk. Before he'd moved here, he'd never even tasted tea with milk, what they called 'builder's brew' but he'd grown quite partial to it over the years. It was just one of many British peculiarities.

Arriving at Waterloo station he was hit by the smell of grease, rancid bodies and hot air. As usual the underpass smelt of, well frankly, piss. He hurried to the departure information board. Noting the first train, a slow one at that, would not leave for another twenty-five minutes, he called his wife from the payphone, then decided he might as well wait on the platform.

He seated himself on the slatted, hard railway bench, the big round-headed bolts studded to it digging into his bottom and back, causing him to shift around uncomfortably. It was testament to the fact that the Brits rarely liked to do things the easy way. Another idiosyncrasy of their stiff upper lip.

When he'd arrived with his family for his second stint in England that cold foggy January night, the country, which had admittedly fought and won a noble war, albeit with more than a little help from its special friend America and now arch enemy Russia, had only recently joined the Common Market. It had only just come out of a recession more than partly caused by crippling unions. Half the country had been on strike! He still remembered the coarse toilet paper, the regular power cuts at night, when they'd have to stumble around the house in candlelight, boiling the kettle on the Aga to fill their hot water bottles in the absence of central heating. To be honest, the country, even if it had created the welfare state, which he conceded was a marvel, had been a disaster, its people hunkering after the days of the Empire where Royal Britannia ruled the waves and world.

It had to be said though, that Britain had come a long way since then, veering away from Blue Nun, prawn cocktails and trifle as European culture and EEC funding firmly took hold.

"The train on platform 11 is the 10.53 to Portsmouth, stopping at, Wimbledon, New Malden, Surbiton, Esher, Hersham, Walton on Thames, Weybridge, West Byfleet, Woking ...", the announcer's voice jolted Joe out of his reverie.

For seven and a half years he'd heard this same voice announcing his destination, one of the main stops on the Portsmouth line. For seven and a half years he'd made this journey to and from the office, reading his book in the morning or chatting amiably about life and the weather, and if he could get a seat, dozing, or working if he wasn't too exhausted, on the way back.

He checked his watch. Already 11.25.

The constant delays of this nationalised service were par for the course: leaves on the track; slippery rain; the wrong kind of snow; even strong sunshine. But he'd learnt to be grateful for small mercies – at least the train had hauled itself into the station.

He found a seat in the non-smoking section of second class and slid open the window with a considerable effort. He then sat back in his chair, surveying the emptiness of the carriage bound for Portsmouth. Evidently, mostly everyone was at work and the daily influx of shoppers with their off-peak returns had only just arrived, disappearing into the bowels of London, down the stairs and escalators bound for Knightsbridge. It was strange that, as he rode out of twenty-five years of his life, everyone around him was going on as normal, as if nothing had changed.

But at least he'd had a good run, at the forefront of the energy industry, the forefront of computing. Who would have thought at the start of the century that everyone would be relying on gas and oil for heating, cars, or air travel? When he was a little boy, if he'd counted even five cars on the road as he walked to kindergarten, he'd considered it a good day.

The still mostly empty 5 carriage train suddenly jolted into activity. A welcome warm soft breeze now caressed his skin, as they bumbled past office blocks, council flats and terraced houses, passing the grey suburbs of Vauxhall, Clapham Junction and Earlsfield, all indistinguishable from each other with their Sainsbury's, Boots and M&S. Then they entered the wide-open space of the green belt, suddenly jerking to a halt just before Weybridge.

"Probably due to a points failure," the ticket collector, passing through the carriage, informed him.

"The tracks often expand during times of hot weather," he was enlightened.

The collector checked his season ticket and handed it back, continuing, "a rarity."

Joe had read somewhere that British Rail painted the tracks white at critical points so they absorbed less heat. He looked out of the window to see only black. Sighing, he put his season ticket back in his wallet and returned his thoughts to his career.

It had been thanks to the little leather-bound Bible he'd received from his wife, his then girlfriend, on his 23rd birthday, that his career took off at all. Eager to please, he'd read it from cover to cover, twice, and it accompanied him everywhere, almost like a talisman. It was the first thing he took out when he arrived at the office, and the last thing to be packed at five p.m.

He'd been tasked with solving a problem involving seismic magnetic tapes, which recorded the vibrations from seismic P-waves made by underground explosions to assess subsurface conditions captured by the receivers placed underground. Each magnetic tape had contained about two hundred records, each of about 120Kb, a huge problem as the computer's memory, being only 4Kb, meant it could only read the tape in sections. It then had to be stopped and partially played back to find the start of the program to read the next section. It had been laborious and timewasting, taking over an hour to read one tape, far too long, especially as thousands of tapes had to be analysed.

It was a problem Joe too had been stumped to solve.

Frustrated, he'd picked up his Bible, hoping the Word would give him insights and wisdom that might help. It had opened to Ecclesiastes and a passage about Gibeon, the one where the Lord appears to Solomon in a dream and tells him 'Ask

111

what I shall give thee?'. Of course! As Joe had read, he'd suddenly understood that there was no point in busting his balls 24/7 at the office, when he would receive all he needed between the sheets at night. He'd gone straight home and early to bed, where in his dream he was given the piece of code he needed for the computer to work ten times faster. All he needed to do was insert this tiny piece of two-byte code at the point between seismic tape sections, amend the program to detect these intervals and the tape would process continuously.

He'd awoken from his dream, jumped into his trousers and Peugeot and raced to the office. He'd thrown anyone working on the computer off it, took over all administrative rights and had by 7am that morning programmed the machine in accordance with his dream, getting it to process data in five minutes, at twelve times the speed, not ten. This too was no coincidence, he was convinced, as twelve was the number of faiths in Christianity. The physicist in him also thought it was a neat way to represent the fractionating of unity. Thus, it was symbolic of the creation of the universe or in this case the creation of North Sea oil, which would be up and running at least two years earlier than planned.

The train was gaining traction and chugging along faster and faster up and down the tracks, when it stopped in the middle of a sea. It was dark, but the water was lit, so he got out and walked to a large mainframe beckoning him ahead. When he got there, however, he was suddenly pulled under water into the pipes and flushed out into the HP of what he recognized as the Aberdeen office. He reached out for punch cards strangely floating in the air, but when he caught one, he saw it was really a tiny computer, no larger than his hand. As soon as he touched the dark screen of the miniscule device a line of code lit up. It wasn't anything he could decipher or recognise but he knew instinctively what it meant: that he might be exiled but he was not alone, that all he needed to do was unlock the code. He gripped the little computer tighter, and began frantically typing with his free hand. It almost slipped out of his palm when Bergsma loomed behind him, his long fingers lashing out, jeering, "and this is meant to produce an invoice?" ….

He awoke with a start by a snort, his own snort, jerking his head, which had fallen on his chest against the hot carriage window, back up. He wiped the saliva protruding from his mouth with his handkerchief, the sweat from his brow with his cuff, felt it down his back, dripping into his belt. What a nightmare. He wondered what it could mean. Bergsma of all people! It probably meant nothing at all.

They were still stationary and without the breeze of motion the carriage was close and sticky. God it was hot. He checked his watch. It'd been 47 minutes exactly now. He was thirsty. His wife would be waiting, although she should be used to the unpredictability of British Rail. At least she wouldn't have to do the twice daily run to the station anymore, even if his overpriced one-thousand-pound season ticket was still valid until the end of the year. Another benefit Shell had afforded him when he started on the

North Sea Oil project, but one he would now rarely use.

That project had been the end of Seismic for him and his new job had been to set up a pipeline administration system and write a computer program that worked out how much oil belonged to each of the various companies linked up to the joint pipeline to the Sullom Voe terminal in Shetland.

He'd had a team of four and a nice office overlooking the Thames. He reported both to the Head of Production and the Shell Board. This was with respect to his relationships with other oil and gas companies, who tried to reduce the interference of the left-wing British government, which saw North Sea Oil as the country's last good chance, perhaps her only chance to save herself from economic and social upheaval. He'd spent so much time liaising and preparing documents for discussion and approval of the project he'd codenamed 'Genesis' at the monthly meetings, which went on and on, that in the end he never completed it. But he'd learnt a lot about licensing and contracts and he'd certainly enjoyed the work.

That is, until Shell Venezuela bled out, sending more than a hundred employees, overpaid and underqualified, in his opinion, to his department in London. That had been after Perez had announced his 'La Gran Venezuela' plan, which called for the nationalization of oil in the country. One of these, that pale bastard Friesian Bergsma, had been placed over his head as his boss.

When they'd first been introduced, Bergsma, who reminded him more than a little of a taller Aryan version of Himmler, with his round little glasses, albeit significantly less talented, had seemed to be a religious man, a good Christian. 'Seemed' being the operative word, as he soon proved to be uncharitable, envious, lazy and mean.

Joe had no time for him and the feeling was mutual, especially after he'd put in a complaint about the new apathy in the department, illustrating it all by drawing a little man, his elbows on his desk, hands under his chin, eyes closed, softly snoring as reams of paper floated into his in-tray. A copy of it had fallen into Bergsma's hands, who with silent red-faced fury had scrunched it up and tossed it into the bin, before stomping off, a murderous look in his eyes.

It had all come to a head when Joe discovered the newly released HP desktop 9835 in the department on the floor below. It stored data on floppy disks instead of tapes, was able to do operations much more quickly and was easier to program. In three weeks, Joe had been able to write programs which on the main frames would have taken up to six-man years! He'd demonstrated its capabilities to Aberdeen who'd hired in an HP especially for the occasion, using the British Gas invoicing system to illustrate the speed with which invoices could be delivered in accordance with gas and oil delivery regulations. Aberdeen had been wild about it, seen the program's potential instantly and wanted to put in an order to buy the machines straightaway.

Bergsma had called him into his office after his return the very next day, demanding angrily.

"What on earth do you think you're doing! Do you want us all to lose our jobs?"

"Well …," Joe had begun, standing a little more upright for what he realised would be another predictable onslaught.

"It's a ridiculous idea," the loathsome man interrupted, "that the whole of our production administrative programs could be made to run on such a tiny machine! And in three weeks!"

"But we're already using the machine in other departments. Just have a look next door …," Joe had countered.

Bergsma had slammed the desk with his fist, and venomously raised his voice, "you're nothing but a con-man!" He was almost hyperventilation by now.

"Of course," Joe had responded calmly, "I made sure that Finance in Aberdeen checked it all and approved the new way forward."

"There will be no new way," Bergsma, whom he was sure was close to a heart attack, had roared. "You're to leave it alone. I don't want to see you operating an HP machine, anywhere for anything, at any time. Do you understand?"

Joe had understood well enough and was livid with Bergsma who, lacking any talent, was thwarting his efforts for progress merely so that he could continue to justify his six-figure salary.

He could have drowned his dissatisfaction in a few extra glasses of Harvey's Amontillados before his dinner or Shiraz with it, even a tipple of Johnny Walker after. He drank all these, of course, had always done so, but as was his norm in times of stress he'd turned to the little Bible in search for answers. He'd suddenly realised, that Abraham, Isaac and Jacob had had a much simpler, more relaxed way to follow God, without the constrictions of prayers or commandments. They just chatted to Him instead. Joe decided to try this the very same evening during his walk on the golf course with his retrievers. Perhaps that would provide a solution.

As he'd looked up at the thousands of stars that lit the city of God, he'd asked out loud, feeling a trifle silly:

"Are you there?"

"Certainly," had come the surprisingly instantaneous reply, "what can I do for you?"

"Nothing special really," he'd responded, "I just felt like a chat."

"Great idea," he'd felt God's easy smile upon him," I just wish more people would do so. Most of you just kneel and pray and beg for favours. Why can't we just be friends?"

Joe had looked up at the bright vastness of the universe and nodded fervently.

"I only have one proviso", his new Friend had continued, "as my friend you're not to ask for anything. And as your friend I'll make sure you get everything you need."

A few weeks after this talk, he'd been called to Bergsma's office, where he and two of his cronies from Venezuela had been waiting, and told him to resign. He'd naturally refused,

"You might not like me and my methods, but Aberdeen appreciates and requires my skills, even if this department is mostly redundant."

117

The trio had shifted uncomfortably, Bergsma glaring at him until he'd suddenly lunged,

"In that case, you're fired!"

Joe had burst out laughing:

"Try it. You'll soon find out you have absolutely no justification for that."

And off they'd gone to human resources, who, even if they didn't know about Joe's special Friend, must have told them that he had other influential colleagues higher up from the days he'd worked with the 1401 mainframe. Told Bergsma he'd need to change his stance if he truly wanted to rid himself of Joe.

So here he was, a few months later, chugging into retirement at the age of fifty-two, to be paid 75% of his final salary every month, plus a golden handshake equivalent to a full year's salary for 25 years of service, tax free. His wife might laugh at the idea of his big Friend, but as had always been the case, He had made sure he was alright. It might be ironic that he, who'd always told others advances in technology would not make them redundant, was the one to lose his job because of it, but they would have a life without financial worries for the rest of his life. He fully intended to make it to at least 88 and with advances in medicine and technology, he might even stretch it out to 99, 110 or even 120 like Job in the Bible, all of it funded by Shell.

The train finally pulled into Woking and Joe gathered his jacket and bag.

With a hop and a skip, he landed on the platform, emerging in to the bright sunlight and looked around for his wife. It really was one of the worst places to live, useful only for having good train links to London. A cheerless place with a surfeit of concrete and red brick structures around the centre, a Sainsbury's and the multi-storey car park.

As he started towards his beautiful wife, waving to him from her MGB convertible, he happily considered that his retirement would finally allow them to move.

"Joe," she began as she opened the passenger door for him, "there was a call from a company called Redwood, asking if you're interested in project somewhere in Australia."

The Wasp

by

Stephanie Thornton

Waspish didn't begin to sum him up. Maurice Mercure had long honed his style as a critic of fine art both verbally, visually and in prose. He didn't spare the punches. Some thought him a great wit, others, a great pain in the proverbial.

First of all, he looked extraordinary. Marcel waves crimped one side of his hair and flowed down to his collar. On the other side, his head was shaved and a painting by Picasso from his 'blue period' was tattooed on his skull. A curl styled with gel decorated his forehead.

He liked to wear a waist-length cape of velvet draped across one shoulder. Tight black trousers with a stripe of vivid emerald green and a matching emerald shirt completed trying to be Oscar Wilde. And his famous face appeared on the tee-shirts of the masses.

Of course, all this effort was a complete contradiction in terms, as he told everyone that he wished to be anonymous. His rule was, not to make a fuss and 'do not observe my visit'. Gallery owners had become quite used to his eccentricities and warned their visitors in advance. But getting him to attend any Vernissage was a total make or break affair if a gallery or artist were to be successful.

The fact that he would arrive an hour after everyone else, pause dramatically in the doorway, usually under a bright spotlight, hand on hip, striking a pose, a long cigarette holder and fake cigarette adorning it, only added to his visibility. He would thus stand and wait for long minutes allowing those within to notice him and whip themselves up in a frenzy of excitement before he entered the room.

Of course, it followed as the night followed the day – his write-up produced pithy words of approbation or rejection. He could bitch and snarl and conjure up such brutish comments, that people cowered in his presence, wondering if they would be singled out and ruined. His pen could have the bitterness of snake venom, create an allergic reaction to his wasp sting or could be as angelic as a feather.

That evening, he perused the pile of invitations that stood to one side of his desk. They were in date order all begging he would come. He sighed. Why did the top one have to be tonight, when he had so looked forward to an early night and a glass of well chilled Chablis? He already felt annoyed and bored at that. He stifled a yawn. Maybe he was losing his edge. Maybe he should take a holiday in the sun? Or maybe the time had come for him finally to retire. Should he?

The opening was at a brand-new gallery called 'Rennards' in Bruton street. They were showing the latest works of Damien Hirst and it promised to be a rave. A rave to everyone but Maurice. He yawned again. He was gradually becoming immune to vast canvases covered in myriads of spots, which everyone would describe as totally important and pretend to understand. They all looked so alike and he had to write something different each and every time. He thought the doting public worthy of the crowd in the story of "The Emperor's New Clothes' when no one dare say what they really thought. He decided that tonight he would be very spiteful. He would denounce the latest works even though he had yet to see what they had on offer.

He noticed he was even more waspish as of late. He was sick of people choosing paintings for their value. Those that chose them as they matched their latest colour scheme and those who bragged about understanding art in order to impress.

His latest foray, to view the new collection at 'Tate Modern', was a critique of an artwork called 'Richard's Jumper'. It had an interesting history. Richard, a double-glazer had taken off his sweater, smeared in putty. It had been seized by Richard's client who was a dealer 'in the know'. He described it as superb and entered it in 'Tate Modern' where it went on to win first prize. The year before, it had been even worse, when 'Robert's Foot' – a sculpture of a poor man's leg, who suffered cellulitis and suppurating sores, went on to win. Now he had to go to 'Rennards' and think of something witty and thought provoking at the viewing.

He arrived an hour late. The gallery was not an easy one to find. Bruton Street was changing. The Arabs and Chinese were making inroads into London and several of the galleries were under new ownership. Some were boarded over waiting for the re-design of front windows and a new, trendy name above the door. He felt a twinge of irritation, already in full waspish mode. 'Rennards' he noted was not yet finished. Bright lights within, but the front had still to be completed. He paused in the doorway noting the modest crowd start to gesture to each other as they spotted him. The volume turned from soft murmurings to that of fever pitch.

He waited for the customary catalogue until new owner Bertrand Miller came over to him apologising that the printers had failed to deliver them. He had complained to his solicitors and expected money back.

"Do come and see dear Damien's work," he said, gesturing for Maurice to come inside.

"Damien won't be with us this evening," he explained, "the poor man has gone down with a dose of food poisoning this very afternoon." The solicitors had been told of this as well.

Lucky solicitors, thought Maurice, underneath his breath. He had a sudden desire to leave.

"Just let me observe. I will look at what I want and then leave quietly without fuss," he told Bertrand, waving away the offered glass of champagne. He was already bored, but at least would do a customary walk around the hangings.

The Wasp minced towards a painting, hung on a wall of palest green, before coming to a sudden jerky halt, almost losing his step. He took a sharp intake of breath and two steps backwards.

What was this? What was this new and vibrant thing before his eyes? There before him was a landscape of such vivid intensity, it took his breath away. Instead of the usual calculated paint spots all across the canvas, accompanied by some posturing description, was a field of corn with poppies under an azure sky. The colours swirled in cloudy masses, and seemed to vibrate, lifting themselves off the surface of the canvas. It was a style totally new in execution causing deep sensations in his brain.

At last! It had happened. It was so different. My God, Damien had decided to deviate from the norm and develop this wonderful alternative. For the first time in several decades, Maurice felt exhilarated when looking at the painting. Perhaps Damien had had a Damascene moment and decided to paint something that had real meaning. He felt a frisson of excitement. He walked towards the next, his brow furrowed in intensity.

The next painting was even more glorious, a child and its mother, walking on a road in summer heat. He could almost feel the heat bouncing off the canvas and it was making his forehead sweat. The colours rippled and shone from the surface of the paint like some glorious communion with God.

After that, a sea scape, with a roaring surf, which made him feel a sudden storm and wind whirling round his ears. He could almost feel the spray upon his face. The other paintings too were sheer brilliance. He wandered round, writing the critique for next morning's papers in the mental filing cabinet within his brain. Behind him stood the crowd watching him observe and wondering. The atmosphere was charged in breathless anticipation.

He drifted to the door feeling almost drunk with pleasure and entered the cool night air, the swirling colours still vibrating in his soul. He stood with his back against the gallery wall in the darkness suffering from shock. He felt as if he'd been hit between the eyes and afterwards, only had a dim recollection of entering a taxi and the journey home.

Once back in his penthouse at the wharf, for the first time in decades, writing his critique flowed from him. There were no pauses, no examining his senses for some actual sense of the usual nonsense. This time it was sheer pleasure. No need for The Wasp to snarl and snipe. The write up was full of sentiments once thought lost to him, now returned.

Soon after the paper was out, the phone started ringing as he ate breakfast in a total mellow mood. He was being congratulated on his write up and people wanted to know his opinion of the value of the paintings. Were they a good investment?

Mid-morning, there was a strange call from the 'Rennard Gallery'.

"This is Director Sir James Forsyth," said a plummy voice.

"Ah yes, I spoke with Bertrand last night and I hope Damien is much better now?" replied Maurice.

"There must be some mistake," said Sir James, "the opening for Damien is next week."

"Impossible, I saw it last night and it was marvellous," replied Maurice.

"You can't have been last night as we weren't open and the re designed front facia for the gallery isn't even erected yet."

"But I saw the new work Damien had done and thought it just superb. No doubt you read my column in the paper where I described what I had seen and the address so everyone would come?"

"Perhaps we'd better meet in Bruton Street and you can show me what you mean," suggested James.

Maurice checked the pocket in his cloak. Yes indeed, he had confused the date. He must have placed it incorrectly on the pile. He mused perhaps that fate had been at work.

Bruton Street was bustling with life that Saturday morning. Crowds of people were gathering at the front of a window halfway along. The street was also full of builders working on various other galleries and making lots of noise.

"This is it," Maurice exclaimed, pausing where the crowd was gathered.

"That's not 'Rennards'," exclaimed James, "that's two more shop fronts further down and covered up with brown paper waiting for its new frontage to arrive.'

They went inside the unmarked gallery, where Maurice spotted Bertrand amongst a crowd of enthusiastic people. Bertrand forgot to observe the rules ignoring Maurice.

"Ah, Monsieur Mercure!" he exclaimed, rushing over to shake his hand. "Just look what you have done. Damien is just thrilled."

"Damien – Damien who?" asked James.

"Damien Parker. Our gallery is called 'Unknowns' and specialises in neglected, overlooked and starving artists, funded by a charity. We can't tell you how important your write up has been to our opening and the location of our gallery. And of course, to Damien. It has made him as an artist and we have now sold all his paintings."

"But he's not Hirst – I've never heard of him and this will interfere with our opening at 'Rennards' at the end of next week. It could ruin the paintings Hirst is so famous for," came James's furious reply, "and why did everyone come thinking it was 'Rennards' and that it was the work of Damien Hirst?"

Maurice didn't wait to see what next transpired. He would write a follow up in the paper explaining all. He slid backwards through the pulsing crowd.

There was a flow of energy and love of art singing in his pulses. It was his own Damascene moment.

He felt he had been reborn. The way forward was now clear. He would celebrate all the new and wonderful. He had been liberated and could write true and worthy words. And refuse to pander to the idiots of art. He would retire and then he could do just whatever came to mind.

He pondered: Maybe he would write a book called, 'The Wasp becomes a Honeybee' – would that work? And with it, he would change his hair and style of clothes which now seemed to him as ridiculous as so-called modern art.

Travel

Wherever you go, go with all your heart
- Confucius

Not all those who wander are lost.
- J.R.R. Tolkien, The Fellowship of the Ring

The world is a book, and those who don't travel
only read one page.
- St. Augustine

Traveling – it leaves you speechless,
then turns you into a storyteller.
- Ibn Battuta

Perhaps travel cannot prevent bigotry, but by
demonstrating that all peoples cry, laugh, eat, worry,
and die, it can introduce the idea that if we try and
understand each other, we may even become friends.
- Maya Angelou

The Journey for New Life

By

C. I. Ripples

The little plane nose-dived into the clouds, plunging towards the ground at an angle so steep Maske felt her stomach lurch. Her throat tightened and she squeezed Nico's hand even harder, inwardly muttering another little prayer.

He patted her hand reassuringly, the engineer in him marvelling at the plane's technology, this phenomenon of physics, the way it defied the gravity of the planet, staying aloft with air and kerosene.

Of course, Maske too was by now used to all sorts of travel, in all forms of transport.

Her first flight had been with KLM, first class, which flew them smoothly from Amsterdam to Lisbon, from there to Venezuela, with a short stop in Ponte Delgada, then on to Curacao, where they spent a few very pleasurable nights, before transferring to an Avianca flight destined for Barrancabermeja, via Barranquilla. Avianca hadn't been as luxurious, but as long as the plane stayed up in the sky, the weather was clear, the flight without bumps, she loved it.

Even during the last years in Colombia, where a lack of road and rail infrastructure meant flying was the most rational form of transport, she'd taken many a small plane, to Bogota, Cartagena, Bucaramanga and Barranquilla for sight-seeing and shopping, but more recently in her search for a child.

Never however had she experienced a journey quite as arduous as this, not only in terms of what she considered several near-death experiences, but also her anxiousness whether they would even make it to their destination within the deadline. A deadline, which if met, would result in the culmination of a journey begun that summer of 1957, when Maske learnt they were unlikely to ever have children, at least of their own.

Was it only two days ago that Nico received a telegram from the convent in Medellin? Only two days since he jumped into the jeep, drove home from the oilfield and raced into the garden where she was writing letters, listening to the short-wave radio, watching the parrot taunt their monkey, Pedro? Only two days since he told her that a little girl had been born, that they'd been chosen to be her parents? That they had four days to collect her? Two days since he lifted her out of her chair and swung her around in his enthusiasm? It seemed a lifetime.

They immediately sent a telegram confirming the collection and booked flights and train tickets.

It wouldn't be an easy journey, there being no direct flights to Medellin from Casabe for the next four days. They would have to charter a private plane and fly to Puerto Berrio, about 150km further south on the Rio Magdalena, which traversed much of the length of western Colombia, where they would board the train to Medellin.

She feared it would be touch and go whether they would arrive in time.

The next morning, one of Nico's colleagues took them to the harbour in Casabe, to catch the Shell Ferry to Barrancabermeja on the other side of the Rio Magdalena, from where they took a taxi straight to the airport. It was early afternoon when their small Cessna T-50 took off for Puerto Berrio and landed in the jungle on a slippery landing zone pitted with potholes, east of the Magdalena. It took less than fifteen minutes for the pilot to unload the plane and by the time Maske and Nico found someone to tell them how to get to their train on the other side, where there was civilization, he was off again.

They discovered that the only way to cross was by boat on the bend of the river, where the current flowed a little slower. Maske, used to Shell ferries or sometimes motorized speed boats, was horrified to learn that what they called a 'boat' was really a type of canoe in the form of a hollow tree trunk, or as Nico told her 'a dugout'. He assured her that dugouts had been used to cross rivers since the earliest of times, but her fears did not abate when, after their luggage had been thrown on and they'd stepped into the long and narrow tree, she barefoot holding her heels, the dugout proving very unstable, swaying from side to side. She struggled to keep her balance. They were instructed to sit on a plank in the middle, which Nico told her would reduce the 'tippiness', but as they plonked themselves down, she was sure they would sink as the water slopped in over the sides. From the corner of her eye she saw what she thought was a huge grey crocodile enter the water, which only heightened her terrors.

"It's probably a green iguana," the seasoned old boatman calmed them, as they set off and he laterally ferried his craft across the current in the wildly gyrating vessel, the water only a few centimetres from the edge.

She felt huge relief when they reached the opposite bank, and even happier when they secured their tickets for the train to Medellin the next morning.

"Tomorrow's journey will take at least ten hours, so we may as well make ourselves comfortable whilst we're here. We should get there with plenty of time to spare. Plenty of time for unforeseen events."

They checked into the nearby hotel Magdalena, which they learned had emerged as a necessity from the construction of the Antioquia railroad in the 1870s. Maske considered the hotel, which had 48 rooms for travellers just as they, all waiting for their train, charming with its wooden ochre and cream yellow walls, zinc roof, and earthen floor. It resembled a stable rather than a hotel, but to her it was an oasis.

"Did you know," Maske told Nico as they explored and ended up by the hotel's deep filter-less pool, "that the chambermaid told me that Olaya Herrera launched his candidacy for the presidency from here in 1930?"

That balmy night, as they enjoyed a drink in the internal courtyard, the stars seemed to shine down on them expectant, perhaps knowing, of the happiness they would soon collect.

Very early the next morning, exhausted from a sleepless night disturbed by the constant crashing of locomotives and trains being moved around, after consuming their Calentado and Chocolate Caliente (*1), they were about to settle the bill, when the duty manager on the desk, on hearing of their onward journey, told them:

"You do know there's a plane that takes off this very morning directly for Medellin. Wouldn't that be much faster and more convenient for you?"

And so, it was, back across the river in the same old log, with the same old boatman.

This time however Maske felt much more confident and even delighted in the crossing, pointing out to Nico the many different catfish in the water, a river stingray, which she knew was unique to the Magdalena. She even spotted a Cauca Molly.

They arrived on the other side at the same time as a Magdalena river turtle slid out of the water, perhaps scattering a flock of Magdalena tinamou, but making little impact on the speckled brownish caimon, lying immobile on the shore, partly submerged in the water.

They were once more guided towards the runway, which had the day prior served as a landing strip, by two young boys, who carried their bags along the jungle track lined with tall Monkey Pot trees laden with river nuts, passing small plots of manioc, corn and plátano.

There they joined three other passengers, who stood with not only suitcases but also boxes of farm produce, waiting for the plane to arrive, accompanied

135

by howlers and other small monkeys swinging in the trees.

The sun had already risen high in the sky, when crowds of children gathered out of nowhere just as the plane touched down. The gruff ex Luftwaffe pilot wanted to know the weight of the luggage. Their two young guides merely shrugged their shoulders.

"Okay," he sighed. "Get in. And you," he pointed at Maske, "can sit next to me."

Nico was forced to sit behind her on a bunch of bananas, next to a woman holding a large pungent fish. The others sat in the back.

The slippery landing strip was very narrow with high grass on both sides which, as it rushed by, the pilot swearing at the children running beside them, whilst they took off on their leap of faith, only just missed the wings. They were about to rise when the pilot suddenly aborted take-off, breaking forcefully, sending them all reeling forwards.

"We won't make it," he barked, followed by a number of expletives, as he turned the plane around, "we'll give it another go."

Maske wishing she could be like the birds who soared freely among the treetops and clouds, resurrected long neglected prayers and reached behind her for Nico's hand.

Then, with full force racing down the three-kilometre strip, the pilot, once it had come to the end, continued on, pulling up the lever to lift off just as it seemed they would fall into the river. The passengers held their breath as the plane pulled up barely high enough to avoid clipping the trees, that rose in front of them, preventing them vanishing into the dense impenetrable jungle below, being swallowed up by its vegetation.

The pilot grinned at Maske. "It's sure as hell dangerous. The slightest problem and this little baby will just fall out of the sky."

Just then a sudden air pocket jolted the machine almost as if in agreement, reminding them that they were soaring above the jungle in what was essentially only a piece of metal with wings and an engine.

Thankfully, after that it was relatively smooth, the plane rising and falling with the still spaces in the air. Maske relaxed a little and almost began to enjoy the flight as she watched the plane's shadow skip over whole sections of the deep green jungles of Antioquia towards their sole focus of arrival, jungles laced with brown rivers that stretched for miles interspersed with an occasional village.

Until now, as it plunged down over the mountains into Medellin of course.

When the plane emerged from the clouds, the city and its surrounding squatter neighbourhoods, nestled into the Andes mountains, stretched out in a seemingly orderly fashion underneath them, revealing grids of houses and roads, smoke rising from chimneys, cars moving in specks from the sky. They were still too high of course to see any detail. But she knew it was a beautiful and pleasant European style city, with lush green vegetation, native fruit trees and an amazing variety of flowers, especially orchids, not to forget the exotic birds and colourful butterflies. It wasn't for nothing that the city with its temperate climate was known as 'la tacita de plata' (*2). She continued to be amazed that she could see no people from the sky, that it was as if humanity did not exist down there, although she knew that in this city the population continued to grow exponentially, having increased six-fold already within the last fifty years.

The pilot next to her whistled a happy tune. Maske admired him for his nerve in holding the stick up and steady, as the ground below them now rushed up at speed, pulling the plane up only moments before the landing strip came into view and they landed at the recently expanded Olaya Herrera airport in the south-west of the city, slewing as it touched down, coming finally to a skidded stop.

She let out her breath and squeezed Nico's hand, her heart beating more normally now that they were finally safe on solid ground, excited that their journey to pick up this new life was almost over.

Still a little shaken, they left the airport and hastened to find a taxi. She breathed the air deeply, swinging on Nico's arm in her exhilaration. The weather was almost perfect, not too warm, nor too cold.

When they asked for Calle 62, then the Hermanas Dominicas de la Presentacion convent by name, the taxi driver seemed to have no idea where it was. Nico was becoming increasingly frustrated with the man, but also with her, because she couldn't remember the directions, only regaining his composure when a friendly policeman came to the rescue and offered to show them the way.

People in Medellin were so welcoming and helpful she marvelled again.

They hurtled through the streets, clean but full of potholes, the policeman hanging onto the sides, weaving their way towards their destination.

Despite the contrast between the have nots and those of rank who had grown wealthy through gold and coffee, all layers of society seemed to mingle, everyone working for the common good.

"I've heard, however," Nico disturbed her thoughts, "that despite appearances, the city is rife with prostitution, alcoholism and high levels of crime, which the Catholic Church struggles to fight with its antioqueño ethos." (*3)

She knew why he mentioned this, concerned that the child they were collecting might come from one of the squatter settlements on the city's steep sloops, where there was no water, education, roads or healthcare. They had no idea as to the baby's genetic, medical or social history. Maske didn't care. What was most important to her was that the child was healthy and without disabilities. She was already full of love, having loved the mere hope of her magical existence.

Just by the Cerro Nutibara, they crossed the Rio Medillin, flowing quite violently, to the other side of the city via the old and very narrow Puente de Guayaquil. They passed the Palaccio de La Cultura Rafael Uribe and then the Cathedral Basilica Metropolitana. Maske recognized it now – they were nearly there. She was almost nauseous with nerves and excitement.

They were invited to take a seat on the hard, wooden chairs that stood against the wall in the dark corridor, whilst a novice of starched habit and dark grey veil went softly to get the Mother Superior. Maske could not possibly sit still, instead focusing her attention on the painting that hung over the chairs. It was of the sacred heart of Jesus, pointing with his finger to the bleeding heart nestled in his open breast, lit up by little drops of bright red blood. It gave her hope, the conviction that their undertaking was indeed a blessing, that the new child would bring peace to her and her family.

She turned to the sound of Mother Superior coming towards her, the filtered light that came in through the stained-glass windows lighting up the folds of her habit and the Christ crucified heavily around her neck.

The plain, smooth faced nun took Maske's hand and looked deeply into her eyes, smiled, patted the back of her hands before letting go, and turning to the novice, gave instructions to get the newly born.

As they waited, Mother explained that the little girl had been born to an unmarried seventeen-year old from an influential wealthy German Jewish family that had lived in the city since the 1650s.

"Nevertheless," she explained, "we cannot guarantee that she's completely of Spanish extraction, despite her pale skin, as over the centuries there has been considerable dilution with the local Indian mountain tribes. And we do not, of course, know who her father is."

"The girl is happy for the sake of her daughter," the Mother Superior continued. "She will soon be leaving for the United States to study and no questions will be asked. Our only condition for the adoption is that you must promise to give the child a Catholic upbringing."

"Of course," Nico consented. In his opinion raising the child with Christian values would more than fulfil that demand.

Maske held her breath as an infant, asleep in a long white baptismal gown was brought in. The young nun touched the newborn's hair lightly by way of introduction and gestured for Maske to sit, before placing the baby in her arms.

The infant, almost as if sensing the momentousness of the occasion, yawned, opened her dark chocolate eyes gleaming with new life, and looked up at Maske, who, as she gazed back, felt her love rise within her like a flood, a love so strong, she knew instantly that this little girl was meant to be hers.

Nico, looking upon the scene, relaxed when he saw the pale skin, allaying his main concern of how a brown baby would fit into their white family. She was perfect.

"If it weren't for her dark eyes, nobody would know she isn't biologically yours," he told her.

"If you're certain you want the child," the Mother Superior intervened, instructing the novice to lift the baby out of her arms again, "you may pick her up tomorrow afternoon." Maske sighed and reluctantly surrendered her daughter for one more night. She could not believe they were already being released into the city again. It had been less than an hour.

Nico hailed a taxi to take them to Calle 52 to buy a bassinet and book flights back to Barancabermeja and then booked them into the Europa Hotel, which was not too far from the convent and famous for its design by Belgian architect Augustin Govaerts for the night.

The next morning, they went back to the convent to collect their daughter, leaving a generous donation before making their way to the airport. Maske could not stop staring at their sleeping infant during the ride to Olaya Herrera and as they waited for their commercial flight, drinking her in with her eyes. This time they would fly directly to Barancabermeja at noon and would be home by early afternoon.

They had just boarded the Dakota DC-3 and settled their little girl, marvelling once more at the perfection of what would be their first and only child, when they were told the flight would be delayed due to low visibility at their destination and asked to leave the plane for the waiting room, until further notice. We may be able to fly, thought Maske impatiently, as she leant over and kissed her daughter's flushed cheeks, but it seems we have not conquered the air.

They finally left several hours later, a smooth flight with only one patch of bad turbulence, which caused the plane to drop an alarming one hundred metres, and were about to land at their destination an hour later, when they learnt the fog had after all not cleared. The pilot, flying blind, made several attempts, one more terrifying than the last.

"At least we have seatbelts and oxygen masks," Nico calmed her, although she noted he himself was almost chain smoking, as they circled low above Barancabermeja to have another go.

Maske's main fear was a mid-air collision or that they would undershoot the landing strip and land in the Rio Magdalena – she could see nothing out of the window.

She thanked the Lord when the plane finally touched down in thick fog and torrential rain, its wheelbarrow wheels bouncing and one set of wings rising worryingly as the other dipped. Maske, looking out, saw there was lots of commotion with cars driving on both sides of the runway with lights on to guide the plane, ambulances at the ready. Her daughter had slept through it all.

They weren't home yet. It was pouring with rain and they still had to cross the gushing Rio Magdalena to get to Casabe, this time in a chartered open speedboat.

Thank goodness Nico had had the foresight to take the tarp with him from his military days. He carefully placed it over the infant to shield her before getting out of the taxi that delivered them to the harbour. They'd had her less than a day, but already they would do anything to protect her, disregarding their own discomfort as the rain lashed at them. It seemed to Maske that danger lurked everywhere, that they'd experienced nothing but, since they left two days ago. She could hardly see across the water, only just making out the outline of the riverbank. At least the wind had died down and the skipper, she noted, did navigate more slowly than usual through the choppy waters. Still, she considered it absurdly fast for these conditions.

"What if another boat comes at us out of the fog? He won't be able to stop in time!" she voiced her concerns to Nico.

"The guy knows these waters inside down and crosses them day and night, whatever the weather."

They arrived soaked but safe on the other side, where a car was waiting to take them home.

The next morning, they informed human resources that they now had a baby, then went to the police, stationed near the oilfield, to register the birth as instructed, giving the name of the hospital where she was delivered. The policeman was astonished.

"Madam, it's a miracle. I only danced with you a few weeks ago and would never have known!"

It was indeed a miracle, agreed Maske as she looked down at their daughter. She was a miracle of life, maybe not flesh of their flesh, or blood of their blood, but she was miraculously theirs.

Author's Notes:
*1 Calentado is a Colombian breakfast of scrambled eggs with tomatoes and onions, served with cork cakes, an egg and a sausage. Chocolate Caliente is hot chocolate milk.
* 2 'la tacita de plata' = 'the little silver cup'
* 3 Antioqueño ethos = work ethics

Sekhmet's Nose

By

Renata Kelly

Maybe travelling around the world, especially by balloon and in eighty days, might provide enough time for learned insights and varied adventures, but in our case such luxury was not an option. Our journeys, as that of many others, were predicated by the mundane need to earn a living and enhance our careers, and by the excitement to see whether the grass was really greener on the other side of the fence. Of course, we didn't have to leave a comfortable life on the Californian coast, but we were young and curious and the opportunities for travel and adventure that a posting to the Middle East, in our particular case, would provide became irresistible. So, we plus our two little daughters, became nomads, and though we did not know it at the time that our travels began, we were to remain untethered to country and continent for more years than we wished to count.

The beginning of our journey, which allowed us over many years to indeed circumnavigate the globe, began in Saudi Arabia. Having grown up in California, where buildings a hundred years old were considered worthy of preservation, my fascination with antiques and antiquities was perhaps understandable. Of course, the Desert Kingdom of Saudi Arabia was itself a fairly new invention, but it encompassed a desert where petrified "forests" and fossilized shells and corals, millions of years old, could easily be found on a casual outing for a desert picnic.

The old souq, or market, which still existed in Riyadh near the fortress in the 1970's, was filled with coarsely carved, painted doors and shutters from the traditional adobe houses that had been pulled down to make room for the ugly four-storey blocks that lined the new roads. Studded, carved chests from Kuwait and carpets from Iran and Afghanistan, sold in transit by the pilgrims that crossed Saudi Arabia on their way to Mecca for the annual Hajj pilgrimage, could be found in the market's dusty, small shops, together with brass and copper coffee posts, incense burners and roughly made Bedouin jewellery. For us and for our expatriate friends exploring the souqs and collecting various local "antique" artifacts became a favourite pastime.

However, it was not until our next posting, seven years later, to Cairo in Egypt, that the true meaning of antiquity, in its cultural and material forms, became stunningly evident. Egypt -- home to one of humanity's oldest civilizations, to some of Christianity's oldest churches and Islam's finest mosques -- remained through the millenniums of its history a magnet to adventurers, scholars, collectors, traders, thieves and indeed, from the earliest times, tourists: that is travellers from other lands who wished to see for themselves the renowned marvels of art and architecture that defined Egypt.

Cairo -- congested with traffic, polluted with fumes and a nightmare to navigate --was itself a museum of Egypt's history. However (and mercifully) we lived in Maadi, a southern, leafy suburb of the teeming city. Maadi, which we were told meant 'garden' in Arabic (but actually was derived from the word for 'ferry'), still at that time lived up to its verdant reputation. Substantial villas, nestled in gardens full of mango trees and hibiscus bushes, outnumbered apartment blocks; wide roads lined with flame trees crisscrossed the area, which, as Cairo itself, abutted the banks of the magnificent Nile.

With children in school and a husband very busy heading a major infrastructure project, I suddenly had the leisure to join a course on Ancient Egyptology which took me and my fellow students to major archaeological sites, such as the pyramids of Giza and Saqqara, and to the Museum of Egyptian Antiquities, a huge neglected building housing untold treasures, located on Tahrir Square. On weekends, I would lead my family to the sites which I had visited or we would explore areas even further afield.

On our first visit to Saqqara, as we entered this vast ancient necropolis, with its famous stepped Pyramid of Djoser, the oldest and first pyramidal structure of this oldest of civilizations, we were struck by a sign by the side of the stony path which we were following: DO NOT LOOK FOR BEADS! It was written in English. We looked at each other and then, as if commanded, looked down to the ground. Not a bead was in sight.

"Why can't we look for beads?" asked our younger daughter.

"There aren't any around, anyway," chimed in her sister, who had darted off the path to survey the surrounding area.

The warning signs continued at various intervals as we made our way towards the Step Pyramid, but not then, on our first visit, nor on any of the many times that we went to Saqqara did we ever spot a bead of any size or vintage. However, the Khan el-Khalili, the medieval bazaar located at the heart of Islamic Cairo, was awash with strands of the small earth-coloured funerary beads. The Khan el-Khalili and its neighbourhood of magnificent mosques soon became another one of our favourite destinations to explore. In the labyrinthine bazaar itself we found beautiful handicrafts, brazen copies of ancient Egyptian gods, plus in the secretive upstairs rooms, above the main shops, some genuine antiques: mummies' eyes, bits of basalt sculptures, and indeed 'genuine' funerary beads, sold for a price far exceeding their modern copies, but quite possibly emanating from the same source.

It was on our visit to Luxor, however, that our search for antiques presented us with the most tempting option and, at the same time, with an ethical conundrum. Luxor, about 600 kilometres south of Cairo, together with Aswan further south down the Nile, are the premier tourist destinations of Egypt. Luxor occupies the site of the ancient capital of Upper Egypt, known as Waset and later renamed by the Greeks as Thebes. Lying on the east side of the Nile, it is the home of the two famous temple

148

complexes of Karnak and Luxor. On the opposite side of the Nile stretches a vast Necropolis, encompassing the underground tombs of the Valley of the Kings and Valley of the Queens, plus temples and monuments, and even the ruins of the workers' village, Deir el-Medina, which throughout multiple millennia housed the artists, craftsmen, and architects who were responsible for the monumental works of art that define Luxor.

Having absorbed the magnificence of the Karnak and Luxor temples on the East Bank, we made our way to the west bank to explore the tombs in the Valley of the Kings, including the most famous one, that of Tutankhamen. On our final day in Luxor we got up early and took a ferry across the Nile to the West Bank. Besieged by eager taxi drivers, assuring us that they were also qualified guides, we finally found ourselves bouncing up the barren escarpment towards the complex of Hatshepsut's temple. On the way, to prove his credentials, the taxi guide stopped at an imposing but largely ruined structure.

"This very, very old temple," he waved his hand encouragingly. "Statue of Sekhmet inside very, very old!" he added.

We got out of the taxi and walked towards the entrance, where a biblically attired and turbaned guard checked our permits to visit the West Bank and then settled himself back on the giant slab that must have belonged to the walls of the temple. Our taxi driver smiled and waved his hand again towards the entrance before joining the guard on his perch and producing a pack of cigarettes.

We entered the temple, which appeared to have no other visitors, and soon in the murky main nave found the statue of the goddess Sekhmet. Huge and sculpted out of dark stone, the goddess with her proud lion's head loomed over us, staring resolutely into the distance. Sekhmet is known to be one of the oldest deities in the pantheon of Egyptian gods. She is the goddess of war and destruction, but also of healing and peace. Numerous statues of all sizes exist of Sekhmet, her feline features painstakingly depicted, right down to the whiskers.

I always had a soft spot for Sekhmet since she reminded me of our pet cats, maybe even in the opposing attributes with which she was endowed, both ferocious and gentle. We stood for a while, admiring the artistry of the unknown sculptor of 5000 years ago, then we moved on to explore the rest of the temple. As we traversed various chambers, we noticed another visitor to the temple, a young, slim man with a soft canvas bag slung over his shoulder. The bag flapped against his leg as we passed him on our way to the furthest chamber which, as we discovered, was devoid of any decoration and missing a part of its back wall. The huge flagstones of the floor seemed to have been recently swept and in one corner we noticed a significant pile of rubble. We approached the pile as we circumnavigated the room and there on top of all the broken stones rested the most perfectly sculpted feline nose. Unmistakably, Sekhmet's nose!

"Oh, look!" I gasped. "Sekhmet's nose! Do you think they're throwing it away?"

We stood for a while, wordlessly examining the exquisite nostrils and whiskers.

"Do you think we could take it?" I whispered. "It's not all that large. It could fit it into my handbag." But as soon as I had uttered those words, I knew the answer.

"Well, well, my dear," said my husband, "taking up antiquities' theft as your hobby? Will grave robbery come next? You're at the right place, but not at the right time. Just a few millennia too late!"

I smiled. "Bet someone pinches that nose, and it ends up in the Khan el-Khalili!"

With a last glance at our tempting find, we left the chamber, and as we stepped out, we again passed the youth with his canvas bag. We made our way once more to the giant statue of Sekhmet, nose intact, in the central nave, then left the temple, gazing at its damaged but impressive façade. Our taxi driver jumped off his perch, offered another cigarette to the guard, who also stood up, expectantly. We gave him a few coins and he saluted us with a broad, somewhat toothless grin. As we were about to get into our taxi, we caught sight of the young man; he was exiting the temple and his canvas bag was no longer flapping; in fact, it was very visibly weighed down with something substantial.

"Look," I said, nudging my husband, "he's got something in that bag!"

It was obvious to both of us that the bag was no longer empty. We stood by our taxi as the youth passed us, following him and his heavy bag with our eyes as he followed a footpath that led toward the distant shimmer of Hatshepsut's sprawling funerary temple.

"Oh, no!" I groaned. "It's Sekhmet's nose, I'm sure!"

Shoestring Luxury

By

Sacha Quinn

Well that's day one nearly over. What a day! Not quite as hot as yesterday but perhaps we've acclimatised quickly. Can you acclimatise in a day between UK 15 degrees Celsius and USA 95 degrees Fahrenheit? Doubtful, my logic was telling me.

Yesterday, in case you're wondering, was travelling day, so not really a day, though, if the truth be told, it was quite an experience. In fact, we could still be sitting at Gatwick airport since the flight to Cincinnati was cancelled indefinitely. But good old Delta had a flight to Atlanta available instead. It apparently wasn't going to cause any sort of problem with an onward domestic flight to Orlando.

In a whirlwind we by-passed all the queues for security and passport control, much in the same way as royalty and big celebs do, checking in in half an hour with only five minutes to spare.

Phew!

Alas no hanging around duty free to review reading matter for us. Which I was a bit pissed off with as to me this is part of the holiday. Even if I don't have huge amounts of spare cash to spend, it's something I think of doing and it's the thought that counts. I was grateful for small mercies though, for effective travel booking systems, so I didn't have to spend three days perusing, whilst awaiting another Cincinnati flight.

Atlanta airport was really something. From landing to getting to the next departure gate took sixty-one minutes, non-stop. Well non-stop apart from standing a few seconds, mouth agape, watching the Japanese Olympic team going in the opposite direction, to catch their flights home in a very disciplined manner. It reminded me of a group of infant school kids, on a school trip but stopping shy of holding hands. Very smart they looked in their red uniforms. Just think, I was within inches of a gold medal winner. Yes, I'm sure they got one or two, so I must have been.

Waiting for a connecting flight must be one of the most boring things on earth. No, correct that, the second most boring. Listening to the National Express coach staff for seven hours non-stop from Bradford to Gatwick took the prize. Jesus, they could talk for England, no question as to who the gold winners would be there. Absolutely no contest. Actually, I'm quite proud of myself, as they are still alive and able to bore some other poor travellers, in another time and place. This is because apart from my uttering, 'which is more than can be said for us tonight' in response to the driver's statement, 'I got a good night's sleep last night', I stayed remarkably quiet and kept my violent thoughts to myself. Practising my stiff upper lip, I told myself, ready to impress the Americans.

We finally got here, travel weary, but not for long. It instantly dissipated upon sight of the hotel. It's one of those grand affairs which the Russians, during 'wall' standing days, would not have allowed the populace to know existed, lest it caused an uprising of the masses not having recourse to such opulence themselves. But how many do anyway, anywhere in the world? It's certainly not something we're likely to experience again unless I can start picking a more favourable set of numbers on the lottery.

The first glimpse of the Orlando World Centre, or center as they put it in American, is gained from route I-4 and it's impressive even then.

"Twenty-four storeys high," they said at the car hire place, "so you can't miss it."

Very true! It's certainly the tallest building around and if a shape was to describe it, it would have to be triangular. A tall tower in the middle, going down in stages at each side. Access is gained from the freeway, up a long dual carriage way drive, tree lined with palms and masses of foliage at their bases, giving a riot of colour. Car parking is two-fold: valet parking for the affluent, nearest the hotel of course, and guest parking for the cheapskates like us.

Pity the poor. It makes carrying two sets of golf clubs and assorted luggage that much more difficult and tiring but the air-conditioned room that awaited us that little bit more welcoming.

What a room!

Talk about a room with a view.

Our room, befitting a Marriot Hotel Platinum Card Holder – that's me I acknowledge proudly – is I assume one of the best. The little ticket on the back of the bathroom door declares $250. That's per day, not as I would usually expect, the week. $250 PER

DAY! That is worthy of shouty capitals. A moment's panic hits us when we think we might actually have to pay the 6% local tax. A frantic scrutiny of the small print on the award redemption certificate ensues. Panic over, on a big sigh of relief, to find room related taxes are covered. Suddenly faced with an unbudgeted bill for £100 is not my idea of a start to holiday fun. It might well be 95 degrees here but there is still the gas bill to pay when we get home.

I digress. Back to the view.

I must say I didn't expect quite so much forestation. Perhaps it's that which contributes to the huge humidity rather like in the jungle. But without knowing anything about weather or jungle conditions I was only guessing. We can see for miles and miles, from our 18th floor balcony. It's the 10th really according to the lift buttons. Goodness knows what happened to floors two to eleven, but presumably that's American logic for you somewhere.

A vast area spread out before us was covered in trees: hardly any buildings but masses of greenery. It's ace. I would say cool because that seems to be the in phrase at the moment but I'd be lying because it's hot, so ace it is or even buzzing. I'd heard that a few times and I'm sure that is quite apt being amongst trees, what with flies, mozzies and other creepy crawlies. They must live somewhere. Since there is very little evidence of them around the hotel, maybe due to some evolutionary development about buildings being hostile territory, they do stay in the trees. I'm certainly hoping so as I know from other foreign holidays, I'm good for insect fodder.

Having said that we did see a cockroach. At least I think that is what it was. Could have been anything really since I'm no bug expert. Anyway, we saw a huge bug land on our balcony wall. I've never seen anything like it before. Obviously, a clever bug too because it buggered off and thus avoided certain death if it had come into contact with my shoe, which I'm sure would not have complemented the cream coloured walls at all.

Our balcony is brilliant, we can see directly down to the, 'kidney with a few bits cut out' shaped pool, dazzlingly lit by sunlight during the day and by twinkly fairy lights at night. In the distance to the right is the pink Disney World Magic Kingdom, with the golf ball of the Epcot Centre slightly further to the right. Even further to the right is the Pleasure Island, unimpressive by day but beautifully laser beamed by night.

Nine pm is the time to be sitting on the balcony when the Magic Kingdom is delighting the multitudes with nightly firework displays. Ha muzzles! We get it for nothing. They've paid nearly £30 each for the privilege. Though I'm sure it's more impressive near to it, we wouldn't be shelling it out on our meagre budget.

I note there are four roads visible from my vantage point. Traffic is non-stop, but it's so far away it's not a distraction. I'm guessing the trees absorb a lot of the noise, thank goodness otherwise it would be awful, probably resulting in sleepless nights.

Though breakfast is free with our room, providing we have the healthy start option of cereals, fruit and skimmed milk, we opted to go out to Shoney's eat all you like for $4.99. We woz robbed! Down the road or rather drive, International Drive to be exact, there was another 'eat all you like' for $3.99. But we would have been robbed there too because even further down it was $3.49. No one beat that though. So, it must have been the bottom line!

Shoney's was quite an experience. 'Eat all you like' said the bill board and the citizens of the U.S of A we encountered in there, certainly did that. A plague of locust in a crop field has nothing on these people. The combinations and concoctions had to be seen to be believed. OK I did put whipped cream on my scrambled eggs but I did at least think it was cheese.

I had a sudden flash back to being in the canteen on the first day in a new job. A colleague asked what I'd put on my dinner. I replied, 'cheese sauce'.

"What cheese sauce?" he asked.

"That over there," I responded, pointing to where I'd found it.

"Ah," he laughed, "you mean the custard for the pudding."

These people I don't think would have cared. I noted them ladling maple syrup onto a plate of bacon, eggs, sausage and hash browns with pancakes, melted blackcurrant jam and sweet waffles on top of that. Quite extraordinary. What I had trouble understanding however was, why they didn't clear the savoury first and then go back for the sweet. It was 'eat all you like' after all. Not just one visit. But no, they piled everything on one plate, then went for a repeat of the same. Hmm. Bacon with treacle? Try it sometime? Ugh. I think not.

Where to next? I had this brilliant idea. We would go to Orlando shopping. Alas, in America you don't go to the city centre, park your car and then walk around the shops. Oh no. Downtown Orlando I was informed, and actually Down Town Anytown, consists of malls. Areas of parking around which there are a conglomerate of stores. If you think they sell what you're looking for, jump in your car get the aircon blasting, cool down, drive to the mall, park up, brave the searing heat between car and stores and if it's not there, move on to the next. Which is exactly what we did, since not wanting to take the nice fluffy peach coloured towels out of the bathroom in the hotel, we were in search of beach towels. $15.00 for a Mickey Mouse/Power Rangers/Florida/Sea-world towel was out of the question. $29.00 for a wonderfully sculptured unusual Bug's Bunny one, regardless of uniqueness, was equally out of the question. $10.60 for two plain common or garden green ones, which will match our bathroom at home, were just the job, purchased at a closing down sale. Same the world over. If you look hard enough you find what you want, at a price you're prepared to pay.

Now that day two is looming, it's time to cash a traveller's cheque. Not that it's a difficult thing here. Not like in some countries where you have to go to bank and jump through identification hoops to get your cash. Here you just sign it in the presence of a cashier. If the bill total is less that the value of the cheque, you get cash back. Simples. But why do we need to resort to traveller's cheques so soon? Simples again. Only $23.45 left out of our budgeted $151.

$53 at the liquor store took a big chunk, but considering the price of beer in the hotel is four times as much it was definitely money well spent. Then there was sun cream, after sun and a John Francome novel since I wasn't able to get 'Men Are from Mars, Women Are from Venus' which I really wanted in paper back from duty free at £6.99. At £16.00 here for hardback, I decided unravelling the mysteries of men and women could wait a little longer.

We had to resort to our flexible friend for the purchase of golf balls. I'm dreading the bill when it arrives since personal liability for car insurance went on the credit card too: can't afford the risk of a law suit here. God, I'm never going to get my hall carpet at this rate.

Still, a once in a lifetime holiday, with free accommodation at a luxury hotel and no travel costs was fabulous, even if we didn't have the spending money to match, coupled with everything being just so expensive. For years, friends had told us America was cheap. How come it all changed when we got there? Oh well, we would still make the most of it, grateful for this break, only possible after collecting air miles and hotel points, as week in week out I commuted to Scotland for two whole years. Yes, now it was pay-back time and we were after all expanding our horizons and 'worldly-wisedness'. OK the sleep button has been pressed. Time for bed.

The Sun Shines Brightest on Shallow Ripples

By

C. I. Ripples

Taking another slug of his Singha, Noah looks out over the water, collecting the memories of his loss. If water was ever a symbol for emotion, he thinks, the darkness of the Andaman Sea ahead represents the heaviness of his soul.

He would be leaving Thailand in the morning, relieved to see the back of it, vowing never to return, never to be confronted again with the events of that afternoon. He feels for the passport, which the authorities had only returned back to him that morning, in his breast pocket, comforted by its existence, the freedom it provides.

The quiet, serene beach he has chosen for his final day is a stark contrast to that of the accident. That one in Kata had been busy, filled with overly colourful flashes of fleshy tattooed tourists, crowding around efficient lifeguards, practising pointless CPR, before handing the stretcher up to the waiting ambulance, sirens shrieking.

Even the heavy clouds hanging low over the water cannot be further from the clear, azure blue sky he remembered from that afternoon. The forlorn softly swaying muslin of the makeshift wedding chapel he now faces, seems to mock him, reminding him that a love gained could be lost in an instant.

Noah sighs, finishes the bottle and orders another as he replays the video of that day in his mind's eye for the umpteenth time.

Has it only been a month since he'd plucked the early morning frangipani, as delicate, pure and perfect as she, and tickled her chin to stir her to wakefulness? Only one month since he'd lent over her, gently pushing aside the blonde hair to whisper in her ear that he loved her and wanted so wake up to her beauty every day? Only one month since he'd taken her slender left hand and placed the aquamarine ring on her finger, telling her he'd be there for her no matter where she went or what she did?

Her laughter full of promise still echoes in his head. Her naked bronzed body had rolled over him, her breath caressing his skin, her beach bleached hair in his mouth as their bodies fused as one, with her teasing him to the brink of ecstasy, until she let him explode inside her as she clung to him.

They'd gone out to celebrate their future together at Kata Rocks overlooking the crystal-clear waters. The treat cut further into his apprentice savings, but he wanted to impress her with his ability to look after her in a manner to which she was not accustomed. The smile that reached her eyes told him he'd succeeded. She'd been totally overawed by the romantic setting, the stunning scenery, the lavish surroundings and superlative service. It had been worth every hard-earned cent. They'd downed a bottle of Dom Perignon and shared oysters as they delighted in each other, the momentous occasion, vowing only to inform the families upon their return to Kyabram.

Noah almost groans, struggling to retain his composure as he watches how the buoyancy of the champagne made them reckless, invincible together as they ran hand in hand across Karon beach. Breathless, they'd stopped at the jet-skis, Noah cajoling her into having a go. She'd never been the adventurous type, pointing out the dangers, the environmentally unfriendliness of it all. He'd teased her mercilessly, her reluctance to try anything new secretly annoying the hell out of him. Perhaps it was Dutch courage, perhaps it was fate, perhaps she was feeling particularly generous, but he was exhilarated when that afternoon she for once let him sweet talk her into it, unaware that in one moment, everything would change.

Soon they were whipping around the bay at high speed, messing about and spraying each other while riding side by side. He can still see the big grin on her face, her white blonde hair flying behind her in the wind, as he showed off his moves and slalomed around her. The next thing he knew the bottom of his ski had slammed into hers at high speed, throwing her into the water, as he on his own ski started to sink.

Noah wipes the sweat from his brow, pulls himself back from the memory, sits up and fast forwards.

He had wept himself dry, as Mia comforted him, insisting that it had been a tragic accident, that two drowning people cannot save each other. Her family too had embraced and wept with him as they flew into Phuket to collect her body. They assured him that he was without blame, yet he felt their silent recriminations keenly in the knowledge they were justified. He alone knew the truth. The dazzling sun reflecting off the sea may have been blinding, but it was his reckless, drunken bravado that had blinded him to danger. And in the instant of her existential need, unconscious in the water as her head had hit the ski when she fell, he had made only cowardly efforts to save himself, escaping with minor injuries, whilst letting Lizzy be dragged down.

As he sits staring at the bay, silent in the westerly breeze, creating soft ripples across the water, Noah considers that drowning a death might actually be preferable to this drowning in an eternal ocean of guilt. His two years suspended sentence for reckless driving causing death is a relief, but it cannot assuage his remorse. He wishes to be taken back, to start over and undo the moment of his loss. Stop at the second glass of champagne, when he had continued drinking. Turn right on the beach, instead of left towards the jet-ski operator. Ride responsibly, where he had been wild to impress. Save his ray of sunshine, when he had saved himself.

Any thoughts of returning home are almost unbearable. He had been headline news in both Phuket and Australia. It had been all over the Internet and newspapers, even on television. There would be a sea of expectations that he knows he and his guilt cannot live up to – to work, to shop, cook and wash, go out with friends, to act 'normally'. All the while he will have to endure the pitying, accusing, questioning glances of those passing him by. He will not be able to bear it, knowing that every time he meets someone, they will think of Lizzy, wondering how he had let it happen, whilst making conversation about everything and nothing, ensuring that the accident never leaves his mind.

With time their curiosity will fade and they will cease to remember. Yet, for Noah not remembering will be another loss in itself. He is not ready to recover from his grief, to forgive himself. He may never be ready. He does not want to lose the ghost floating alongside him everywhere he goes, filling his soul with accusations, even if he is drowning under its weight.

As Noah pays, then walks towards the water, he wonders why it is only on the shallowest ripples that the sun shines brightest.

The Traveller

by

Stephanie Thornton

He could have been regarded as a traveler. Not the sort that walked from John O'Groats to Land's End or walked the 'Lyke Wake'. Nor was he a student in a gap year who walked down Koh San Road and took inspiration from 'The Beach'. And he didn't have a caravan; neither one with a curved roof made of corrugated iron nor one of giant size which had a least three bedrooms and running toilets in the rear. But he was the sort of man things happened to and this usually involved travel of some sort.

To look at him would have been a glimpse of some ordinary man. Average height, around 40 years of age, dark haired with little blond streaks now grey running through it. Trim and prone to wearing jumpers with the occasional motif on the front – just to add variety. You could read 'why have pâté when you can have fois gras' on one his Mum had knit, but where he lived, in quite an ordinary house on the street named 'Mr. Average', most folks wouldn't know what fois gras was anyway. They would understand such phrases as 'It's time for tea, or sex if you prefer it?' and other such nonsense.

It was the 'happenings' themselves which were unusual. He would have been at work in Kuala

Lumpur for a week and at the airport about to return home, when he'd find himself sitting in the toilets when there was a sudden rumble. This wasn't caused because of something he had eaten. He was sure of this. The cubicle started to shake and in the far reaches of the toilet block, one of the partitions fell to the floor. He was in the middle of a small earthquake. This was not the thing that happened to ordinary people. He just happened to be in the wrong place at the right time.

In India, he was staying at the Neemrama Palace Fort hotel just taking tiffin at the four o'clock daily ritual, when a large hornet fell out of the sky and took a large bite out of his cheek. A grown man, shrieking his head off, was something the other guests had never seen before and they thought it was an act put on for visitors. Afterwards, he would relate the tale, saying it was carried out every day for visitors in celebration of us losing the British Empire there.

His Indian driver, who drove like some lunatic on speed, hurtled down a side road in the middle of which was a tiny lump of concrete and nearly ran down a cliff where the road wasn't finished. Everyone was supposed to know that a tiny lump of concrete meant a six-foot drop in India.

Each time he'd had a lucky escape. Like when an elephant ran amok around a spice plantation whilst he was riding it. The fact the elephant had the name of 'Lucky' was perhaps just that.

In Jamaica, he asked directions to 'Port Royal' at a way side café. His intention was to visit the lonely archaeologist working there. They asked him to sit at a table. This was somewhat of a puzzle. They said they'd come back in a moment, and did so - only to deliver a full English breakfast which they announced was called in fact 'A Port Royal'. And on the way back, he was surrounded by an angry mob around his car and only just managed to escape by running over some of them.

But the biggest happening of all was in Thailand. He got bitten by a mosquito and ended up with the dreaded dengue fever. It wasn't the low grade one where everyone got better after a raging fever and flu like illness, his was the worst sort of all. It could be a killer.

The hospital gave him a five percent chance to pull through. After deliriums of such intensity his heart had had enough and stopped. He died.

Or so they thought.

This is where his travelling turned into an altogether different kind.

He felt himself rise out of his body which remained lying underneath him on the bed and he floated down the corridor outside the room. There was a large fan in the ceiling which some technicians were attempting to make work and they were standing on bamboo poles. One of them wore a tee shirt which said 'I love my teddy' on it. He smiled to himself – the small Thai man must surely have borrowed it from a child? He also smiled at them working on the electricity so typical of third world countries with no idea of the dangerous way they were working. Further down the corridor, a woman sat with a little girl on her knees and the girl was wearing bright blue pyjamas and bows to match at the ends of her pigtails. The corridor ended at a double door without windows and across it was a safety bar with a padlock on it. Just as he thought he must stop, he seemed to dissolve through the door as if it were made of jelly. And then he was outside.

He could see all around. Not just straight in front of him, but to the side and backwards too and he was soaring rapidly down the street and high into the air towards the stars. It was so interesting. He could see the world spread out below him, and all around the world at once. There was America and India and Australia all at once below him and beyond that, a bright and warming light encouraging him to come to it. But just as he was about to enter, he felt a whooshing feeling and there he was on the hospital bed again shaking with delirium.

They said he had been dead but that word seemed trivial and absurd to him. It was a poor excuse for the wonders he had seen. And they verified his account of the men working on the fan and the woman with the child. But instead of saying this was a most curious event, it seemed to make everyone most uncomfortable. Perhaps no one was meant to know such things or experience them and thus pass on knowledge to others that would be best to remain a mystery.

It should have stayed as such but the travels didn't stop when he eventually got home. He would find, each night, that instead of sleeping and waking up at morning light, he now would rise from his body and drift upwards into the clouds swirling round the earth. At least they seemed like clouds. They were made of strips of coloured lights of all things harmonious and shaded with swirling sparkling blue of the palest shade to deep purple and of darkest indigo.

Glittering strands of cord-like threads linked all the shades together. It seemed in a flash he could be anywhere he wanted. If he thought of the plains of the Serengeti, which he had never visited, he would be there in a flash. If he thought - I'd like to see the slums of Rio - he was there. Or the market stalls in Indonesia. And all the while, his body remained in the bed at home, though he was attached to it by a thin and wispy rope, like an umbilicus which unravelled out of his body in a misty, silvery sheen.

He was very attached to his cord and felt it was as necessary to him as every breath he took. And where ever he travelled, it would stretch as long as he required. He knew he was always in some high place far above the earth and on returning, must fall back into his body as if from this great height. If he was sometimes fully conscious of this, he would experience a sudden temporary fright that he was going to fall and would jerk as he came back to his sleeping body on the bed.

When it was time to travel back to sleep from whichever place he had visited, he would think home thoughts and the cord would bring him slowly back like a reel re-winding itself. It was there in the etheric beyond the world of earth that all things felt known to him, but on waking, he had only a hazy recollection of his nocturnal travels. He decided it must be a way of reporting to God. After all, so little was known about the reasons or mechanics of our sleep.

Scientists had as yet no knowledge of why we really sleep and what happens to us in those unknown hours. Do we report to God our events of the day and are we given advice by sentient beings? The travelling was a gift, but he knew it must be secret and not open for discussion. If he met other travellers whilst travelling on the etheric, they would mentally swop their thoughts, but no one ever spoke.

Was he changed by this? The ability was obviously a gift left over from the experience called dying. For him, it stretched into his daily life by showing kindness and a more enhanced gentleness to others. If they had thought to describe the 'new' him, they would liken it to having had some sort of spiritual encounter. A Damascene moment which now governed all aspects of his life. Could he heal by the laying on of hands? Could he prophesy the future? Could he give advice of such profoundness that other would come to seek out his gifts? Was it a blessing, or a curse? Did it become deeper in the passing of time? Could he teach others how to 'travel'?

There were no answers to the 'why?'. It was what it was. Unsolvable and as elusive as a vapour trail dissolving into air. He was a traveller but a traveller of an altogether different kind. It was his fate, his destiny and not to know the reasons why. All would be revealed at life's end when he entered the other place, he knew with certainly was there - just around the corner, in another room.

He had faith it would be so

Children and Learning

Your children are not your children. They are
the sons and daughters of Life's longing for itself.
They come through you but not from you. And
though they are with you yet they belong not to you
- Kahil Gibran

Children must be taught how to think, not what to
think.
-    Margaret Mead

"Tell me and I forget. Teach me and I remember.
Involve me and I learn."
- Benjamin Franklin

Teach your children they're unique. That way, they
won't feel pressured to be like everybody else.
-   Cindy Cashman

The essence of our effort to see that every child has
a chance must be to assure each an equal
opportunity,
not to become equal, but to become different –
to realize whatever unique potential of body,
mind and spirit he or she possesses.
- John Fischer

A Curious Encounter

by

Stephanie Thornton

I felt as if I had been walking for hours. The temperature had reached an uncomfortable 34 degrees and it was also very humid. The sort of heat that made the pavements seem covered in a sort of sweat. Almost human, almost breathing.

You had to watch the surface. It was very uneven, full of hidden cracks and ruts where the slabs had cracked and there were bits of rotten vegetable waste left over from the early market. And the pavement edges full of broken curbs. No sign of health and safety. No one seemed to care and just got on with living. It's strange that when you are away like that, it doesn't seem to matter. You only realise how conscious you have become of danger when you return to the mother country and then look for every pitfall just in case 'you have been hurt in an accident' and have to phone a lawyer. How silly it seems.

But here, the atmosphere buzzed and crackled with vibrant energy. It was way too early for the monsoon which is just as fierce in Thailand as it is in India. But some days it just feels like it's coming early, and the sky will go a weird sort of yellow colour. On days like that, there's lots of smog from taxi fumes and tuk-tuks and you'd go anywhere to get cool.

You'd avoid all the tourist traps like the Koh San Road – although cute – been there, done that, many years ago now. Now you would go native like a full-time resident familiar with the city. And your Salwar Kameez would cling to your body albeit the coolest choice to wear in such a climate.

It was now late afternoon, so I decided to take a short cut through Soi Five where it joined onto Four, by going through the side passageways that linked them. This was an Arab quarter. You almost felt you were in Cairo, not in the teeming streets of Bangkok. The passageway was full of perfume parlours. Their glass flagons and sculptured stoppers gleamed under myriad lights on ceilings and plate glass windows – a real Aladdin's cave of treasures. And there was a smell of leather too where shops displayed racks full of glittering sandals with beaded thongs, Ali Baba shoes and leather belts and handbags.

There was a café there, covered in mirrors of chequered black and silver. Like a glittering version of a motor racing flag. It gleamed like some sort of glorious sultan's palace and I thought of the hookah pipe I had smoked with my dear friend Vijay in that café in Jodhpur a long time ago. His father, a devout Muslim, would have been red with rage if he had known what his son got up to.

"It's only apple," Vijay said, but later, I found we had smoked tobacco too. How naïve I was.

This café in Bangkok was full of pipes scattered around the floor – vast silver and gold affairs with their pipes coiled around each base like snakes. The men in flowing robes of white or beige were watching the world go by and sipping the sugary mint tea that I love so much, in highly decorated glasses trimmed with gold.

One of them broke off drinking leaping from the table to bar my way. He tried to sell me a fake Dior watch, but his salesmanship was a little lacking. And I suddenly had a feeling I was going to have a little adventure. A sort of premonition?

I told him no, and we laughed.

There was a suggestive look on his face. Selling the Dior watch had changed. Now he asked if I would like him to give me a personal massage? Then he grinned. There was a mischievous sparkle in his eye and I declined it. We laughed again and his eyes were bright with humour. His friends sat around the café table shouted out encouragements. At least, I think that's what they meant!

I am always a success where Arabs are concerned. They love ladies that have some flesh on them. It's something to do with value – or maybe the price of camels, which are likened to the value of larger ladies. The bid for me stands at 20,000 camels at today's date. I told him this and he laughed again. I was still smiling when I left the café and waved at them goodbye.

When you reach the end of this Soi, you are suddenly in an eight-lane highway doing a dance with death as the green man on the traffic lights starts to run as the lights change. The clicking noise that accompanies him also changes to an irate speedo version. It's never wise to wait or to get stuck in the middle………………

So, I arrived at the modern store, which was full of glass and chrome, panting for breath in the soupy air. The coolness of the air conditioning was an unexpected shock to the senses. And the vast space in contrast to the bustling traffic rushing past the door. It was all open plan inside – no walls at all and in the middle, an escalator rose up to the next level.

Tucked under this, was my familiar nail bar run by a Thai girl called Kim. They all seem to be called Kim.

"I suppose you are from Isan?" I asked and laughed. It's the north east region of Thailand.

She giggled back – they all seem to come from there too.

I sat on the chairs. They were pouffes covered in violent turquoise and equally violent pink. Interior design is not perhaps best known to general Thai. It tends to be a mixture of all things bright, which clash together outrageously, in some sort of mental boiling pot.

The other pouffes were covered in faux pony skins. But here the nails are works of art with the most amazing paintings known to man. To go there is my treat.

I had just started to relax, as the busy day ended, when a very exotic woman arrived and sat down next to me. She had the sort of looks and hairstyle that made you look twice, and she was reed thin and very tall in comparison to usual Thai girls who were considered tall at 5 feet 2 inches. She wore a figure-hugging mini skirt and thigh length suede boots in black with very high heels. She also had the most immaculate makeup. Perfectly drawn lips and blushed cheeks. The sort that made you want to have a makeover and where women rush off to a mirror to check what they look like too. Not to impress or attract a man – just being part of the female psyche.

I couldn't resist having a second look. Her hair was jet black and rough cut but with such style it stuck out at every angle arranged to look that way, not in the sort of style wrecked by Yorkshire winds. It was what could be only be described as 'orderly messiness' and I said I thought her hair looked great.

"I'm so glad you think that," she replied, but this came over as a little shock as her voice was deep and low. But then she turned towards me and in doing so, the lights caught her eyes and she had the most amazing eyes I have ever seen. They were gold with tints of copper and yellow streaked through them. Like the centre of a 'Crunchie' chocolate bar. I gave a little gasp and Kim giggled.

The woman must have seen me take a breath.

"It's OK," she said, "don't be worried. My name is Katharina and I'm a man." Just like that! As if she was saying, I'll take milk in my tea or how much does the bus cost? No more, no less. And I could see that my earlier thoughts of a little adventure had just become reality.

"You can't be," I gasped, and was so astonished for a moment that I hastily added, "you've got breasts."

She was wearing a very clinging top and could see the nipples pointing through the fabric. And there was no sign of the tell- tale 'Adams apple' on her throat.

"I know," she said, and laughed, putting one hand under each. Then lifted each one up and jiggled them around.

"Aren't they gorgeous," she declared.

"Yes.... but No!" I said, "it can't be true?"

"Yes, aren't they wonderful. Would you like to see them?" And without further ado, without an affirmation, right there, right then, in the middle of the huge shop she stood up and stripped off her top.

I gasped.

"Would you like to touch them?" she invited Kim and me.

How could we refuse such an unusual offer? Curiosity got the better of us both.

So, we both leant over and cupped them in our hands. And whilst this was happening, I was thinking I had arrived in an alternative universe and it couldn't be happening. I must be having some sort of dream. I wondered what I was doing. Then I remembered. It was certainly not the sort of thing that would ever happen in Harvey Nics in Leeds. Could you imagine that? We'd be arrested on the spot and it'd be on 'Look North' that night and on front pages in the morning. Headline, 'Woman gropes man'. No, I was having some small adventure right there, right then. And even stranger, no one passing by was taking any notice at all.

"They feel just like the real thing," we said, "and there's no sign of any scars."

"That's what my boyfriend says," she proudly announced. "I'm actually a man from the waist down but all woman waist up."

I held my breath and hoped she wasn't going to take off her skirt as well…………

I laughed, "it must be a bit confusing for him?"

Then I wondered how I'd got so risqué. Having this matter of fact conversation with a half-naked man, who is a woman, in the middle of a hypermarket, and just as if it was a normal every day sort of affair. Like discussing knitting patterns or how to bake a cake.

"Well, I'm intending to have the op' next year but have to save up first," she continued. "The main problem I have is my arms; I can't get them smooth."

And she showed me where the hair grew, the hair she'd shaved off leaving a trace of stubble. I noticed her hands and arms were large and didn't match the rest of her. I felt a little sad for her.

"I work in a bar at night. Come and have a drink or just pop in for coffee at my flat when you're passing," she said, handing me a card.

And as I left and went on up the escalator to visit my friend Max, the tailor on the floor above, we both waved and blew each other a kiss and shouted a goodbye. And people in the area below looked on in puzzled wonderment. This was strange when they'd never shown any interest in her earlier strip tease.

As for me, what a nice woman/man, I thought.

I must confess it totally altered my previous perceptions. I had thought I would be horrified. That I would have difficulty accepting this alternative life style. I thought I'd think it like a Drag Show, which I don't care for, or liken it to some outrageous Gays that have worked with me in the Fine Arts world. But now, I had a different take on this world of hers. It

181

was both an enlightenment and an enriching experience

I went back two days later and left a tube of 'Immac' for her arms.

Many months later, when back in France, my American friend Dana, who writes for 'People Magazine', was told the tale. She was furious.

"I've always wanted to meet a real Thai Lady boy and now you've got there first," she said, with great annoyance.

"This was not a Thai Lady boy. She was something else indeed. So, Nah, nah, nah, na, na," I said.

"Not only was she trans-gender but she was Iranian too," I laughed.

Finding the Light

By

Marion McNally

March 2018

She had no idea how long she'd been slumped over the hospital bed; she was becoming vaguely aware of slivers of light streaming into the small sterile room. She looked at her watch – 6.45 a.m. Time of death had been recorded as 5.15.

"There's nothing else you can do," said Dave as he left the room with her mother. But Maria felt compelled to stay, trying to piece together the events from the last few days.

Nurse Terry interrupted her jumbled chain of thoughts saying, "Mrs. Thompson, you have to go now – we'll take over from here. Go and get a cup of tea with your mum and your husband in the visitors' room. I'll keep you in my prayers."

Maria couldn't bear to leave her sister. She held Jo's hand one last time and whispered, "I love you, Jo." Tearfully she picked up Roddy, Jo's stuffed rabbit she'd had since she was a new-born, hugging it to her chest before putting it into her shopping bag with all the other bits and pieces that had been given to Jo since she'd been rushed to the emergency room.

Her last conversation with Jo was still vivid in her mind: "I'm so sorry to put you and mum through this again," she'd whispered to Maria. "I know I'm dying Maria. But I don't have the strength to pick myself up again. Tell Nathan I love him so much. Give him Roddy for me." Those had been her last words.

In the visitors' room her mum, Agnes, sat crumpled in an oversized chair and Dave stood waiting for the kettle to boil again. Maria entered the room letting out a pitiful, soulful cry - as if she had been storing emotions and was only now able to release a tiny particle of this frightening dark presence that had embedded itself inside her body since Jo's overdose.

"Who's going to tell Nathan?" whispered Agnes. Maria hadn't even thought about her eight-year old son, the only grandson on both sides of the family, adored and spoiled. Jo had been his favourite aunt; they had so much in common: answering questions with more questions, laughing until they almost cried at corny jokes - and the way they both tilted their heads slightly to the right and stuck their thumbs under their chin, just as they were about to challenge something that had been said – well that was just uncanny.

Maria had only ever wanted one child. After an arduous 35-hour labour and several months of post-partum depression she had never been more certain about anything in her life. She wasn't prepared for the depth of love that would consume her though once the depression had lifted. Now she lived for Nathan's smiles. Even teachers loved Nathan and he loved them back – 'a model child' they would say; 'a great influence on the naughtier children in the class'. Her heart would sing every time someone complimented her little boy.

"Let's go collect Nathan. Agnes, you come to us and stay for a while," said David. Agnes, wiping another tear from her cheek nodded saying, "What am I going to do without Jo?"

"We'll get through this somehow, Mum," said Maria shivering, as she thought back to a year ago.

Jo had met a young man at a friend's party and he'd made it very clear to her he was serious about their relationship. Within two months they'd moved in together. Although the family had been shocked at first, they were delighted that George had a steady job and a stable family. He wasn't a big drinker, had never done drugs though he did smoke a few cigarettes every day.

Maria however was worried. One evening after a family dinner, when George went out for a smoke, she confronted Jo asking, "Have you told George about your addiction?"

Jo stared at her plate and sighed. She tilted her head slightly to the right placed her thumb under her chin and said, "I'm getting there – no need to rush anything. It's still early days. Look, I haven't had even a joint in four months. I'm clean and confident that I can keep it that way – especially now that George is with me. There was silence around the table for a few seconds, then Agnes, proud as a peacock about her daughter's recovery, said: "That's fantastic news!'

Throughout this conversation Nathan had been playing on his i-pad. He'd known for some time that

Auntie Jo had a problem: when he was seven, he'd heard angry conversations on the phone, and his mum who'd always wanted to read bed time stories to him now found excuses not to. "I've been so busy at work today Nathan," she'd said often or, "let's leave the story tonight."

Nathan was listening intently to the conversation at the dinner table. Auntie Jo looked happier than he'd ever seen her – still, there was something in her voice that didn't ring true. He'd no idea how he knew this but he did. This 'knowing' was something Nathan had taken for granted during his short life; his father had called him 'intuitive' and Agnes always said 'he's been here before'; Maria found this aspect of Nathan's character a little difficult to deal with so she generally ignored it – preferred not to think about it at all.

Nathan was at the door waiting for them when they arrived back from the hospital. "How's Auntie Jo? Gran said she was feeling sick…"

Maria grabbed him and held him in a bear hug. "Come inside and we'll talk about it."

Dave's mum went into the kitchen to put the kettle on; Dave's father decided that this was a good time to return some e-mails.

Dave and Maria sat at opposite ends of the small couch Nathan between them. Agnes sat in an armchair. "Why do you all look so sad?" he asked. Agnes took another paper tissue and pressed it to her eyes. "Grandma, don't cry – what's wrong?" At this, Agnes let out a loud sob.

Maria took Nathan's hand He looked desperately from one face to the other. "What's happened?" he asked, his little cherub face crinkling as he spoke.

"Auntie Jo has died."

"Before she died," said Dave, "she told us to tell you that she loved you very much."

Maria went into her bag and pulled out Roddy. "She wanted you to have this," she said, handing it to Nathan.

"Roddy Rabbit…I love Roddy," he whimpered, hugging the stuffed toy tightly.

He dashed to the corner of the room and continued to hug Roddy tightly.

As Dave's mum came into the room with tea and biscuits, Nathan, who still sat huddled in the corner suddenly asked: "But WHERE is Auntie Jo now? I want to see her."

Maria, not knowing how to respond, sat next to Nathan on the floor. "When can I see her?" he asked. Maria cuddled him tightly and said, "We're really not sure if that will be possible Nathan. There are some people we need to talk to first. Go collect your things and we'll all head home now."

Nathan, still with Roddy hugged tightly in his arms followed the adults as they walked desolately towards the car.

That night, after Agnes had gone to bed, Nathan sat with Roddy on his lap watching closely as his mum and dad worked quietly at the dining room table. He loved that table – it was where they had the best family meals, where they laughed and told each other stories when mum and dad came home from work. He especially loved that table when the family came every Sunday for dinner. Jo and Nathan always sat next to each other – even when Jo was with George, Nathan had insisted that he should sit between them, so that he could tell Jo his latest stories and jokes.

On the day of the funeral the small-town community church, where Agnes had prayed over the years for Jo's recovery, was so full with friends, family and neighbours, people were standing at the back and in the aisles.

Nathan sat at the front of the church staring at the coffin. The wreath on top of the coffin, said 'in Loving Memory of my daughter, Jo'. Nathan, had seen the wreath in Gran's hand before she placed it on top – it seemed to be there just to convince him that Auntie Jo had indeed gone.

He thought back to what his mother had told him about seeing Auntie Jo one last time – it was probably for the best that he hadn't seen inside that big casket. He began to imagine what she looked like in there right now - then stopped – realising she couldn't possibly look the same as she did when she'd been alive.

The priest spoke candidly about the problem of drugs in the community and the heartbreak it caused. The congregation, listened with heavy hearts when Father Flynn talked about the Jo he'd known as a child. Nathan listened intently and bravely sang 'The Lord is My Shepherd'.

"It's sad that George didn't come to say goodbye to Auntie Jo," said Nathan once they returned home, where he sat next to his grandma with Roddy sitting limply in his lap.

"Well," said Maria, "maybe he was just too upset or maybe he couldn't get time off work." Her eyes showed Nathan that this wasn't in fact the truth; he knew there was something they weren't telling him.

Nathan didn't know that Jo had just discovered that she was pregnant - three days before the overdose – or that George had been devastated when he discovered that she'd gone with her friends to the pub that day after work. He'd heard a known local dealer had started chatting with Jo. Somehow, she'd ended up in the alley at the back of the pub overdosing on the pills she'd been given.

"She was pregnant, Maria," he'd said in a phone call the morning after the overdose. "We were both pretty shocked to hear the news. But, Maria, this is what I'd wanted all along - to have a family. I knew that we'd get married, so it wasn't an issue for me that we'd tie the knot sooner rather than later. I can't bear knowing that she's taken our child's life along with her own."

Time dragged on. Maria returned to her job two weeks after Jo's death feeling completely heart broken. For the first time she understood that the expression was literal; when her father had died three years before, she'd been broken, but this was different – this was a piercing, excruciating pain. She couldn't sleep and ate little; at times she could barely breathe.

One Saturday morning, three months after Jo's death whilst having breakfast at the big table, Nathan announced that the mother of his friend Colin was pregnant. "She's going to have a baby in four weeks' time," he said as he chewed a piece of toast adding, "could we have a baby, mum?"

"Don't be silly, Nathan. Colin's mum is much younger than me," she said, "I'll be forty in a couple of months." She stared at Dave, her eyes pleading with him to join in this conversation. Dave shrugged. Nathan could see that there was a tiny hint of a smile hiding behind Dave's lips.

"You know that dad and I only ever wanted you Nathan – don't you think our family is just perfect the way it is?"

Nathan cocked his head to the right and stuck his thumb under his chin.

"I think that it would be good to have a little sister or brother," he announced matter-of-factly.

"Look, Gran is going to be here in twenty minutes to take you for ice cream. Let's talk about this later. "Go get dressed now."

"Thanks for the support," said Maria sarcastically, when she and Dave had gone upstairs to their bedroom.

"What did you want me to say?"

"Well, for a start, it would have been good for Nathan to know that we have a perfect little family right here right now."

"Well…" she could see that Dave was playing for time, hesitating,

 "If you want to know the truth, I don't think that his suggestion was such a bad one,"

Maria, who was sitting in front of the mirror straightening her hair, stared at her husband. "I can't believe you're saying that," she cried. "After all I went through delivering Nathan and post-partum depression. "You have a baby if you want. I can't do it." She threw the hot straighteners on the chair and ran to the bed.

Dave rushed across the room to hug her. "Look, let's just leave it. We can do the weekly shop, pick up Nathan and Agnes from the ice cream shop then head to the beach."

Maria, felt her soul shrivelling, sensing her already unstable mind was about to take a turn for the worse.

"How are you feeling today?" Dave asked as he opened the door to Agnes.

"Same as usual." she replied popping her head through the living room door saying, "Are you ready for chocolate chip ice cream?"

Nathan rushed to his gran and gave her a big hug. "Can I have sprinkles and Gummy Bears too?" he asked.

"Okay," said Gran.

"I want Roddy to come with us today. Is that okay Gran?'

A tear appeared in Agnes's eyes. "Of course, Nathan. I'm sure he'll be good company for us both."

The Ice Cream Factory was Nathan's favourite café. After ordering their favourite ice-cream they chose a table by the big window, where Nathan liked to sit and watch the traffic. He put Roddy on one chair and sat himself down on the one opposite his grandma.

"How are you feeling now Gran?" asked Nathan, popping a Gummy into his mouth.

"Well Nathan the pain is still very bad and I still think about Auntie Jo every minute of the day. Not sure when that will stop, my love."

A grief counsellor had explained that it was best not to hide any strong emotions from children – so that they too could voice what they were going through.

"And what about you Nathan? How are you feeling?"

Nathan finished his first scoop of ice-cream, "I'm really sad, Gran. I don't think about Auntie Jo all the time but I do think about her a lot. Mummy cries every night. That makes me sad too."

Agnes looked at him and wiped her face with a handkerchief. She was trying her best not to show Nathan how upsetting it was to hear that Maria was suffering as much as she was.

"Remember that the counsellor told us that it's okay to cry when we feel really sad?"

"Of course I do," said Nathan. "Colin's mum is going to have a baby. I asked mum if we could have one too – maybe mum would stop crying so much if we had a baby. What do you think Gran?"

Agnes looked startled. She lifted Roddy from the chair and started to adjust his little gingham waistcoat. For a moment she thought she could smell Jo's perfume…

"Well," said Gran, "If mum and dad both want a baby that would be fine, but I think your mum only ever wanted you, Nathan. What did Mum say when you asked her?" Nathan was finishing off the second scoop of ice cream.

"She said that we'd talk about it later. I think Dad wants a baby though…"

April 2019

Maria couldn't remember exactly when she decided have a second child. At some point in the dark months that passed, a tiny little light had appeared in her soul. She couldn't name this feeling but she knew she was moving through the stages of grief just as the counsellor had predicted.

She sat up in the hospital bed cradling her new-born in her arms. The labour, this time, had been remarkably short and the delivery straightforward; her heart ached holding this little bundle in her arms. The ache was for Jo, but it was also for her new baby.

At visiting time Dave walked Nathan gently towards the bed whilst Agnes went to sit in the visitor's chair.

"Nathan, come and say hello to your sister," said Maria.

He gingerly stepped forward and peeked inside the shawl. There he saw the tiniest little human he'd ever seen. The baby's eyes were tightly closed, her arms and hands were hidden behind a shawl and a tiny pink hat sat on her little head. Just then she let out a whimper. "Can I touch her?" he asked.

"As long as you're gentle," said Maria. Her heart melted when she saw him gently caress her little cheeks in his hands,

"Hello little sister," he said, "I'm Nathan, your big brother. I'm going to look after you and I'm going to be the best big brother anyone has ever had."

Nathan stared at this little baby knowing in his soul she was the one that would bring happier times to his family. He knew his Auntie Jo would want this for everyone.

"What do you think we should call her?" asked Dave. Nathan touched her little nose and her little ears saying. "Should we call her Jo after Auntie Jo?"

Agnes looked at Maria and Maria looked at Dave pulling the baby closer to her and thought for a second. "You know, I think we'd all get confused if we call her Jo – we won't know if we're talking about the baby or Auntie Jo."

Nathan moved away from the bed and sat on Dave's lap. Everyone could see that he was thinking.

"Well, maybe we could take the J and the O from Jo and D and the Y from Roddy - and call her Jody?"

Silence. A minute or more passed. Maria, overcome with love for her son, let out a sigh. "Dave, what do you think about that?"

Hugging Nathan tightly, Dave said, "I think it's the name our daughter is supposed to have. Jody – what a great name for your new baby sister."

A few minutes later a nurse stepped into the room asking if it was okay to allow another visitor in.

"Who is it?" asked Maria.

"He just said he was a friend of the family, shall I let him in?"

"Yes sure."

George walked in. Nathan bounced across the room grabbing him by the hand.

"George, come and see Jody, my baby sister," he said, explaining how he'd decided on the baby's name.

"I didn't know what to do Maria. I'm so sorry that I didn't go to the funeral. I'm ashamed that I haven't been in touch since…"

"It's okay George. We've all been through hell. I can't imagine that yours was any easier than ours."

George reached into his backpack and took out a present. "Nathan, do you want to open this up for your sister?"

Nathan dashed across the room and tore open the paper. Inside was a stuffed rabbit. It wasn't the same as Roddy but everyone knew that this present had been chosen with love and care.

"Wow, Jody and I both have rabbits to play with now George."

"Now you have to find a name for this little guy," laughed George.

Finding Henry Moore

By

Stephanie Thornton

Bertie rushed into the house without stopping to close the door. In his hands he held a small box.

"Whatever is the matter?" Mum asked, as she did the washing up.

"I've got some clay and I have to make an egg."

"So that's what's in the box."

"Everyone's got some in our school. Miss Jenkins said we are to make the egg at home, bake it in the oven and bring it to school just before we close for Easter. And we can choose our own design."

Bertie was panting with excitement and shuffling from foot to foot.

"Well, you'll have to cook it when I'm baking something else, we're still on rations," Mum smiled at Bertie. "Why are you so excited?"

"I don't know why. It feels so good just to touch the clay."

Mum knew her son was different. He seemed to have an extra something special and his bedroom was full of objects he had made.

"Well when we go to Temple Newsam tomorrow with your Gran, I'll show you the sculpture made by Henry Moore. It may give you some ideas.

Everyone is talking about it. Mind you, it's quite unusual and I don't really think you'll like it."

Saturday came. It was a cold and windy day but Bertie felt a buzz of excitement at what his mother promised. As they walked down the path, they could see an enormous object in the distance.

There it was, at the side of the path where the giant rhododendrons were just beginning to flower.

An enormous piece of polished bronze lay upon a block. He peered at the title. It said "Mother and child" on the plaque. It was really very curious. He was interrupted by some friends of Mum who stopped to say hello.

"Go sit on that bench and just look at it. I need to talk with Gran to my friends a while," suggested Mum.

He perched upon the bench, next to a man who was sitting there with his coat collar high up to his chin. Bertie shuffled round trying to fold his legs under the front bar as it was too high for him. On the path in front of him, two women stopped to look at the figure.

One sniffed, "Huh, call that mother and child!"

"It feels like me when I've been on my feet all day," the other laughed, and they walked quickly down the path away from it.

He found he couldn't take his eyes off the strange shape in front of him. He gazed at it and found he felt quite hypnotized.

"What do you think of the sculpture?" the man asked, breaking into his thoughts.

Bertie blinked, was it OK to talk to strangers? But his mum stood there so he was sure it was all right.

"Well it makes me feel a glow in my tummy. I suppose it's the way the light shines off the lady and the baby laid in that sort of curvy shape."

"You can see that, can you. How old are you?"

"I'll be eight next week."

"Do you like sculpture?" asked the man. He really seemed most interested.

So, Bertie told him of the egg he had to make.

"If you like," offered the man, "bring the clay to me in the park tomorrow and some water in a pail and we'll have a little go at it, shall we?"

"My mum won't let me talk to strangers."

"Perhaps we can ask her to bring you or you could come with a friend if you like."

Bertie said his mum worked on a Sunday at the church, but he'd see if Donald could come.

"Donald has spots though, so he doesn't look very nice," he added.

It was agreed Bertie would come with Donald and Mum had said it was OK so long as they were together.

Sunday was a little warmer. Bertie carried the pail into the park, water slopping over its side, and Donald held the box, a hand towel and a football under his other arm.

"I don't know why you think this man can help. I think it's a silly idea," said Donald, always the pragmatist.

When they arrived at the bench, Bertie sighed with relief. The man was there. Donald rushed off to kick the ball.

"As it's for a competition, it must be all your own work," said the man, "otherwise it's cheating. Feel the clay within your fingers until you feel it's part of you and only then begin."

Bertie felt the clay change underneath his touch. It didn't feel cold or clammy, it seemed to fill him with a sort of pulsing feeling.

"That's your energy running into the clay," explained the man. But Bertie didn't understand this, only that for him the clay felt alive within his hands. He worked at the small piece until he felt happy with the shape, then they covered it with the cloth within the box and kept it wet.

"When you've baked it slowly in the oven overnight, ask your mum for a nail file and make sure it's quite smooth before you colour it. What colour will you choose?"

Bertie explained his idea to the man who nodded and approved, and they sat and looked at 'The woman and child' until Donald said he'd had enough of football and wanted to go home.

During the following week, Bertie was consumed with all things egg-like. His mum had supplied him with an old emery board, and he filed away until the egg was smooth as silk and ready for the Easter egg competition.

They had a large table laid out for the judge and egg cups donated from each family on which to stand each egg and a name card, giving a title for each one.

The judge was a famous artist who was a friend of the school governor. Privately she was quite dreading how to make wonderful comments about some gaily decorated eggs.

The usual sight greeted the judge on that Maundy Thursday. Row upon row of brightly coloured eggs covered in spots, and swirls and flowers.

All except one.

There amongst the mass stood a most curious pure white egg which glowed with a brilliant sheen. Even more a curiosity, carved out within a hole that ran right through, was a golden yolk like pearl connected to the chamber. The card in front said, 'Mother and child'.

The judge said it was impossible a child of eight could do this, but Bertie got the prize.

It was a book on sculpture, by the artist Henry Moore.

Donald sniffed, he thought the prize quite stupid, but Bertie didn't.

"And look," Donald said, pointing to the photo on the back, "that's that geezer in the park you were talking to last week."

(Author's note; In the 1950s, Henry Moore used to sit on a bench in Temple Newsam to observe what people said about his sculpture)

Rockets on the Playground

By

C. I. Ripples

Mrs. Gottfried pulled Donald off the boy, who was lying flat on his back with a bloody nose. She sighed,

"Donald, this time I will have to call your parents. At the very least I'm sending you to Principal Guterres."

She knew full well this would have little effect, seeing as Donald's parents were major donors to the little school. Nevertheless, Donald lacked boundaries and had gone too far. She could not, would not condone physical violence, even if his father was Chairman of the Board.

"But Miss," Donald cried angrily, pointing at Justin with stubby bloodied fingers, "He said I was the stupidest in the class!"

"Is this true Justin?' she asked the boy as she sat him up, holding a handkerchief under his nose to catch the bleeding.

He merely shook his head, too stunned to speak.

Mrs. Gottfried looked questioningly at the children gathered around the scene.

"Angel," she asked the girl she considered the most reliable of her class, "did you see what happened?"

She shook her head,

"I was working on our refugee project with Seppe Miss."

Jean Michel stepped forward confidently, a good-looking boy, he proudly informed his beloved teacher,

"Donald accused Justin of taking his biscuit and then threw his lunch in the bin Miss. Justin then called him a stupid bully."

"Liar, liar, pants on fire!" Boris, bright but lazy, the joker of the class, the darling of many, stepped forward confidently.

"I bet Enrique did it," he announced, pointing at the tall weedy Latino boy.

Mrs. Gottfried knew the boy's family was struggling, the father having recently lost his job, spending his days knocking on doors, but she also knew Boris had a propensity to sandpaper over the truth, having herself too often been taken in by his deadly charm. She ignored him.

Mary had always been best friends with Donald and recently jealously found he was paying a little too much attention to Kim:

"Actually Miss, it was Kim who took the biscuit," she piped in.

"Kim?" Mrs., Gottfried turned to the rather obese little boy.

"No Miss, it weren't me. Or it were, but Jin told me to do it."

"I did not!" Jin jumped in absolutely denying the accusation:

"He's lying Miss. I was making soda rockets with Vlad. See?"

He proudly showed the vinegar and soda, as well as the bottles they'd brought to school.

"Kim's just angry we wouldn't let him play with us after he nearly hit Abe."

"You know you shouldn't play with rockets in the playground," Mrs. Gottfried scolded the boys, "I've warned you before. You could have seriously hurt someone!"

"But Donald plays with rockets too. He and Ben were the first to launch theirs when break started," Hassan sneaked in, "but they got bored when the bottle broke."

"We've got plenty more," a smug Donald added, "I've got more bottles than anyone here!"

"You're to leave your bottles at home Donald. You too boys," she gestured to, Kim, Vlad, Jin and Ben.

"What about Hassan and Tayip Miss?" Mohammed asked slyly.

"You're such a snitch," Tayip hissed, giving him a punch in the back, before informing Mrs. Gottfried innocently, "I don't own any."

"I have only one," Mary sighed enviously.

"Enough," Mrs. Gottfried clapped her hands, "everyone inside. Break is over."

The boys shoved and pushed their way back into the classroom ahead of the girls. Only Enrique lagged behind, waiting until the teacher was at her desk before making a dash past Donald's desk.

When they were finally settled in their seats Mrs. Gottfried informed her pupils as she wrote on the whiteboard:

"I want you all to copy this into your exercise books":

We are kind
We are sharing
We are caring
We do not bully
We do not lie
We do not play with rockets

The children dutifully copied down the text as Mrs. Gottfried circled the classroom. She noted that Donald was as usual the slowest to copy it down, the tip of his tongue pressed between his lips with the effort. His handwriting was atrocious. It didn't help that he had such short fingers, such little hands, but he couldn't help that. She'd given up on trying to improve his script long ago. Just as long as he completed the exercise. She would wait until he was finished.

Then she told the children to stand up and asked them in unison to repeat the words on the whiteboard. Finally, she added to the bottom 'agreed and accepted' and asked them if they knew what it meant.

Angel raised her hand, "It means that we agree that we should not do the bad things, only the good things."

"Very good Angel", Mrs. Gottfried praised, "but what does 'accepted' mean?"

Sania raised her hand, "does it mean that we agree that we agree?"

"Exactly!" Mrs. Gottfried smiled happily. They got the point after all.

"Donald, Vlad and Boris. Do you understand?"

"Of course, Miss!" Boris and Vlad called out in unison.

Donald looked a little perplexed, thought the whole thing stupid, but it was best to pretend and nod.

"I want you all to come to the whiteboard to write your name. That means that you really do agree to keeping to these class rules. Please stand up and come forward one by one, starting from the back," Mrs. Gottfried instructed the children, pleased with herself for her brilliant idea, for the progress made that day, at least in terms of behaviour if not necessarily academic achievement.

Donald, who's desk was closest to the teacher's, jumped from one foot onto the other as he waited his turn for the whiteboard, trying to trip up Jae, then Enrique, as they filed passed.

"We never get to do anything fun," he said under his breath to Ben, when he finally got to the board to write his name.

Just as he finished, the bell went to announce the end of school.

"Donald, you're to stay behind and go to the Principal, just as soon as I'm done here," Mrs. Gottfried instructed, before she turned her back to him to stand by the door to shake the hand of each child in turn.

Making an obscene gesture using his middle finger, Donald snuck up to the board to erase his name, then grinned stupidly at Kim, who winked back knowingly as Boris gave him a thumbs up.

Kieran's Colours

By

Sacha Quinn

Edwina Salt really didn't know what to say, which was very unusual for her. Most of the time she had lots to say on many things, but this time she was stumped. Kieran, four years old, a delightful child and a very popular member of her nursery class was somehow showing some unusual traits.

She hadn't noticed them herself but to be fair, for the last few weeks, she had given over most of her class and duties to a student teacher, Mina Edo. Mina had proved herself invaluable, being far more competent than Edwina would ordinarily expect. So, for once she had been glad to let Mina take over in the driving seat whilst she took a back seat, to contemplate retirement, leaving this increasingly bureaucratic education system behind.

"So, what do you think Edwina?" asked Mina as she presented the artistic masterpiece from her nursery class.

"Well, it's very colourful," was her first reply, not knowing quite what else she should say other than, "but is there some significance, apart from the fact that it looks more like a seven-year old competency rather than a four-year old?"

"There is that." Mina offered, "Yes, this child is certainly beyond what I would normally expect for his age in being able to articulate drawing a family scene. But what I'm puzzled about is why all the people in the picture have different coloured faces. Normally people have skin tones, regardless of whether they are black, white or somewhere in between. This child gives them vivid rainbow colours, and I say that to distinguish from flesh colours, regardless of usual and readily acceptable skin colours."

Mina started to look a little uncomfortable raising her eyes to Edwina, but Edwina simply nodded a 'carry on'.

"You see he colours people in shades we wouldn't expect. I mean how many people would paint their father's face blue? Sorry Edwina, but if this was a one off, I wouldn't have said anything. The fact it appears a number of times is more of a concern."

At that point she brought out a few more artistic renditions of the now seemingly problematic Kieran. Father was always blue; mother was a mixture of pink and peach and his sister was a kind of lilacy-purpley shade.

"What about anyone else? You know apart from his family? What about his class mates or outside friends?"

As well as trying to get a bit more insight to what was being presented, Edwina was playing for time, because there was something at the back of her mind that was just not coming through, but she knew was there.

"I don't know," replied Mina wishing she'd thought of those questions herself, so she could have presented a fuller picture and information to her mentor. Ever ready to do so, she said she would get onto it straight away.

"Oh, by the way," Edwina continued her mind still multi-tasking and not fully with Mina, "Does he ever say anything about the colours, you know like, my dad is blue or my mum is peach?"

Mina pondered the question, looking up as if searching for the answer on the ceiling, then lowered her eyes back to Edwina before replying.

"Actually, I only remember asking him twice, once I realised there seemed to be a pattern. I asked him why he coloured his dad blue and he said because he is blue. I asked the same about his mum and sister and the reply was the same. He appears to colour them as he sees them."

"OK, Mina, I really don't know what to say. But for now, I suggest we just humour him and basically ignore it. It might be a bit like those kids who invent an imaginary friend, that actually may only appear to be imaginary to us but to them is real. With those we tend to just ignore that too and after a while it runs its course and the friend disappears as reality and understanding of the real world takes hold."

As Mina left the tiny nursery office Edwina, still thoughtful, picked up her smart phone and went to her Facebook page looking for inspiration. It didn't disappoint. Almost as if it was meant to be and Edwina was certainly in the 'meant to be' and 'happens for a reason' schools of thought. There it was. A post from her former school friend Gladys.

Gladys had always been a little bit odd she'd thought. She had on many occasions said she 'felt' things and had a keen sense of premonition. Not in the foretelling of fortunes or being able to predict lottery numbers but of happenings with people. Of course, no-one really believed her and because of her inclinations people would make fun of her which had then turned her into the classic 'misunderstood problem child' who rebelled, ultimately becoming a teenage runaway. Nowadays she was just thought of as a dotty or eccentric.

But what if it was all true, she mused as she picked up her mobile, searching her contact list. Edwina, now fifty-nine years old, had seen a lot in her life. So much so that she now was convinced there were so many things she didn't know, couldn't know, would likely never know and what's more would never likely be able to explain. Just like at that party Gladys had invited her to. She had overheard Gladys telling the niece of another old school friend Ali, that there was someone in her empath group who saw people in colours.

Edwina's first thoughts had been what the hell is an empath group and then dwelled on the thoughts of someone being able to see people in colour: Is this the same as Kieran? Is he the same as this person Gladys knows?

There was just so much that was unknown in the world. Who was she to say whether Kieran actually seeing people in colour is the true way or whether somehow everyone else had been conditioned, somewhere through evolution, to understand the regular skin tones that almost everyone else in the world saw and were accustomed to?

She was still philosophising these self-imposed questions when her call connected. "Hi Gladys. It's Edwina."

"Hey Edwina I was just thinking about you!"

"Of course, you were. You always did have a bit of that sixth-sense, didn't you?"

Gladys laughed and agreed, asking, "So how can I help. I get the feeling this is not just a social call.'

"Your feelings would be correct Gladys."

When she disconnected the call, Edwina folded the scrap of paper with the information she had written down during their chat. She put it for safe keeping in her phone cover wondering how long it might be before she needed to retrieve it.

Not as long as she expected! Kieran's classmates, as children do, had started to notice things about Kieran too. Just like Mina had wanted to know why all the people he drew had bright coloured faces, now so did they. But children being children, they were not in any way discrete and word got to other children and classes and teachers and parents and squabbles had started.

Edwina along with Mina, who had by now been accepted as a newly qualified teacher, found themselves having to sort out the discontent until finally the headmistress, a sour faced individual, aptly named Miss Lemon, decided enough was enough. Such was her seeming intolerance of children, many times people had called into question why she was actually in the teaching profession, where she had to devote her life to them every day of the week. It was thought that maybe it had actually helped to secure her position as headmistress and management rather than teaching, positions in which the children didn't have to face her every day either. However, there was no doubt that she ran a tight ship and if some little upstart from primary one was causing disruption, it didn't usually take her long to make sure that the situation was remedied one way or another.

This was the reason Kieran's pinky-peachy faced mother, Martine found herself with his lilacy-purple faced sister, Lucy on her knee and blue faced father, Andre sitting by her side in Miss Lemon's office. She didn't know it but she was actually yellow faced and Edwina Salt, who had asked for this meeting, was very much lilacy-purple just as Lucy was.

Kieran had told them.

Not in so many words, since they had tried to discourage him from drawing attention to himself in this way. But he drew his mother's attention anyway when he coloured a picture of them with vivid rainbow skin colours rather than skin tones and then explaining in furtive whispers who they were. Sitting before her, Martine easily picked out Miss Lemon, Edwina Salt and the young Miss Mina since their colour on Kieran's picture exactly matched what she was seeing herself.

She drifted back to what Miss Lemon had to say hoping Andre had been paying more attention. Her head was buzzing and had temporarily distracted her. She still held hopes that as Kieran had never mentioned this buzzing, which she suffered as she absorbed the emotions of people around her, he had been spared this additional burden. That he wasn't quite the same as her gave her some blessed relief.

"So of course, I feel there is no option but for Kieran to try and find someplace where he can get both the needs of education and suitable treatment for his delusions about people being in colour," said Miss Lemon with a certain finality to her speech.

Andre could see tension rising in Martine. It didn't happen often. Mostly she kept her feelings under control. He reached out to try and offer a sympathetic touch but he knew this time it wouldn't help. This was a mother fighting for her child.

"Delusions, delusions, treatment. What are you talking about? There is nothing wrong with Kieran."

"But I don't think you understand Mrs. Rossi. He is not normal. He can't be. He talks about people having colour or always draws people with vivid colour faces. That is not normal."

"Normal, normal, what exactly is normal? I'll tell you what normal is for me shall I?" Martine now in full flight stared straight into Miss Lemon's eyes declaring, "you, Miss Lemon are yellow."

Without giving a chance for response she turned to Edwina saying, "You, Miss Salt are pinky-purple, whilst you, Miss Mina are a lovely shade of pink. And I know this how? Not because Kieran painted a picture but because I see exactly the same as he does."

Without giving any chance for right of reply, Martine stood up. Directing her words to Andre she said, "Come on, time to go. We are not going to get anything from this woman, my buzzing head is telling me so. Her defences are up, her feelings are hostile and uncompromising and she is giving me a headache with her intolerance and prejudice as well as her rising feelings of indignation no doubt wanting to dispute everything I have said."

Now directing her words back at an open-mouthed Miss Lemon, challenged,

"Tell me I'm wrong!"

Silence.

"No because you can't."

With that she hugged Lucy closer to her and taking hold of Kieran's hand declared,

"We are leaving now. Kieran deserves better than this, better than anything I ever got. There was no one to fight for me and my differences, but I'm here for him and we will not put up with this intolerance of people who are different."

During this outburst no-one noticed Edwina take out a piece of paper from her phone and, as the Rossi's left the room she quickly stood up to follow them, for once ignoring the command of her superior to come back.

"Mrs. Rossi, Mrs. Rossi wait."

Martine and Andre turned and waited as a breathless Edwina caught up with them.

"Here take this," she continued as she handed over the scrap of paper,

"It's the name of a school that claims to cater for every child however different or challenging they are. Not that Kieran is challenging. He's actually a delightful child," she hastened to add, taking hold of Kieran's hand and giving it a tight squeeze.

Martine's buzzing started to abate as she noted Edwina was quite calm with no bad intentions. She felt a modicum of peace hoping it would continue.

"Thank you, Miss Salt. I'm guessing from the colour of you, you too are different and have not had an easy life."

Edwina looked at her, deciding for once not to be in denial but instead look questioningly at Martine.

"Miss Salt you are pinky-purple. Pinky-purple to me usually indicates that someone is gay. Or lesbian, or bi-sexual. It's not always clear. Yes, Miss Salt you too were regarded as different in your day no doubt. Probably got no support as a child, teenager, young woman or even now. Very sad how, as children, we are not accepted for what and who we are and how it affects our lives. But Lucy here, who also shares your colour and Kieran, who is true blue straight like his father do have their individual differences and I will not see them suffer like I did and I suppose like you did too."

Edwina, eyes moist, felt choked.

"Yes, it would have been good to have had support. Kieran and Lucy will certainly have support at this school too. It's not close to here, it's in a place called Chanley Green about fifty miles north of here. A friend of mine gave me the details."

"Chanley Green?" questioned Martine, "I'm sure I've heard of that before."

"Yes, I'm guessing you have. And further guessing, you're in the same empath group as…."

"Gladys!" they said in unison.

214

Georgiana Does Paint

by

Stephanie Thornton

Her mum, Miriam, had been gazing into the bottom of a tea-cup, for a long time, reading the tea leaves. Mum was worried. In the bottom of the cup was a sort of hazy swirl and through this she could see the outline of a small child – one with pigtails stuck out at an angle and bright blond hair – and it meant trouble. With a capital 'T'.

Mum's family were all white witches. Not the black sort that rode around on broomsticks in a pointy hat, with a black cat perched pillion on the rear. Just plain ordinary ones. The sort that could 'tell' things and to whom people came for wise advice. For hundreds of years, witches had run in the family through a strange and rather weird gene pool that seemed to have given them a little bit of extra when it came to talents and to prophesies.

"Beth," her mum called out (her real name was Bethesda), "bring me that magnifying glass so I can look a little closer at the leaves please"

"Sorry Mum, I'm going to be late for school and you need to take me in the car."

Her mum gave a little sigh. It wasn't good to be interrupted when the stream was flowing from her powers. At the school gates, Miriam just missed running into a large and gleaming silver Bentley which had just pulled in around her.

"It's Georgiana, my new friend," Beth excitedly exclaimed. "She's only started school this week – and I want her to come for tea"

Miriam looked out of the car window as her eight-year-old daughter ran towards the other car. A door opened and a little blond girl got out at which Miriam caught her breath. It was the girl she had seen in the bottom of the leaves. Her bright blond hair was parted in a precise line right down the middle of her head with not a wisp in sight. It was so immaculate, so precise, it could have almost been a wig. Pigtails stuck out from this, at an angle, with huge blue bows of red and yellow decorating the ends. Her dress matched these with layers of petticoats, which also stuck out at an angle and were trimmed with yards and yards of lace. Her face itself was like a porcelain doll with a cupid mouth, short and puckered in the centre, over which a button nose and huge eyes, totally out of all proportion, rounded it off. It was a startling face but also rather chilling. Just too perfect, too symmetrical, too tidy. Miriam hated her on sight. The thought of Georgiana coming to tea was just too horrible to think about. A friend tapped on the glass just as she was about to drive away.

"Did you see that Bentley?" asked the friend. "That's the gorgeous Georgiana's parents and guess what, they're both psychiatrists!" she continued, as if that explained everything.

"We'll have to watch ourselves," she giggled.

Miriam gave a little shudder. Psychiatry was the other end of the scale of what she excelled at. If they found out what she did, they'd probably lock her up – so they could study her, or even have her burned at the stake. And sell tickets to compete with 'Get me out of here' and other such nonsense.

During the following week, Beth pestered her mum daily, saying she wanted the dreaded Georgiana to come for tea. There was nothing for it but to agree. Miriam prepared the pretty tea with pride; finger sandwiches and dainty cakes to fit in with the vision of the girl in the petticoated dress. Georgiana had come to tea, even more be-ribboned. This time the colour scheme was paisley green with scarlet polka dots. In contrast, Beth was wearing leggings and a tee-shirt with the phrase 'I love my cat' printed on the front. At this, Georgiana sniffed.

"Mother says all pets are parasites" she declared.

Beth changed into another. This one said 'Pigs may fly'. Georgiana then said pigs were dirty filthy beasts. She liked the one with 'Beethoven rules' on the front and explained that she thought that they ate that sort of bread at home. At this, Miriam turned her face away and grinned, hoping Georgiana hadn't spotted her.

The dainty tea went quite well, apart from the fact that Georgiana didn't eat cheese, or ham, or chicken and only ate the radishes that decorated the plate, saying, "Mummy wouldn't allow the rest". She refused salt to accompany the radishes, declaring salt was bad for the heart. Mummy had told her so. Good old Mummy, Miriam thought sarcastically, underneath her breath.

After the tea, they went to Beth's room to play. Georgiana looked at the pretty room and sniffed.

217

"Mummy wouldn't like these colours," she announced, "she would say they would disturb the balance of the mind".

Miriam thought she sounded just like a miniature professor and fled the room before she said something she would regret.

There followed, a long period of silence. Whatever were they doing up there, she thought, as she looked up at the ceiling?

At 6pm the Dr. Mrs. Georgiana arrived to take her home.

"Do look, Mummy," cried Georgiana from the top of the stairs, "come see what I've been doing."

She had been decorating Beth's bedspread with poster paints.

"You're SO clever, my darling, "said the doctor, and turned to the horrified Miriam, "She's just been expressing herself. How precious! And look at the dolphin and the butterfly she has painted"

All Miriam could see, was a horrible dauby mess covering the spread. Even Picasso couldn't have explained the scrawls. The doctor was taking a picture on her phone. "I shall write of it in 'The Lancet," she declared.

You would have thought that Beth would have had enough of Georgie after this disastrous visit. No, she would have her come again, but Miriam insisted it was to be outside in the garden. Surely it would be safe out there.

Dr. Mr. Georgiana came this time, where he was shown Georgiana's latest 'work' of a picture made of flower heads from Beth's father's prize chrysanthemums. And the newly decorated bunny!

218

"She's so expressive, such talent, so creative. Of course, she must, with parents like us. How can she possibly not?" the proud father exclaimed. He clapped then hugged her close, after taking another picture to show the Dr. Mrs. and no doubt add it to 'The Lancet' feature.

The bunny hated being washed and ended up at the vets.

The third visit seemed to pass without a hitch and Miriam drove the precious Georgiana home in her new car. They arrived at Dr. Mr. and Dr. Mrs.'s house and Georgiana said she had had such a good time she had left a present for Beth's Mum in the back of the car. Miriam tipped the seat back and found the gift, which was a series of puncture marks in the soft leather covering the walls of the new car – and in red at that. Miriam was mad to boiling point and marched to the front door. And there, only to be told, after showing them Georgiana's gift, that it was more than wonderful this time and that Georgiana had really excelled herself.

"It really is as good as Picasso!" exclaimed both doctors. "You're so lucky to have it in your car. It will be valuable one day when our daughter's famous. We'll take a picture and publish it in 'Psychiatry Today'. But whilst you're here, do come in and we'll show you our newly decorated house. We are developing it to give a positive and welcoming attitude for all our clients who come to us at home."

Miriam's curiosity got the better of her. This she must see. Inside, it was a vision of deep depressing greys and midnight blue with touches of black thrown in for effect.

"It is so calming for the mood, so it helps our patients if they have to visit here. So restful, so serene, and look at the subtle touches on the ceilings," they announced. In the niches in the drawing room lit up with spots, stood black basalt urns swathed in dark green velvet on the walls behind.

Personally, Miriam thought it was like going into a funeral parlour and couldn't wait to leave. She wondered if patients going there got better or if it made them worse. If the latter, more fees would result. But as she drove off furiously down the road there was a little gem of an idea beginning to form and she started to smile to herself.

It was finally time for Beth to go to tea at Georgiana's. Miriam had planted her idea in Beth's head whilst she was asleep, and Beth woke up on that day with a fun idea to do there. She whispered it to Georgiana when they got to school, but by tea-time Georgiana had forgotten where the idea had come from – she thought she'd thought of it herself.

They got home from school some time before the doctors came home from their consulting rooms to find the housekeeper had left a tea ready for them. It was the sort of tea considered 'suitable' for ones concerned with health. But the idea of radishes didn't appeal to Beth. Neither did plates of carrots sticks and lettuce leaves. But at least the housekeeper, who felt sorry for the girls, had left two slices of cake she'd brought from home.

Beth ate some cake. Georgiana ate some too. She wasn't used to sweet things and a sugar rush ensued, and whilst Georgiana tore around the house, totally out of control, Beth just sat and watched her. She was slowly going off her 'new best friend' and had begun to think she was an idiot.

Miriam and the doctors all arrived at the same moment when the time came for Beth to leave. Dr. Mrs. Georgiana was the first to enter the house. She screamed at the sight that greeted her and put her hands up to shield her eyes as she staggered back in horror. The newly painted walls were covered in enormous swirls and daubs of yellows, reds and greens and covering the velvet drapes and urns.

"Aren't I clever, I did it all myself. I knew you would be pleased and I wouldn't let Beth do any of it. She was only allowed to sit and watch!" Georgiana exclaimed, holding up the paint brush.

"Oh, how very lovely," stated Miriam, "What a clever daughter you have and so expressive too. It's quite as good as any 'Turner prize'. My Beth isn't clever enough to create like this." She turned to the Drs. whose faces were an angry red. They looked at her as if she were quite mad. "You'll be able to put this in 'The Lancet' too. At this rate, you'll have a very famous daughter on your hands. And we can say we knew her when she was so young. I'll just have to take a picture to remember this and put it on the notice board at school," and she quickly took one on her mobile phone.

Both Doctors started to object. Fast action was now necessary.

"So sorry, but it's time for us to leave," Miriam said in haste. "I promised Beth a hamburger from McDonalds' on the way home. She's just won an art prize at school – it's of Loch Lomond – and we're going to hang it on the wall. Thanks so much for tea. It was such an honour for Beth to be invited here. Goodbye!"

And they fled off down the path.

Relationships

Assumptions are the termites of relationships.
- Henry Winkler

Relationships are mysterious. We doubt the positive qualities in others, seldom the negative.
- Christopher Pike, Remember Me

What we know of other people is only our memory of the moments during which we knew them.
- T.S. Elliot, The Cocktail Party

Seldom, very seldom, does complete truth belong to any human disclosure; seldom can it happen that something is not a little disguised or a little mistaken.
- Jane Austin, Emma

You don't develop courage by being happy in your relationships every day. You develop it by surviving difficult times and challenging adversity.
- Epicurus

Odd Folk

By

Stephanie Thornton

"Do the work that's nearest,
'tho' 't'is't dull the whiles.
Helping when you meet them,
Lame dogs over stiles"

I was given this poem in an autograph album from
my teacher when I was ten years old. It must have
had some deep impact. Either that or she must have
been a really great teacher. But the result was that I
took to looking after 'Lame Dogs' big time
afterwards.

At the time, I thought this teacher huge and pretty
scary. She had a large wart on her chin too, with little
hairs sticking out of it which wobbled when she
talked. You stared at it when speaking to her, in total
fascination as to why it didn't fall off. She wore large
heavy rimmed spectacles under a head of grey and
wiry hair that stuck out sideways. Just the sort of
person Roald Dahl would love to meet for
inspiration.

There's no doubt about it. I attract Lame Dogs -
also known as 'odd folk'. Not the sort such as the
vertically challenged. Like when my son Jake, then
aged four, saw a dwarf get off a boat down the

gangplank. He'd shouted at the top of his voice, "Who's that little man, mummy?" He went on shouting it at the top of his voice until I could hush him up and explain. No, it's the sort you can't spot at a glance. The sort that don't have bright pink eyes and teeth like Jaws, or strange cone shapes coming out of their head like aliens. It's the sort of folk who look quite ordinary – on the outside.

They are attracted to me like magnets. I think I must have an invisible sign that says 'MUG' flashing on my forehead. But there they are, homing in. Or perhaps we're already dead like some people say and this is heaven already. If so, is this some sort of biblical task the Archangel has set of me? Or maybe it's just because I am odd too.

In Yorkshire terms, I would be called 'a fettler upper'. This is a bit like whittling (carving wood) but this time with peoples' psyche. In other words, someone who fixes things. If I don't catch myself, I do this big time. If I hear a child having a temper tantrum in a super market and hear it saying, 'I want' and 'I won't' and having a screaming fit, I can feel my feet, firmly fixed to the floor, start to turn in its direction. I then start walking towards the sound – you know, like Zombies do when they smell blood.

I did it on a boat in Venice once. This French kid was climbing all over everyone's feet and being a total pain. I shouted at it in French and it sat for two hours after just staring at me with a look of terror on its face. Perhaps I will now be recruited by M15 and save the use of weapons. I had never thought my fettling could be so useful. But perhaps the terror was due to my French accent?

I also acquire weird friends that I will fettle without asking. The ones that need a housekeeper as the fiftieth one has just left. The wife who moans about ironing her husband's shirts that I will listen to and sympathise with for the millionth time without actually curing anything. Instead of telling her to tell him to do them himself. Why do they do this moaning then, not take any notice of anyone who tries to make things better? The answer must be that they actually like being this way. A sort of washing machine that only ever empties water whilst the clothes remain within the drum. Or forever on the spin cycle of being dependent on moans?

There's a medical condition for it which I have found is called co-dependency. So, I attract all the needies. These include ones with marital troubles. Ones with money troubles. Ones with sex troubles. Ones with a daft dog. Ones with children, who will show me endless photos of the whole tribe in difference poses, saying Johnny is wearing a blue shirt in this picture. Groan! Yawn! And just when I think I've made a new friend; they will turn into some monster with all sorts of hidden issues.

I also observe that I will spend lots of time in someone's company and realise that they either got me to talk about myself in minute detail for several hours which leaves me totally exhausted whilst they've drunk seven cocktails, whilst they had a great time doing mental gossip. Or they've talked about themselves for several hours and never asked how I was doing.

So, I joined a 12-step programme to try to sort out my CD problems. I would 'share' what my problem was – the whittling, the fixing and the fettling – only to find out everyone was doing the same. We were all boring each other ridged with 'tales of the totally expected'.

The lesson to learn is to detach. That way you go off into a sort of mental drift sideways, scanning the floss out of all the dumpings. But just when you've learnt this, another friend comes along and spots the 'mug' sign flashing on your forehead. Before you know where you are, you're into full fixing mode again. A sort of mechanic for the brain of others. They bring their brain in for a mental service at your garage, they have a quick grease round, before they go off, literally, sparkling and new, leaving you with swarf on the floor.

But didn't they say that 'mad dogs and English men go out in the midday sun?' – that's because the lame-mad dogs and the men are really all the same person and they're all mad. The trouble is, spotting them.

Great leaders have also been examples of the master fettler. Included are the great religious leaders: Mohammed, Buddha and Jesus. Jesus gets the biggest A-plus ever for effort, but whilst followers then cherry picked what they would choose to do from his wise words, no one told him to stop fettling or he may end up getting crucified.

Modern day leaders probably learnt to fettle at their mothers' apron strings. Margaret Thatcher learnt hers young, over gossip at the counter of the grocer's shop. Then later used it to fix bin men and the miners. Mao Zedong listened to his neighbours, when counting grains of rice with chop sticks. Hitler painted portraits of a house, whilst the owner recanted tales of woe about their life.

Scientists tell us how to save the planet when we moan about how hot it's getting. Then, Reagan removes the solar panels off the White House roof. The public adopt snippets of advice that best suit their life style, reserving the thought of Armageddon to a later date.

The truth must be that we don't want to get fixed. We just want to have a good moan.

Men do it too. Look at Mark Darcy who must have wanted to fix Bridget Jones big time. Just look at him, a big shot lawyer taking on all that neediness. Just typical. His earlier example, the other Mr. Darcy, fixed all Miss Bennet's too.

I am now on marriage number two, thinking I will get some great in-laws. Perhaps Liz Taylor thought the same and as far as I know, she was a fixer and fettler too. I could have saved her lots of trouble, and all those expensive divorces.

The answer is that new marriages don't fix things. I have had two mean lots of brothers and sisters – penny pinching doesn't come near it. At the birth of first child, I was given a little piece of guest soap from a hotel and for the second nothing at all. However, I had learnt to make the soap last and was still using it two years later when the second was born. It taught me thrift and economy – what a great gift it turned out to be.

When I'm not fixing and fettling others of course and have run out, I can always fix my children.

The eldest one has been a bit depressed recently. Too much work and no time off. So, in his spare time, which he hasn't got much of, he has been decorating. The chosen choice of colour is grey. So fresh, so modern, so depressing. Tip: If you want to heighten your depression and get more pills, colour it grey. However, I realise I must please my daughter-in-law and not try to fettle her too. She likes grey. If I try it, she may set her dog onto me, who is a soppy spaniel, now looking at me with mournful eyes. I see that he too is just right for a fettle. Instead I scratch his nose. He likes this and comes to me for more. At least someone is now fixed.

I will look at my history of the fettle. It dates back to early teens when my mum was always ill. She wasn't really ill. Just a little bit ill. But a career was made of it which lasted 70 years. Would I have been different if not for that? Or am I doing what the shrink would say? If there is no cure, blame the parents?

It's no good saying this time it will be different when you meet someone new. These people are very clever at hiding the real 'them'. They should invent a 'Sat. Nav.' to guide you to the right ones.

I would be the one Norman Bates would seek out to talk about 'mummy'. I'd be so keen to fix him, when he gave me that little boy stare of his, that I'd probably invite him in for tea so we could have a little chat. I'd think he was quite normal as he sipped his tea, even though he really was an 'odd ball'.

On hospital visits, I will try to be most kind.

"I have a bad cold so can I please have a mask, so others won't get it?"

The nurse looks at me with pity. "We don't do masks," she declares, giving my gift of cold to all the others in the ward. How kind. She is obviously a fettler too sending all the oldies to an earlier grave speeding up the turn-over of beds and reducing the waiting list.

Now, just when I think I have written this tale and all is lost and I am beyond hope, a friend comes to visit. She asks me all about what's ailing me. She asks me this a lot. Every day, every minute - for a whole week. Then, just when I've started to feel a bit confused, the penny drops. I've been sussed. She's a fixer and fettler too. This time, it's my turn to be fettled. Finally, I can have a rest. Someone else is at it. Wonderful!

Agent Nineteen

By

C. I. Ripples

Agent Nineteen to MUV Planetary Council – Earth time ET2100:

The climate wars, which have wiped out all but twenty percent of the human population are still ongoing and unlikely to cease until total eradication has been achieved.

We warned humans about the relationship between human activities and climate about 100 Earth years ago. We informed them about the indirect relationship between CO_2 emissions and global temperature rises – that a reduction in emissions would not lead to a proportional drop in temperatures, due to the extremely long cycle of CO_2. We told them that it would take centuries for climate change to reverse. We showed them that there was a relationship between global warming and rising sea levels. That the sea expands as temperatures rise and the carbon balance is altered. That they will continue to rise.

As outlined in our detailed ET2000 report, we already gave humans the basics of our language, to code their own predictive models, one hundred and fifty years ago, in the belief that humans were more likely to believe predictions they produced themselves. When human scientists discovered the catastrophic consequences of human actions, and not only for the human race, of destabilizing the relationships of the natural world, in good time, well over a century ago, we were hopeful for corrective action as scientists such as Keeling and Manabe tried to warn the human race.

When our hopes proved erroneous, we highlighted our concerns in our ET2005 communication to the Council, who asked our agents to step up their efforts. Our eons therefore infiltrated great influential minds, such as that of Lessing, Gore, Hansen and Dyer. The last was inspired to write his great book, 'Climate War', which although accurate in most of in its predictions, failed to stem the

tide. Dyer, influential then, in ET2010, was ridiculed. Even our whisperings to Greta Thunberg a decade later, heeded by many, at least for an Earth season, were ridiculed by others as the ramblings of an autistic girl, ignored by those with the most power to change things.

Of course, there were those who listened and understood, mainly grassroots but also international organizations such as the IPCC and the UN, that collaborative organization that was disbanded in ET2036, which tried to influence human governing bodies. There was even a time when they were successful, as demonstrated by what became known as the Paris Agreement on Climate, signed by 194 countries, setting global targets for emissions. We thought our work was almost done.

Until ET2017 that is, when the USA, led by Donald Trump, then President, who himself died from over rather than undernourishment, ceased all participation in said ET2015 Paris Agreement, insisting there was no relationship between human emissions and climate change. Of course, he was playing to the coal, oil and gas industries, powerful campaign supporters. Then came ET2018, when a US administration led full-scale cyber-attack on climate scientists was largely ignored by the masses, who preferred to believe it was fake news, preferred to believe their lack of blame as they drove their cars, ate a meat filled diet, flew to their holidays, continued to reproduce. Not soon after came Bolsonaro, brought to power by Brazil's powerful agribusiness block, who encouraged further burning of the Amazon for logging and cattle farming.

Only in ET2030, when Earth's temperature had increased by 1.5 degrees unleashing a crescendo of deadly storms, floods and droughts, were our warnings finally taken seriously. By then it was too late as the window of opportunity to drastically reduce global emissions to safe levels had closed ten years prior and Earth's temperature continued to rise as we predicted, by 2, then 3 and finally in the last decade 4 degrees.

As anticipated, once Earth had warmed by 3 degrees, the relationship between human activity and climate change was severed, as the methane and CO_2 released from the melting Arctic permafrost overwhelmed human emission cuts. Humans had lost their ability to control the weather, leaving Earth on the road to no return.

By ET2040 cities like Dhaka and Florida were drowning. A decade later much of Jakarta was underwater. Tens of millions were fleeing the rising sea waters of Shanghai, Lagos, and Mumbai, coastal areas with huge populations. Even London is seven meters under. More recently, one billion tried to flee the Middle East and Africa, because living conditions have become untenable, the heat unbearable, the lack of water unsustainable. Today, even in the tropics and subtropics, the increasing drought and shorter growing seasons, have severely reduced the availability of such dietary staples such as rice and maize. The human world is either starving or drowning, which as predicted has resulted in civil unrest.

Of course, humans have been faced many times in history with the consequences of food or water shortages, yet they fail to link it to conflict and don't learn the lessons of history, although the relationship has always been clear: for every degree of temperature rise, the number of climate refugees rises, the number of failed states rises, and as a result the number of wars and conflicts. Please refer to our ET2020 communication to the Council which highlighted that the absence of water and food would lead to one community fighting another for mere survival within a matter of decades.

This was demonstrated in Syria, where a drought that lasted several years beginning in ET2007, resulted in crop failure as arable land became desert, leading 1.5 million migrants fleeing from rural communities. This was a major factor that helped destabilize the country. Please refer to our ET2020 communication for further details.

No lessons were learnt, we would go as far as to say they were persistently ignored, as humans continued to drive climate change, steadily making the whole eastern Mediterranean and Middle East regions, including Lebanon, Jordan, Israel, Iraq and Iran, more arid. African states such as Somalia and Sudan also descended into drought fuelled conflicts, as did Central America, particularly Mexico.

In Central America, where drought became the new normal, crop failures and the breakdown of governments led to increased attempts to emigrate to the USA. Despite the fact that the border had been fortified by a wall of 5G antenna placed 300m apart along its borders. Relatively harmless for other 5G users, the antenna wall had a gigahertz strength well over 95 to deter migrants, who as they approached the border fell back, believing their faces were on fire. Those who persevered were faced by automated machine gun posts and anti-personnel mines. This in turn led to an outcry by the 60 million or so Hispanic Americans, with resultant disturbances and violent demonstrations. Again, the military used 5G technology as a form of crowd control. The government justified its actions on national security grounds as extreme weather, droughts, heatwaves, flooding and storms reduced its own food production.

Such views and individual countries' fight for survival by ET2050, meant that human rights conventions were no longer abided by and all hope of international collaboration went out the window. It wasn't long before other countries followed the American model. What was then India, for example, closed its borders to refugees from sinking Bangladesh, placed its military on the border and landmines beyond, resulting in large scale loss of life.

Those countries that could still feed their populations and had enough might, too closed their borders to the masses of climate refugees using a 5G force field. These included Greater Russia, The Northern Union, The Devolved Kingdom, Greater Pakistan and Iran. There was one thing most of these countries had in common – they, like the USA and starving China, all owned nuclear weapons with consequences almost as serious for humanity as climate change itself.

Already back in ET2006 what was then the United Kingdom had established the connection between the use of nuclear weapons and climate change. As demonstrated when the USA attempted to threaten one of the Northern Union countries with a nuclear strike in ET2055, unless it allowed the USA to seize the melting resource rich Greenland. Greater Russia, which is an ally of the Northern Union, defused the situation by warning it would retaliate if it detected any incoming missiles. Another example was Pakistan, which only won the Indus River war, provoked by India when it cut off rivers Pakistan depended on for irrigation, because it didn't have the 'no first use' nuclear policy as did India. It was a short-lived nuclear exchange, that destroyed much of India's nuclear bases, but as a result, those who weren't wiped out in the blasts, died from radiation poisoning, which spread from Jaipur in Northern India as far as Faisalabad in Pakistan. The winds carried the fall-out as far as Myanmar and northern Thailand where millions died. When Israel refused to share water supplies with Palestine, and started a war with Jordan over access to water, this evoked a nuclear response from Iran, with an inevitable retaliation, which apart from large scale loss of life in Iran and Israel itself, left what remained of many of their already drought stressed neighbours uninhabitable due to radiation poisoning.

Earth's population is now at ET1945 levels, but the climate crisis, further compounded by radiation poisoning, has not been resolved. Still humans have not come together to deal with these calamities, nor helped each other survive. Humans continue to starve, but the climate wars will not cease any time soon.

We predict that China, which can't feed its famine reduced population, now at ten per cent of ET2019 levels, from its increasingly arid farmlands, and which continues to be swept by famine and civil unrest, will be the next country to choose the nuclear option. It has had its eyes on fertile Siberia for a long time, is desperate and has little left to lose.

In light of the above, it is our opinion that despite our best efforts we have failed to save this planet, perhaps because in the process of our unrequited efforts we lost our faith in humanity. We failed, because we were unable to persuade humanity to rise above that essentially human characteristic of egotistical short termism. We failed, because in giving them the language for good, we also gave them the language of destruction. We failed, because we did not recognize that black forces opposing us had already occupied the planet, had festered and grown too strong to counter long ago.

Our advice to the Council therefore is to sever all relationships with Earth and to let matters take their own course. Even if this leads to wholesale destruction. There is nothing left here for us to do.

One Summer's Day

By

Stephanie Thornton

Why did she go back to that place? The one with the name that reminded her of him. Perhaps his relations owned it and she would find him there. But then, what would she do?

Everyone was eating fish and chips. Haddock! Many places only served up cod. Ugh, it may have fluke worms. Or so her husband told her.

She must have been there half an hour and still the lunch had not arrived. It was raining heavily outside. The promised summer heat had not begun. It had disappeared, replaced by a steaming journey in a bus with all the windows misted up.

In the distance an elderly couple arrived with two children. Grandparents? She did a double take looking at the man. Perhaps she was already in that sort of mood, searching for the boy from long ago. Was it him? She ate alone that day, which always made the situation worse. She had nothing to accompany her, other than her thoughts. She would fiddle with the menu and move the items on the table around a little and then move them back again, just to keep her fingers busy. Hoping people didn't see.

Thus, she could sit, perusing, people-watching, looking for that time when he would walk in through the door. But what would he look like now and would she even recognise him? His mouth would be the same, - mouths didn't change - even if his face had – and he may be slim or fat, lined or smooth, bald or bushy now. He may even have a beard. She smiled to herself. In fact, he may even be dead too. That would be of help.

If this man turned out to be him, would she confront him or start to sob? Maybe she would scream and then everyone in the café would come rushing or pretend they hadn't seen the mad woman sitting at the table by their side. This time, she was so sure she knew him – that he was the one –time seemed to slow. The clock on the wall paused. People seemed to freeze before her eyes, with drooping slices of pale white bread halfway to their mouths, and the crunch on the batter of the fish stretching into a long metallic sound, as if the fish had turned brittle coating to wage war on chomping teeth.

She had only been eleven the last time she had seen him. He was the leader of her gang and she worshipped him. He was the best, the smartest and the kindest. She gazed at him in wonder rescuing a fallen bird, when the rival gang, the bad ones, had shot it from a tree. Her gang built the biggest bonfires, had the grandest fireworks and a den – a worn out wooden shed - the envy of the kids around the block. She would cook mud pies for her hero and practise playing wife of sorts. She was also the only girl to play cricket and jump the wall called 'Everest'. That was until Linda came along from time to time.

Somewhere around ten, things started to change. A time of confusion and transition. She and best friend Linda did a sort of strip tease for the boys, with layers of strips of cloth draped around their fully dressed up bodies. Make believe pretend. After that, it was the dance of the seven veils. With not an inch of flesh exposed. But she'd stopped going to the den after that, as it was covered in graffiti chalk marks with ugly sketches on the walls – nothing romantic. Quite the opposite – obscene in fact. It frightened her. In fact, anything to do with sex was something hidden in the back drawer of her mind, refusing to be consulted. It wasn't time to end the make believe.

One Saturday, she discovered that the air was suffused with heat when she went out to play. The sun shone strongly in its golden orb. There was only Peter there, kicking stones along the path. She felt proud he was there for her. She had him to herself. She considered it romantic.

He had found an ancient insect spray. It was a metal affair with two rusty chambers on either side of the head which made it look like a blown-up frog. At the other end was a plunger that drew up the liquid from the chamber until it sprayed out in a mist. He had filled it with water and was using it on walls and gates all along the row of terraced houses. They were linked by a cobbled street down the back where pavements lay, made from huge cracked slabs of Yorkshire stone.

There was not a soul in sight. The track was rough. Easy to fall over. Strewn with weeds amidst the cracks. He was teasing her. The sun boiled down, turning faces brown. Gritty knees and sweating hair. He was laughing in the sun.

What a great feeling to be sprayed with water from the gun. She was with him. Her hero.

At the end of the cobbled road was a large neglected area that rose up a banking, where residents had tried to start allotments. They failed. Here and there, clumps of grass mixed up with neglected vegetables and trailing brambles grew, binding everything together. They called it 'The Tanks'.

He put a hand out to help her climb on higher ground. It was wonderful. But then he didn't let her go. She felt proud. His grip got tighter. His fingers bruised her skin. He started to drag her up the grass away from the cobbled road. Confusion! Romance spiralled into violence like a non-existent mist. The Cinderella girl in her shrank and disappeared. The glass slipper shattered into bits of clay.

"What are you doing? Let me go!"

"I'm going to do you. And you're going to let me. Just like Linda does," he said.

He got hold of her hair and started pulling on it as he dragged her up the path. His strength was enormous and his manner brutal. He was so strong; he had pulled her now almost to the tangled crops. Her hero dropped to dust before her eyes. She started to panic. How could he be so strong? He was only twelve. She must get back to the main road at all costs, but she was slowly losing. His power was far greater than hers could ever be.

Her feet caught on a rock. Precious time to get some leverage and prise herself away from his grip

243

and a foothold from the slippery grass. As she fled off down the bank, his fingers grabbed and pulled. He clutched her over and over. She flailed around like a fly in his spider's web. His grip failing and yet still clasping and clawing at her. Catching, then losing. Catching and losing.

At the bottom of the bank, a steep pavement stretched down to the main road on the other side of the houses. If she could reach there, there would be people, she would be safe. He ran after her, all the way down the steep, steep path until she turned the corner at the bottom. A man was there walking towards her in the summer heat. She would remember him. Her face must have been twisted up in fear – eyes and mouth crumpled up in pain, like a wounded animal. He looked at her, concern written on his face. His hand stretched out to stop to ask her if she was alright. But she escaped his questions. Four houses further on was her house. She slowed down and held onto garden walls until her breath had evened out. She could walk back to the house now at a normal pace and everything would look alright. No one would know. No one must know.

Her father was washing his car in the drive, his arms, in suds, already summer brown. He smiled at her.

"Have you had a nice time?" he asked.

"Yes, Daddy," she replied, quickly skirting round the soapy car avoiding further questions.

She sat on her bed for an hour until she could pretend all things were normal. They weren't. She tried to rationalise what had happened to her hero.

Would he always be a violent man? Had he learnt this from his father?

Sixty years had passed and now she was looking at the man in the restaurant.

"Is your name Peter?"

She wondered if she should dare ask these words. What sort of a plan should she arrange within her mind as to what should happen next? If 'yes', she'd ask him to leave the woman she presumed to be his wife, and talk to him alone. She could hardly blurt out those words, in front of people eating fish and chips, and tell him she remembered that day and ask him if he did too. If he did say 'yes', would she say she had forgiven him. Or had she? As she left the café, she knew she must ask the question.

At last she posed the question pondered at so long.

"Is your husband's name Peter?" she asked the woman, "I may have been at school with him."

"No, it's John Wood," replied the woman. He was not the man she sought.

Perhaps she would never find the man. History had filled in some of the answers to her questions. But nothing healed the hurt, of the hero who was lost to her, on that hot summer's day.

Toxic Relationships

by Sacha Quinn

Dear Nico,

I never thought I would ever be writing this letter. In fact, I'm quite surprised at myself for doing so. After so many years together I thought we would be forever. But alas it is not to be. You give me no choice. Hmm actually you do in a way. Which is, I suppose me making this decision now. My choice.

Why you may well ask? And why now?

Well, I have come to realise that the hold you have over me is unhealthy. You are that drug that even the most passionate of lovers cannot match. A habit that I just find so irresistible that I keep coming back to take you into the whole of me. And you continue to abuse me. Why? Why can you not be gentler, and a good choice? Abuse is never good.

You were always such a good friend at one time. Or so I was led to believe. You were always there for me in my hour of need. You gave me that comfort I craved. You were always reassuring, always by my side. Well mostly. There were some exceptions on some rare occasions when you ran out on me. When you would be with another and I would have to seek you out. Then when I found you, you would hold me in your thrall again and all would be forgiven.

I guess I was lucky that the others never minded sharing you. And I was happy to reciprocate. I don't think you were much better towards them than you were to me. You still aren't. You never will be. Some of them would tell me about their relationship with you too. Sometimes we'd have a discussion about you and decide whether to end these stupid relationships, offering each other support, to get over you. We would try so very hard, so as not to weaken and return to your ever-welcoming embrace. We knew it was so difficult when we loved you so much. And we tried many times to let you go. Yes, we. So, you see it's not just me.

I loved you so much through the years. Yet, you literally took my breath away and were at the same time the very air that I breathed. You tightened my chest, you made my heart pump harder, making my blood race around my body. Every single time we met. Since that first kiss in fact, when you touched my lips, signifying your offering. I was a hopeless victim right from the very first day we met. It was the start of that fifteen year on-off relationship which continued throughout, with that persuasive pull of yours and false assurances. Now I realise the empty promises and that there could be no good result by continuing to be with you.

You see, many people reject me when I'm with you. They send me pitying looks. I never want to be the object of pity. I never did. But it started to happen more and more. They too, knew you are doing me no good, never did, in fact that you are a danger to me. They cannot understand why I stay with you. They ask me and I have no answer. They don't want anything to do with you, nor me, when we are together. They reject you too. And I know exactly why. But for so long I was in denial and I just could not give you up. It's not easy to give up those things that make you feel good even if it doesn't always last for very long.

I should be feeling really down about ending this relationship. Feeling sad that it has ended this way. But no. I'm not. Instead I am trying very hard to be positive, knowing it is the right thing to do.

In my heart of hearts, I know that this relationship, this actual toxic relationship, has to end. I have to end it because I know you never could. I know you will always be there and should my need ever be so desperate I could come back. You would willingly take me back. Begin poisoning me all over again.

Know this: I have come to realise; I do love myself more than I love you. I love others in my life more than I love you. People who genuinely care for me and want the best from me and for me. People who have put up with you for too long now on my behalf, often being deprived of my company because of you. Deprived of wealth, deprived of health and in so being, deprived of happiness. Deprived of a future happiness that only being without you, can surely bring.

No, that badness has to stop. Here and now. With you in my life I cannot change anything. But I am changing. I am starting a new happy, healthy life without you. For to stay with you any longer you will surely be the death of me.

Oh, by the way remember that companion of ours, Al? You know the one we all had that three-way relationship with that seemed to work so well. Yes, boy oh boy, I know it was quite a threesome we had between us. Good for a very long while and nice whilst it lasted but in reality, that was not good either. When I finally realised how destructive we were together I knew you would have to be the first to go. Why? Because Al is not quite as abusive as you and is far easier to control.

Oh, I know what you are thinking. You think if I stay in a relationship with Al, you might be able to sneak your way back to us, with your tempting ways and Al egging me on, finding a weakening on my part, so it can all start again. But no, you are wrong Nico, you will never be allowed back into my life.

And what about Al? Well we're going steady at the moment. There are of course those times when we get a bit silly and overdo it, but overall, Al is more controllable than you.

So, for these reasons I say goodbye, Nico or to put your name in full Nicotine – goodbye.

Yours, no longer faithfully. In fact, yours never again.

Sincerely? Absolutely.

No love from

Penny Bacon.

P.S. If Al gets out of control it will be another relationship that goes down the drain, because Al, or to put the name in full, Alcohol is not going to control me any more than you did and will also be deserving of a letter of dismissal.

The Nosy Parker *

By

Stephanie Thornton

Ernest had been born nosy. He was even examining the birth canal as he arrived into the world, crying before he'd even entered daylight. His mother broke off from her laboured breath-control and muttered to the nurse that she thought this baby would be 'difficult'. It took him several minutes before he exited the womb. His nose had managed to get a little in the way. The nurse frowned. She observed his nose was slightly bigger than the normal baby button one, but his mother didn't seem to mind. Mum declared she thought his nose was cute.

From then on, it was downhill all the way. Nosiness ruled. He would examine his mother's breast before he had a feed, just to make sure it was warm and comfy and to make sure his nose was positioned at a perfect angle.

When he started to crawl, he drove all the other kids mad by picking up their toys and seeing what they were. Then he'd put these in his mouth, just to have a final check and return them covered in stickiness and goo.

By the time school came, he had turned this into an art form and would hover round the back of a crowd of kids, chattering together in the yard, to find

250

out what they were up to - and if it was something naughty, rush to tell the teacher. No wonder he had social problems. He especially liked to spot the tell-tale signs of smoking, seeing a tiny puff drift his way from around the nearest corner, and creep up on the culprit and shout this out for all to hear.

By the time he was a teenager, his thoughts had changed to those of sex. How could his parents possibly do that dreadful thing? After all, his Dad was all of 36 and way too old to carry on such nonsense. It was all so disgusting anyway. He was cheered when he failed to discover any signs of condoms or sex toys that may have been concealed within his parents' bedroom drawers.

Not so lucky, his parents' friends, the Entwistles. His mum had asked him to return some flour to them which she had borrowed earlier. A most excellent opportunity for Ernest. Mrs. Entwistle asked him if he'd like a drink, and while she made it, gave him the ideal chance to wander into the library adjacent to the lounge. There he could look at the spines of all the books.

Bingo, bulls-eye – there was "Lady Chatterley", "The Karma Sutra" and "The Hite Report" standing side by side in clear plain sight for everyone to see. Disgusting! His parents were their friends, so they must be disgusting too. What immoral people!

It gave him a good excuse and afterwards, to gossip secrets and make sure everyone else knew about them too. Soon people in the village were giving Mr. and Mrs. Entwistle funny looks and they had missed out on several invitations as people thought they may be perverts. Later, someone managed to enlighten them.

Then he heard that the neighbours opposite were re-decorating their front room. Once done, they would hold a surprise party to show everyone their new colour scheme they were so proud of. Oh dear! Ernest overheard this, climbed the tree in his garden and could see the new colour above the partly covered windows. He told everyone it was a quite hideous green and everyone kept away trying to be tactful. The party was a no-show.

He'd also developed the ability of reading documents upside down. He took great delight in looking at the files spread out on his doctor's desk. He already knew some of the complaints other patients had come there for and would mention this to anyone of interest, albeit always in a confidential manner. He also found out Mr. Entwistle had to take Viagra. Before long, everyone else knew Mr. Entwistle's little secret.

He felt a flicker of irritation when the doctors decided to computerize the surgery. How very annoying when the paper files changed to files on screen. He couldn't see the words there. But he could ask for a glass of water and whilst the Doctor had gone off to supply one, quickly have a furtive look. All he saw were his own records and at the top of them a note of caution stating Ernest was a busy-body. Obviously, someone else had sussed him out. He was more than just a tad annoyed.

By now, Ernest was driving everybody mad. He had become a total pest.

He lost every girlfriend by controlling them and interfering with their lives. He stuck his nose into everything. He would jump out to instruct people how to park their cars making them grind to a sudden halt or almost run him over leaving the driver shaking like a leaf. Then he'd tell them they had overrun the parking lines. He'd tell the supermarket cashier how to do her work if she was having an idle chat with a customer in front of him. He'd stop in the supermarket's aisles to adjust the labels and line up all the tins and complain if they were wrong.

One day, he found a dog tied up outside and returned it to the address on the dog-tag leaving the poor owner beside herself with grief, thinking her dog had been stolen when she came out of the shop. This same elderly owner was even more distraught, when she paused at the pelican crossing looking for the missing pet. He marched up to her and hurried her across it. She didn't want to cross and hit him with her umbrella.

In church, he would position himself near the back, to note the ones that turned up late and give them a most superior look. Then, he'd make loud tut-tutting noses which could be heard over the sermon and made the priest forget his calm demeanour and turn an angry red.

At the side of the confessional, it was possible to eavesdrop the conversations made within there. He had become a mine of information but then mis-construed the facts. The priest found out about his snooping at the box and had a screen put round it to stop him getting near. The priest went to visit him at home to complain, noting the twitching of the net curtain covering the window, whilst Ernest nosed at who had come to visit. If it had been Victorian times, Ernest would have had the proverbial Aspidistra in a plant pot on the window to give him extra camouflage. The priest failed to stop Ernest's busy-bodying ways. Even praying he would change, had no affect at all.

God must be on holiday!

It was at a parish meeting that Ernest's annoying habit was brought up for attention. Everyone was sick of him and his long inquisitive nose. They hatched a plan.

Later in the week, he spotted Mr. Entwistle entering the pub. He would join him at the bar so he could watch how much he drank.

"Hello Ernest," said Mr. Entwistle. "Not very well, I've heard."

"I'm perfectly fine," Ernest said, feeling rather confused.

"I'm sure the operation on your nose, will turn out to be quite simple," Mr. Entwistle continued.

"There's nothing wrong with it!" Ernest was even more confused.

"I heard you caught the NP bug – there's a lot of it around," Mr. Entwistle continued, "and looking at your nose, it is very funny colour."

Ernest felt the end of it with his fingers and wobbled it around. It felt just as it always had but he rushed off to the toilet to make sure. He saw a tiny spot.

"Are you all right?" said Jed Norbit, who was washing his hands.

Ernest explained he was checking his nose in the mirror and Jed came over to have a look.

"Oh yes, it's looking as if you've got NP," said Jed, quickly covering his face with a handkerchief, whilst he peered at Ernest.

"I don't know what NP is," said Ernest, frowning at Jed who had taken several steps backwards away from him.

"Well, you can look it up on the internet, but it's only recently been diagnosed, so I doubt you'll find much on there. I hear it is infectious and you may have to go in quarantine," Jed informed him.

Ernest looked at his nose again. Yes, it did look a little odd and the tiny spot had grown.

"Your nose is bigger than when I saw you last," continued Jed. "I really will have to leave you as otherwise you may give it to me too. Go to the doctor without delay."

Ernest had very little sleep that night whilst he worried about his nose. His parents who were not in on the plot, told him there was nothing wrong and he became quite angry with them. He had rung up the surgery only to be told he could be seen in four weeks' time.

"Don't be ridiculous," Ernest crossly told the receptionist, "I have been told I have NP and must be seen at once, do you hear?"

"Oh, in that case, if you think you have NP, you must be seen at once," declared the receptionist who had been at the parish meeting, "come and see the doctor this afternoon, but meanwhile, keep clear of everyone else, otherwise the town will have an epidemic."

At the surgery that afternoon, the doctor typed copious amounts of notes on his computer screen listing Ernest's symptoms.

He had been pre-briefed all about NP, following the local parish meeting. In fact, he could say he was the world's expert in all things symptomatic of the condition called NP. He gave Ernest a most pitying look, which made Ernest shrink into his chair, cowering with fear.

"I'll go get you some water and a calming pill," announced the doctor. He made sure Ernest had plenty of time to look at the computer screen.

Ernest was horrified. The notes said that his nose would fall off within the next few weeks unless Ernest responded to the treatment given and that the treatment would fail if Ernest didn't use it all his life. The prognosis was appalling.

"You see, the throat, ear, nose and the eye sockets are all linked together," explained the doctor when he came back into the room. "You must be very careful when you are in other people's company and not come too near them in case you pass it on. With care and attention, you will keep your nose but must take great care not to make it bigger. The main symptom is that it makes you extra sensitive and this will agitate you. Because you are so sensitive you will need to help and try to fix other people's problems and talk about them too. Sadly, this will only make your condition worse and aggravate it. So, you must take several steps backwards mentally and keep a very low profile and not interfere with anything."

"Yes," agreed Ernest, "I think I have been behaving that way all my life. Have I had NP since I was born?"

"Yes, it's most probable, but they have only just diagnosed the condition and even now are doing research. There may never be a cure. The only people that will not be affected will be any future wife and children, and your parents, who will all be immune to you."

"Thank you," Ernest said, as he exited the room. As he passed reception, he heard Mrs. Entwistle telling the receptionist a tasty tale about Jed Norbit. At this, he stuck his nose up in the air. He was no longer interested in such things. 'Non sum qualis eram'** he told himself, in Latin. After all, he had the lifelong illness of NP and besides that, there was nothing he could do to help but to keep his nose out of Jed's affairs!

* The nosy parker – a phrase named after Archbishop Mathew Parker in the sixteenth century and his annoying habit of prying into other peoples' lives.

**'Non sum qualis eram' meaning - I am not what I was.

Political Correctness

The greatest enemy of clear language is insincerity.
- George Orwell

The idea that you have to be protected from any
kind of uncomfortable emotion is what
I absolutely do not subscribe to.
-    John Cleese

"You're not allowed to call them dinosaurs
anymore," said Yo-less. "It's speciesist.
You have to call them pre-petroleum persons."
- Terry Pratchett, Johnny and the Bomb

To learn who rules over you, simply find out
who you are not allowed to criticize.
- Voltaire

'Political correctness' is a label the privileged
often use to distract from their privilege and hate.
- DaShanne Stokes

A Matter of Minds

By

Stephanie Thornton

Are you sitting comfortably? Then I'll begin

Once upon a time, around the 1970s, in a galaxy far, far away on a planet called Earth, there lived a very angry white supremacist called Ian Tofear. He was angry all the time.

He even had angry dreams.

One night, when he was having one of them, God appeared to him and said,

"Verily I say unto thee, go forth and find thyself a very angry young black woman and marry her."

Ian Tofear's eyes bulged, his face went red, He was furious. God advised him this was a righteous thing. They would be compatible and happy. But Ian was angry with God and shouted at him. He hated blacks.

God commanded him to stop and listen.

"Together, ye shalt beget a child who will be a Saviour of the World." ('well sort of,' God muttered as an after- thought - God was still thinking about this and wondering if he was making a wise move)

"Thou shalt name thy child Political Correctness*, PC for short. It will grow to be a mighty warrior, champion of the downtrodden and the overlooked."

Ian woke up next morning even more angry. How dare God tell him what to do.

He stormed off to the supermarket and there, proceeded to beat up a row of tinned baked beans which were on a shelf minding their own business. It was no-good, he was still annoyed.

In the distance, there was the sound of something smashing. It was a much better noise than he was making so he ran over to investigate.

Magic! There he found a black woman hitting a pack of frozen Brussel sprouts. He shouted at her an encouragement and clapped and cheered.

"I hate Brussel sprouts, even more than I hate Niggers," he bellowed.

At this, she felt a lightning bolt coursing through her body. Then she saw him clearly, a halo shining above his head. She was totally enchanted with this angry man with the red face. How handsome he looked, shouting and spitting on the supermarket floor.

"My name is Lettuce Sortit," she told him holding out her hand.

Together, hand in hand, they left the shop, walking angrily down the street, gazing into each other's eyes. Love at first sight!

They married quickly, enjoying time shouting at each other and being most compatible in anger. And it came to pass just as God had said. She became pregnant quickly.

But this was not like any other birth. The baby grew to full term after many years of gestating.

It was born at the desk at work rather than in hospital.

Everyone came to gaze in wonderment and awe at the new infant, which they called 'Political Correctness' just as God had commanded.

It was such a cute thing. It had wonderful little hands and toes which wriggled with delight when tickled, and a smiling face and a lovely red and brown plump body – inherited from both parents and enhanced with genetics honed from communism. But the baby was a curiosity and something of a puzzle. It had been born without gender and nothing lay between its legs. Nichts, nada, rien. Absolutely nothing!

Angry Lettuce was pleased. It would save a fortune in nappies. There was no need to add to the terrible billions of them lying in land-fill sites all over the western world. After all, Lettuce was green-minded, like her name, and supported the hypocrisy of the 'Green movement' trying to save Planet Earth, as it selectively cherry-picked what turned out to be convenient.

But there was yet another problem. Ian Tofear and Lettuce Sortit were even more angry when PC refused to drink milk and spent all day and night wailing and howling without respite. Perhaps it was genetic? At least they thought there was no mistaking the baby's parents. One week passed and PC still refused to drink.

Ian angrily read his daily paper, trying to concentrate above the howls. He covered his face with it, trying to avoid seeing the bright red baby face puckered up in rage. Too late and too near, the baby grabbed the paper in one tiny fist and a piece of it tore off.

PC stuffed the paper into its mouth and swallowed it whole. The crying stopped. For a moment Ian forgot to shout. The baby was gurgling and making happy sounds.

On its face was the widest grin showing a row of pearly white baby teeth. Its little crumpled fists stretched out for more. Maybe they should try it? Its row of teeth chewed the print with ease. And it was quiet. In fact, it seemed to have no trouble gobbling up pages and pages of anything in print.

And all the more it smiled and cooed and grinned. Quite adorable.

"It says here that Meryl Streep is now an actor, not an actress," the man said to his wife, "She must have had some bits stuck on!"

"I'll put the kettle on," the wife muttered.

The cute baby had such a gentle and benevolent nature. It offered kind gestures to the downtrodden and neglected by selecting bits of print that featured tales of suffering as its favourite food. They came and worshipped at the altar of their new God in thousands, genuflecting and offering it praise and adoration.

As they did so, it seemed to grow and grow. Like a hydra, it soon grew feelers that connected it to everything else that needed to be fixed on planet earth. It soon sourced Health and Safety rules, politicians with weird and loopy plans and minority groups that would have been previously thought as cranky. It took these only until itself – the saviour of the planet and for a while, all seemed calm on planet Earth. All these hallowed halls where complaints were housed were joined as one in harmony, in attempts to make things right.

Soon, all the inhabitants of earth had heard about PC and decided to copy its example. It seemed to be a healthy diet to adopt. They would pick and choose what matters to embrace and, in order to be helpful, pass laws about them controlling everyone.

Soon the young were no longer thinking for themselves. Everything was analysed. If they thought something was wrong, they had been told to keep it to themselves. The result was great waves of depression sweeping across the lands. Everyone felt very angry. All the time.

It was not a good idea to mention this. It would not fit in with PC ways.

The doctors said the young were trying to be something they were not, which left their patients puzzled. No one dared say what was really wrong. Their thoughts were controlled and monitored, and they pondered long and hard before they said what they thought would be appropriate. They tried to please everyone without thinking what they felt inside.

"What a lovely rainbow," said the man to his wife, looking out of the window.

"I think you can say that," the wife told her husband, "even though rainbows are used for other things these days. Let's have a cup of tea."

Meanwhile, the proud parents tried to feed the baby's ravenous appetite; telephone directories, Hello magazine, Private Eye, The Guardian. But PC was now beginning to change. It would rage and rant if it didn't get exactly what it wanted. Gone was the cute baby everyone adored. It had developing an evil smelling wind and seemed to burp a lot. Now the size of a teenager, it spit out fragments of the papers only eating when it approved of what was fed to it. Now the only way was to edit out the print with a large black pen to see what it would eat.

"Whatever happened to freedom of the press?" the man said to his wife, as he folded up his newspaper covered in black lines.

His wife murmured sympathetically, whilst pouring out some tea.

The doctor declared PC was suffering from Righteous Indigestion and suggested a special diet. How about trying some of the classics but first try simple books like Enid Blyton and Beano comics? This seemed to do the trick, but only after hours of editing took place.

"I wanted to take the grandchildren to the pantomime," the man said to his wife, "but Dick Whittington is now called Richard and we can't take any photos of the school play either."

His wife murmured sympathetically, blowing on her hot tea.

PC screamed with rage at Noddy and his gay curtains, and Big Ears, long term friend of Noddy, gave it indigestion. The defenders of PC killed Big Ears off and buried him.

'The Famous Five' were reduced to two. PC was outraged by Ann who was always in the kitchen, Dick remained but had to change his name to Richard. Julian was a male chauvinist and Timmy the dog, was indigestible – to have a dog in the book was demeaning to the dog. PC did love George however, as a pioneer of everyone transgender. Somehow, 'The Famous Two' didn't sound quite right any more. And Fanny in the 'Far Away tree' had to become Franny or she may offend the little children.

"We have become a world of blue meanies," the man said to his wife, after secretly watching 'Yellow Submarine', which was now regarded as a classic film, but banned by PC.

His wife murmured sympathetically, gazing into her cooling tea.

The politicians looked at the activities of PC deciding this was a good religion to adopt. PC was an inspiration to the world. The saviour, just as God had promised.

"Whatever happened to free speech?" the man said to his wife, when he listened to the politician, who's words were punctuated with beeping sounds.

His wife murmured sympathetically and gazed into her luke-warm tea.

By now PC was an adult, a huge snapping angry monster with gnashing teeth and thrashing body. The angry parents were quite worn out and sent for the doctor again. The doctor announced PC had been indulged far too much, suffering from delusions of grandeur with an inflated ego. It had become totally out of control and untameable. Like a genie out of the bottle, there was no way to get it back in again. The doctor blamed the angry parents saying they should have known better. In turn, the parents blamed the doctor, telling him they knew their rights, PC had told them so. And they all blamed the establishment.

"It's totally out of control now," declared Ian Tofear angrily. "We should never have allowed it to get this way."

"I suggest a pared-down diet will help the swollen head," suggested the doctor and ran off to Barbados for a rest.

"Whatever happened to the dictionary?" the man said to his wife. "It's only a few pages long now."

His wife murmured sympathetically, gazing at her now cold tea.

PC had become controller of the world. The new diet did not work. All they had done was make the problems worse by encouraging its habits and pandering to its every whim.

"I think George Orwell put the wrong date on his book when he put 1984," the man said to his wife.

But the wife had died, frozen to her tea cup.

The world turned and wondered and pondered over the thing it had created. The children stayed at home from school. There weren't enough subjects left to teach any more.

Churches fell into ruin, as children were allowed to choose their religion when they were too young to even follow one.

The population died out as sex education for five-year-olds put them off for life.

The angry feminist movement founded by Lettuce in a fit of rage, took care of all the rest.

"I'd like a black coffee," the man ordered, on his lonely visit to the bar.

"It's not allowed. All colour is banned," the barista explained.

And the world turned grey and stopped.

*   Historically, Political Correctness was a communist concept, born in Stalin's Russia in the 1920s. Now regarded as back-door propaganda after coming to America in the 1970s and thus proliferating.

PC on the Beach

By

C. I. Ripples

"Welcome to our esteemed Paradise Club, Mr. & Mrs. Smith," Vinay welcomed the newly arrived guests.

He took in the plus sized badly dressed woman fully as he beamed at the couple, prided himself on his accurate guess work. Definitely Australian. Who else would wear a flowery stretchy 'boob tube', clinging to rolls of fat, with the straps of a cheap black frilly bra as clearly visible as her superior demeanour! As she turned to bellow something about the unbearable heat to her beer bellied partner whilst fanning her heaving frame, he noted that the elastic flowers had slipped down almost to her behind, giving a hint of her buttock cleavage but a full view of her tattooed blubbery back. It seemed she'd fallen asleep on a newspaper. Guests such as these should really be banned from properties with the PCs elevated rank. These days, of course, he sighed, with occupancy down, they were forced to accept all sorts.

Whilst waiting for his charges to complete their registration, Vinay caught the eye of a well-groomed, evidently Italian, gentleman staring at the spectacle Mrs. Smith presented from behind the potted plant in the café, comforted that the two of them were united in their judgement.

Mrs. Smith nudged her silent slouching husband as the yellow turmeric stained fingers took their South African passports.

"Disgusting habit these Indians have," she muttered under her breath.

She planned fully to complain to the manager about the lack of hygiene and allowing these animals to work in such high-end establishments. She dreaded to think what back of house might look like - surely betel nut spitting stains would be decorating the corridors. She certainly planned to use her UV blacklight flashlight to check the cleanliness of the sheets.

The Javanese front office manager, who was in no way ignorant of the remark, surreptitiously gave a nod and a wink to his colleague. This lot would be relegated to the Chinese wing.

Mrs. Smith snatched the key cards with a clipped, "Thank you," and turned away to rummage with her flabby upper arms in her hand bag for a disinfectant wet wipe, before striding to the lift, partner in tow, snapping her fingers at the porter to follow.

At the café, Johan was as oblivious to eye contact as he was to the check-in occurring at the front desk. Waiting for his espresso, he yawned, mentally preparing the letter he would write to the manager, bad tempered by his exhaustion.

The hotel itself and staff were pleasant, but the place was filled with Chinese tourists, which had made his stay completely disagreeable. Not because it was full, but because it was full of Chinese. They were the worst - far worse than unruly British on a stag weekend, ghastlier than unsavoury Pakistanis or those appallingly arrogant, pushy Russians.

The problem with the Chinese tourist, he reflected, was that they lacked any kind of Western etiquette. Every night was sleepless as they talked loudly in the corridors or the room neighbouring his, until he was so exhausted and pissed off, he got out of bed to make a formal complaint to the duty manager.

At breakfast too, his family's enjoyment was destroyed by voluble Chinese voices, kids running around untamed and loud-mouthed, Face Timing at the table with relatives in the home country. Why were there no rules prohibiting the use of phones for video calls in the restaurants?

At the buffet, 'they' had a habit of taking a bite of everything before putting things on their plate. Often using the same spoon! 'They' stood by the milk dispenser drinking out of bowls for Christ's sake! Even his Japanese mother-in-law, normally not one to criticise, commented on the basic lack of manners as she pointed to the buffet, where a group of said nationality were stuffing their bags with fruit and bread rolls, which they didn't even try to hide as they left the restaurant laden.

"This morning there isn't one banana left at the buffet," she lamented and then shuddered as on the neighbouring table, one of 'them' violently raised the phlegm to his throat and spat, missing Johan's foot by mere centimetres!

"They give us Asians a bad reputation," she exhaled, holding a handkerchief over her mouth,

272

watching dismayed as a waiter rushed over with a bucket of suspiciously murky water and a mop.

As the badly needed double espresso arrived, Johan absentmindedly thanked the demure Malaysian waiter, dwelling once more on his misfortunate visit surrounded by Chinese, directing his thoughts now to the beach. He must not forget to add that experience to his complaint. He had tried to sleep on the comfy recliners, enjoying the soft breeze coming off the sea, when a group of Chinese tourists came and sat right next to him.

Why?

There was a whole beach to choose from! And they'd made so much noise that the two other Western guests, he was sure they were French-Swiss, told them politely to please be quiet. Without any result of course, as none of 'them' understood English. He and said guests had been forced to take their towels to sleep uncomfortably directly on the sand, away from the hotel. Even there, Chinese kids were running around shouting at the top of their lungs, throwing up sand with the pitter patter of their short stubby feet.

His wife had wanted to have a swim in the pool, only to come back aghast.

"I can't possibly get into the water," she told him close to tears, "Most of 'them' can't swim and 'they' clear their noses with one hand over the side of the pool into the filters as they splutter, snort and spit. And I dread to think how much urine is deposited in the pool. It's absolutely disgusting!"

He would have to advise the manager that there should really be signs in Chinese insisting spitting, snorting, and defecating in the pool is prohibited.

Said manager was doing a turn around the hotel, before going to the executive floor for a room inspection prior to cocktail hour. He liked to be visible, his posture upright with a sense of self possession, striding about his property with a purpose, greeting guests with a short nod, or if he deemed them important enough, stopping for a brief chat. The demands of his jobs were weighty, especially as he, who had always believed himself to be quite skilled at delegation, found disappointingly, that at PC on the Beach he was forced constantly to whip the staff, who proved to be antagonistic to even the smallest changes, into shape. If only guests knew the constant battle he waged to give the semblance of effortlessness when it came to maintaining hotel brand standards.

He was disconcerted by the feeble Trip Advisor ratings recently and positively alarmed at the daily steady flow of complaints. Today alone he'd had received a flood of emails about unclean sheets and the state of the pool. There was even a complaint about the weather!

Having satisfied himself that the levels of chlorine were enough to ensure hygiene, he pressed for the lift to take him to his next destination. As he waited, he continued to ponder on the predicament of guest satisfaction.

Of course, it was all the fault of social media, which raised guest expectations above realistically attainable levels. Affordable levels. If only guests would just have a quiet word with him instead of going public. It was always the Scandinavians who complained most, although the British were a close second and non-resident Indians were a rapidly growing breed. Even if he impressed upon his staff the virtue of withholding judgement, it was no wonder hotel groups were starting to segregate their guests into specific wings to mitigate the levels of grievances, as a matter of policy!

Yet, the Chinese, the target of most complaints, relegated to the lowest quality wing, rarely grumbled. He put this down to the fact that they were probably just happy to be out of their own country. Although … even silence could be interpreted as a less than favourable opinion. He had to admit that his guests might have a point when it came to the cleanliness of hotel linen - that's what happens, he was convinced, when you outsource laundry to the locals.

When the lift arrived, it was already full of Orientals, and he decided to wait for the next one, letting a muscular fiery looking Russian with his botoxed devochka and babushka squeeze in ahead of him.

On each floor more Chinese tourists crowded in, packed like sardines, which meant that by the time Anatoly and his entourage arrived on their floor, the lift was so full there was no way to exit. No one moved aside despite him shoving his considerable bulk and the doors closed before they were able to get out. They finally ended up on the lobby floor, where the hoards thankfully swarmed out through the doors. There, he noted with relief as he pressed the button for the now emptied lift to go back down, the suitcases were piled high and two huge coaches were waiting to whisk the Chinese guests away.

He arrived in his room for a well-deserved afternoon nap, after which his wife decided to go off to the spa, and Anatoly decided to go see the sunset and enjoy a cocktail in the relative peace and quiet of the executive lounge. Before getting into the lift, however, they were almost accosted by a group of drunken rowdy Brits, obviously on a stag night, waving bottles of beer and accompanied by a young lady of local origin, who was decidedly not a resident and wrapped so economically one almost thought she'd run out of fabric.

With a palpable sense of foreboding, he planned to warn the duty manager as he was sure it was against hotel policy for non-paying guests, especially of this variety, to stay in its rooms. He had not forgotten or forgiven the unjust treatment of his beloved mother country during the Novichok incident. Like Brexit, he was sure the Brits had only themselves to blame.

He arrived in the lounge to find an anorexic American Caucasian woman in her mid-thirties, in some kind of yoga outfit, making a nuisance of herself, swearing at the staff at the top of her lungs that she wanted another drink. He was sure she didn't in any way conform to the dress code required for the lounge, but as usual the submissive overly polite waiters were not up to such an overbearing hysterical presence. These Americans always thought they

276

were running the show. As she turned to the bar, almost knocking over the waiter with a tray of drinks, which he duly dropped, she proceeded to decant white wine into coca cola bottles and chop blocks of cheese which she wrapped in a tissue and attempted to sneak into her bag.

"And they say Russians drink a lot," Anatoly commented to the waiter.

Things came to a head when she sat on the lap of an unwilling Frenchman, who, he was certain, was homosexual, and began to stroke his crotch. It was fortuitous that the manager arrived at that exact moment and escorted her off the property yelling all kinds of abuse. Peace was restored, but he had missed the sunset.

That night at 2.11 am exactly, the fire alarm went off. Mrs. Smith was awake anyway, the heat and the din that was going on in the room upstairs made it impossible to fall asleep. She'd set the air conditioning at 18 degrees Celsius, but found it deficient and instead was sitting in a cold bath. She was making a mental note to call the duty manager to complain when the alarm forced them outside. She was scantily clad in a towel, wading through the exodus of Chinese guests, some in pyjamas, many in their underwear, who were running chaotically with masks and handkerchiefs held to their mouths. They finally made it to the helipad on the other side of the property. There they waited for what seemed hours in an almost a tropical storm until the local fire brigade established it was a false alarm. Furious and exhausted, they had stomped back to their room soaking wet. It was gone 3.30 when after a hot shower they finally hit the sack. Consequently, they overslept and missed the breakfast spread included in their room rate and which she had fully intended to last them until dinner. She would be adding this fiasco to her long list of complaints and would demand a refund.

Starving, Mr. & Mrs. Smith dragged themselves to the café in their swimsuits and ordered a latte and four sad pain au chocolate.

There was some commotion at the front desk.

"Ah, the waiter informed them disapprovingly, as he took their order, "it seems the fire alarm was set off by a young lady visiting some British guests who had become overzealous in their ardour."

Mrs. Smith recalled that some names had not been responded to during the evacuation roll call and nodded, leaning forward eagerly for further information, her ample bosom on display. The waiter averted his gaze to the potted palm tree.

"The duty manager went to check, and found the guests passed out in their room from beer, vodka, hashish and other illegal substances," he tut tutted, his eyes following the well-dressed European gentleman from the day before, on his way to the lobby.

Gesturing towards the front desk, he added, "they've been asked to leave the property immediately."

She yawned and nodded, craning her neck only to find the front office manager smiling vacuously whilst being verbally abused by a very angry drunk young man who she could only assume was the groom.

Just as she was sinking her teeth into her chocolate croissant which was very mealy, the shit, as she liked to say, hit the fan. Everything seemed to unfold at once. The groom, red faced, smashed his beer bottle on the counter, waving the broken glass in the front office manager's face, then turned and advanced on the guests behind him in the queue, even children, bottle in hand. An agile Chinese woman dove to the floor to tackle the groom's legs, causing him to sway and crash to the ground as an elegant gentleman rescued the beer dripping broken bottle, without regard for his expensive linen suit, the front office manager called the police and a tall muscular man with a to die for six pack, obviously on his way to the pool in the briefest of trunks, held the groom down.

The police and the manager arrived on the scene as Mrs. Smith was mopping up the crumbs on her plate, using her fingers to prise off the melted chocolate. The manager, usually completely composed and of grave expression, was smiling and shook hands with his heroic guests, who in turn were laughing, shaking hands with each other on a job well done, patting the front office manager on the back.

Mrs. Smith, taking the last sip from her excellent latte, mellowed at the sight of such unity in the face of adversity, and almost applauded when the police escorted the groom through the revolving doors into the world outside.

Double Standards

By

Stephanie Thornton

God enjoyed creating mischief. When God had stirred things up enough, God could smite the person of God's choice.

There were millions of folks to choose from. For example, a couple called Harvey Lode and his wife Constance Wittering who lived in little England

"Where are you off to today?" asked Harvey, as his wife got ready to go out.

"It's another rally in Trafalgar Square," she answered pulling on her t-shirt with 'ban plastic' written on the front.

"Well you can't wear that," he said. "You'll have to put on that wool jumper that granny sent last Christmas!"

"Why not?" she angrily replied, "the one I wore last month wore out and all the words rubbed off, so they've given us all new ones."

"Because it's polyester which is made from plastic and it makes you look like idiots."

"What do you know!" shouted Constance, already in the mode for protesting, before she flounced out of the door and drove her brand-new energy efficient car into the city.

On the way, she stopped at Starbucks to grab a drink. It was such a nuisance. The paper-plastic cup leaked, and the straw was useless. The cup was on the new car's seat so she threw it out of the sunroof before any more damage could be done.

At the rally, which was already gaining momentum, she stopped to talk to friend, Rebecca, who had paused to change her child's disposable nappy and was looking for a bin to put it in.

"Just hold the baby for a mo please, whilst I find one. And I'll get rid of the dog's poo bag at the same time,"

"Why don't you use the towel nappies they've just re introduced. Granny says it's such a good idea?" asked Constance.

"Oh, they're such a nuisance – all that washing."

"You're supposed to put them in a nappy pail and wash them all together once a week."

"Ugh!" said Rebecca. "Besides that, the baby will only be in nappies for two years. Grandparents, what do they know, sticking their nose into things they know nothing about?"

She was holding up a flag which the organizers had issued for everyone to carry. Its large letters said, 'Save the planet, ban plastic'.

"I don't think it'll last long in this wind; the plastic coating is quite thin, and it's only held on with glue. But I can get a new one if this one rips."

"Would you like to join me for lunch," Constance asked. "Harvey has paid for a table at a two-star Michelin restaurant. My treat. It will be our reward for our good deeds this morning."

The parade marched until it arrived at the offices of the Minister for the Environment. He was not happy at yet another protest at his door and he was tapping his fingers on the desk. There had been a delay. His printing had not yet arrived.

His secretary was already fuming and in a sulk. She'd broken a nail opening an ink cartridge package and was ranting about it having to undo four layers of plastic wrapping. The outer one was extra thick so it could hang up on display in a shop and could only be opened with a pair of scissors.

The minister was also in a sulk as he'd asked for a reduction of packaging on his breakfast cereal and been told it was essential for employment in China where it was made and not to 'wake the sleeping dragon'. The ink cartridge also came from China.

At the restaurant, Constance and Rebecca pondered over the menu whilst the maître d' glared at the baby on her hip.

"I'll have the roast beef," Constance told the maître d'.

Rebecca gave her a look. "Think of greenhouse gases," she whispered. "I'll have the Atlantic Halibut please," she commanded.

"Isn't it an endangered species?" Constance whispered back, in full point scoring mode.

"I happen to like it," Rebecca countered.

"And a carafe of water?" he enquired.

The women looked at him in astonishment as if he wanted to poison them.

"Absolutely not!" was the angry response.

The maître d' asked if they would prefer the Aqua di Cristallo, Tasmanian Rain or Highland Spring instead.

"How much is the Aqua?" Constance asked, knowing the answer but wanting to impress her friend.

"£50 a bottle," replied the maître d'.

"Which one would you recommend goes best with the roast beef?" Constance asked, and smiled serenely. (*1)

He sniggered under his breath spotting the t-shirts they wore. The only reason they had acquired the table was that Harvey Lode was considered celebrity. The water had come from as far away as Fiji and Japan to get to the famous restaurant and the one they chose, came in a plastic bottle too. At least the bottle was coloured blue which some diners said made it taste better. Some restaurants in fact recycled it from their kitchen taps, re sealed and chilled it in the fridges so it tasted just the same. The restaurants had to guard their profits.

Later that afternoon, the doorbell rang after Constance arrived home. A friendly looking man was standing there.

"I'm doing milk rounds where milk is delivered daily to your door and the bottles are recycled. I wondered if I could sign you up?"

"Well I'll think about it. I don't know how many I will need and suppose I run out? Then you'll want me to open an account with you and it'll take up my valuable time. It's so much easier to just get it from the shop."

283

The man gave her a puzzled look.

"If I don't get enough people to use me, then the round will fail. Here's my card," he said, "I'll leave it on the step to remind you. It's coated in plastic, so it won't get ruined in the rain."

"As I said, I'll think about it," she snapped, shutting the door angrily in his face.

Round at the supermarket just as the manager re-entered the store having put up a large sign saying, 'plastic bags no longer used in this store', he was accosted by an angry customer. The happy, smug smile he had from doing such a good deed, dropped from his face.

"How dare you put up this stupid sign. Just look at all the vegetables in their plastic bags," said the woman waving to the aisles behind her where all the shelves were covered in layers and layers of film.

"They're like that to keep them fresh and make them look nice too," He felt justified with his explanation.

She started ripping at the bags.

"Well, as soon as you open them, they go 'off,'" she shouted. "It's just so you can sell them longer and make more profit."

The manager had to send for the police – the woman was causing too much trouble and other customers had started to mutter too. He smiled. She was given a month's community service sentence, picking litter up from the roadside which the judge considered appropriate. It included the Starbucks cup dropped by Constance earlier. What a good task it had turned out to be.

Constance had pretended not to notice the angry confrontation but did notice they were now employing Muslims at the checkout counters. The woman scanning her items was robed all in black right down to the floor and wore the customary hajib over her hair. Constance muttered something about terrorism to Harvey as they left the store.

"Keep your voice down."

"Why? Everyone agrees with me."

"They do go to the Mosque five times a day," he countered.

"Where they learn to blow us all up! At least you'll get chance to go to *our* church this weekend. Remember your nephew is getting christened then."

"I've no idea where it is," he said, fiddling with the GPS when they returned to the car.

"Humm……. It's not under 'Places of Interest', he laughed. "Nor Historic Sites."

"Try Entertainment," she suggested.

"Don't be daft!"

"I know it is a pretty one. Nice for photos," she suggested.

"How do you know?"

"I passed it a few months ago but I still can't remember where it is!"

That evening Harvey went with male friends from work to a lap dancing club. The women there were very different from the shop assistant. Later on, that night, Constance put on the latest episode of a box set they were watching. It was full of people being decapitated.

"Far too much tomato ketchup," Harvey muttered.

Then came the sex scenes full of sodomy and same sex kissing. Constance said she felt jaded and she yawned.

"It's all so '*samey*'," she declared, and Harvey agreed with her as he drank his third glass of scotch.

"We've seen it all. What else can they find to film now?"

They changed channels and watched Britney gyrating sexually in a tiny hardly existent pair of knickers (or so Harvey named them)

"More a strip of cloth...............a belt perhaps?"

"She earned over three million for that," Constance declared, "and look how hard you have to work to earn your money."

"I heard that other actress," he scratched his head, "I can't remember her name, has brought out another celebrity candle. This one's called 'Vomit'!"

"How sick!"

"Yes," he laughed, "but they say it's wrapped in bio-degradable wrapping and only takes forty years to decompose. That should make you happy."

"Do change channels – put it onto 4 please."

The screen changed to a symphony orchestra playing Bach.

"See that chap in the string section," Harvey pointed to the screen. "I know him. That's Jim Shackleton. He went to Uni then the RSM for four years and now he barely earns a living for all that training."

"It's not fair really is it?" said his wife.

The next day Harvey was showing off his new acquisition to his friend. A vintage bakelite phone. So retro. So cool.

"You see, I too am doing my bit to save the planet, I won't buy a new phone now and I use this one instead," he explained to his puzzled friend. It rang as they were speaking, confirming his fifth holiday of the year, this time to Ecuador.

"You see I save so much money in petrol, which is good for the planet, by working from home, that I can afford all these holidays. Such a wise working practice and it saves mileage on my car to keep its value. If everyone did this, just think of how we'd use less oil."

Constance Wittering was also doing her bit to save the planet. Quietly.

She'd sent off money to a charity helping Africans who were depleting the hedgerows and causing soil erosion, digging charcoal to make fire for cooking and ritual fires where they used the blackened stumps to decorate their faces. Then there was a coup and the same Africans fled to Britain. She was secretly a NIMBY (*2) and horrified when one family came to live next door and made their customary ritual fire from timber made from the adjoining hedge. She told Harvey that the price of their detached would thus fall, losing them a fortune.

At the christening, the vicar gazed at them below spectacles balanced on his forehead.

They had all struggled through the service, apart from Harvey's Mum and the usual parishioners who belted out the hymns that the newbies didn't seemed to know.

"At the last church - thing we attended at the village hall, there were guitars and tambourines and we all sang some jolly songs," Constance complained.

She was disappointed with the organ music and said it sounded just like a movie starring Vincent Price.

"And what is water used for?" asked the vicar, as he pointed in the font.

"To mix with orange juice," the young nephew being christened shouted out.

The vicar sighed, "it's to wash away our sins."

"You'd need a swimming pool," Constance whispered to her husband.

Some weeks later, Constance went to church where the christening had been, to repent her thoughts but her real reason was that such nice people seemed to be there. She thought they were 'her sort', chatting about all the good they had done saving milk bottle tops to send to Africa and making crafts from recycled plastic bottles for the annual bring and buy.

She agreed to take part in the annual McMillan coffee morning but was upset when Rebecca's husband, sick with cancer, wanted to attend. She said it was inappropriate and would only upset everyone seeing him there looking ill.

Meanwhile, in heaven, God groaned whilst considering who to smite. Who would God choose?

288

God didn't even have a gender now. Was God now a he, she, it or even they? So many given names.

God was mightily confused. There was hardly any time to just be God.

There was no doubt about it. God had got it wrong. The cunning plan to test mankind/womankind/ theykind or itkind had failed. Adam and Eve had been a disaster. Perhaps it was time to start again. Perhaps a virus was the answer. After all a virus could be called the new word "woke" which means perfection in every way. Perhaps this would solve all the problems of the world. And the virus wouldn't need a plastic wrapping either.

'Let's see,' said the God person and started getting out the test tubes.

Author's Note:
This story as written in December 2019 just before the COVID-19 pandemic started

*1 Elizabeth Taylor in the film 'Ash Wednesday'
*2 NIMBY – 'not in my back yard'

Money

Money doesn't talk, it swears.
-Bob Dylan, Lyrics: 1962-2001

I made my money the old-fashioned way.
I was very nice to a wealthy relative right before he died.
- Malcolm Forbes

A wise person should have money in their head, but not in their heart.
- Jonathan Swift

Wealth consists not in having great possessions, but in having few wants.
- Epictetus

Money is good for nothing unless you know the value of it by experience.
- P.T. Barnum

Money, Cats and Charlie

By

Stephanie Thornton

'Think of money as if it were your favourite cat.
Stroke it, feed it and guard it well.
For if you do not, it will surely come back and bite you'

S.T.

Charlie didn't like cats. In fact, he positively hated them. The trouble was, they would invite themselves to come and sit upon his knee, if any particular girlfriend had happened to have one, and purr away contentedly, not appearing to observe him glaring at them when the girlfriend wasn't looking. In fact, he hated anything furry. Apart from the fur that lay between a girlfriend's legs. He quite liked that. But what he really liked was money.

His father, recently deceased, had made parsimony into an art form, attributing it to the years of war when 'making do and mend' had been the way to live. His father would dole out little chunks of cash dictating rules of exactly what it had to be spent on and requiring proof of this when purchases were made. Charlie was the opposite. He had seen 'Wall Street' at the movies. He too could be just like Gordon Gekko. However, Charlie was a Catholic and Gordon Gekko didn't seem to have any religious aspirations – other than that of chasing the holy grail of money.

When Charlie's father died, Charlie got his own back, spending money from the estate to give him pleasure so long denied him by his father. He was not going to be like him. He got a job he knew his father wouldn't have approved of either. Charlie decided to become a banker because he could then be just like famous Gordon and have all the trappings that went with it.

First came the trophy wife called Larissa. She was a most interesting character to study when it came to spending money. She really needed to see a therapist.

Let's have a little look at her…………………..

All that Charlie sees is her façade. A true case of a cake in a shop window. Good to look at, but not so good when tasted. He really should be aware that she really hates cats and has a tiny poodle which she keeps in her designer handbag. He should also note that cats don't like cake at all.

So, Larissa falls in love, not with him, but with his Maserati and his bank balance. She doesn't know it, but the balance should have made her most aware of treating cats with care. He buys her an engagement ring which he had thought looked rather nice. Alas, she does not, and during the first five years of marriage, has managed to lose the ring five times and each time buys a bigger one. Its size has now reached epic proportions – it's only one size less than the Taylor-Burton diamond and it seems to drag her hand down carrying the mere weight of it. By now, the insurers are beginning to wise up to Larissa, but she has arrived at the peak of Everest in the size of her ever-exchanged ring.

Five years pass.

Now, she is used to being Charlie's wife and he is used to her. Well, sort of!

She insists Charlie buys her only the very latest fashions from her favourite boutique on Kensington High street. She has to shop in London. Only London will suffice.

Her cleaner somehow manages to wear clothes of similar design, bought at the back of Leeds market. The sweat shop making them in China is careful to stitch the right designer labels on the clothes in the packets shipped to Britain. Same dress but one with a suitable label 'a la Kensington', the other 'a la Leeds'.

Larissa can't understand how her cleaner can wear such nice things that look so similar to hers. Perhaps she pays her too much money for the work? She complains of this to Charlie. After all, cleaners should know their place, shouldn't they? And the cleaner has adopted several cats which she dotes on like little children. Ugh! Occasionally, Larissa has to call on her cleaner at her house and the cats hiss and spit at her cowering whimpering pet poodle who she then takes to a psychiatrist for pets. She is told to stop dying her poodle in the colour of her latest fashions.

To accompany the outfits, Larissa spends a fortune on designer shoes. They are killing her feet, but they cost a mint, so she insists they must be good. In years to come, she will develop bunions.

She will order the most expensive meal on the menu whenever they go out and without regard to whoever may be paying. When it arrives, she will only eat a mouthful or two and leave the rest, whilst trying to look sophisticated. After all, it would not do to choose something less expensive and appear to be quite poor. Or to give the impression of being hungry.

On the journey home after, to the five bedroomed - en-suited house where they live, in the village with no church, as it has been turned into a Pub, Larissa remarks on a street walker standing underneath a lamp.

"Just look at her," she says. "What a disgusting person and fancy having to do that – have sex for money."

Charlie looks over at his wife huddled in her fur coat against the cold and wonders in his heart just who in fact is the hooker.

Still, she is doing her bit for charity and can boast about this to her friends. Every day, she answers TV adverts about poverty in third world countries. She is already sending money to over fifty of them. She feels justified in doing so. Later, there is another coup in one of them. She thinks, they seem to have a lot of guns in third world countries and kill lots of people. She wonders where they got the money from. Still, no matter. She has done her bit to help.

By now Larissa definitely needs to see a therapist even more so than five years earlier.

Tonight, they are entertaining ten at home. Everyone will talk of spending when they sit around the dinner table. They talk of little else. They will speak of holidays and yachts and doing up their houses, which are already done-up to death.

Everyone is living in the land of 'Vanity Fair' where everyone is striving for what is not worth having.

Lately, Charlie has been quite canny in his relationship with the Chairman of the Bank. He has taken him to an auction where Charlie bids a vast sum for a painting. He has no intention of buying it and stops his bid just before the bidding stops. He's had a lucky escape – his cunning plan to impress his boss has worked. The chairman notices Charlie's apparent buying power and offers him the job as the Head of their Banks of South East Asia. Charlie is quite smug about this. He thinks Gordon Gekko would have much approved of Charlie's tactics. He doesn't understand the chairman, whom he finds has several favourite cats. He thinks the chairman is an idiot.

The family relocate to a vast penthouse on Victoria Peak in Hong Kong looking out across the bay to Kowloon. The kids go to the English school where they learn lots about how to spend the money earned by Dad, and how to keep up with the Joneses. The children also learn all about the joys of sniffing coke. The school is regarded as one of the very best worldwide. It must be. It costs so much to send them there.

And so, time passes, whilst they spend the oceans of cash that come in the form of bonuses and gifts.

One day, Charlie is in a café when a nun comes in on her way from a pilgrimage to Rome. "You're a long way from home," Charlie remarks, "May I buy you a coffee when I have so much, and you have so little?"

The Nun looks at him with a strange look on her face.

"Are you sure you have that the right way around?" she asks, whilst the café's cat runs itself around her legs and loudly purrs.

Charlie blinks and over the next few days, ponders on her words. However, in the weekly confessional, he never mentions money or his wife, just a few trivialities which he thinks will please the priest. He has soon forgotten the wise words spoken by the Nun.

He is too busy being Gordon Gekko.

In the years up to Charlie leaving work, money is no object. He plans for his retirement, by buying bonds which will give him an abundant yield of super rich investment cash paid to him each month. He takes ever larger mortgages on all his houses in order to re-invest the money in these bonds with massive high returns. His broker, Gerry, is what's called 'old school'. He has an impressive, cultured accent and trappings full of luxury. He tells Charlie the bonds are much too good to miss.

Charlie is convinced. He doesn't bother reading all the small print. He thinks Gerry is a super chap. He never thinks to ask if Gerry likes cats. Instead Charlie buys lots of expensive cars and jewels. He's so busy being clever at spending money. Later, he discovers his most impressive broker is in fact a former second-hand car dealer from the back streets of scruffy Islington. Lots of cats prowl the back streets of his yard and Gerry keeps them fed. He knows all about the value of his cats and they keep away the mice. Gerry is already Gordon Gekko.

So where does it all go wrong for Charlie? It doesn't turn out at all the way he's planned. He loses everything he worked so hard to acquire and becomes materialistically poor. He is already so in spirit and has been so for many years. He's spent it all chasing things of little value.

So, both his cups are empty.

Should he have decided to like cats and thus look after them like the poem said? Now at eighty years of age, he looks back at a life of total emptiness. The trophy wife has been traded in three times for younger models and all the bonds have turned out to be worthless. He cashes in the watches and the jewels and is outraged they only go for hundreds in auctions which are the only place to sell them. The cars depreciate to the tiniest amounts once they have come out of the showrooms and the housing market goes into the most massive of declines.

Charlie must now live on welfare in an old folk's home run by the council that he used to advise about money. He has not fed his cat, stroked it or guarded it well. It's a pity Charlie didn't liked cats.

Beyond Price

By

Sacha Quinn

A couple of weeks ago I lost another ring. I don't know quite when I lost it. I really don't know the last time I saw it. I don't, as a routine, look at my fingers to see if my rings are there. I kind of just expect them to be there. Then there is that moment when you do something that is totally subconscious, where you automatically feel for something out of habit. When you realise with a start that it's gone.

It was the second ring I'd lost that week.

Both these rings are significant to me. Both are in celebration of the birth of my children, traditionally received as an eternity ring.

They are not the only rings I've lost.

Five years ago, I relocated from Singapore to Thailand thinking I had my wedding rings in a zip-lock bag. You don't want to know how much luggage I had, most of it on its way via a shipping company but some things were just too personal, which saw me over packing them into bulging suitcases, for the flight to Phuket. I was especially strapped in terms of hand luggage, so I tipped all my jewellery into a plastic bag. It didn't amount to much in monetary terms, but in sentiment a whole lot more.

When we arrived in Thailand and I sorted stuff out, the only things missing were my wedding and engagement rings. I looked everywhere but no, they weren't to be found.

I generally put a lot of thought into symbolism and the significance of things. I therefore took it to be, that the basis upon which those rings were given and received had maybe changed somewhere along the way and, as part of our marriage and our vows, was perhaps no longer valid.

It troubled me.

My rings were missing. To me it was a sign. I wasn't quite sure what it was a sign of, and I mourned the loss for long enough. They weren't coming back. There was no sign. There was nothing wrong. I moved on.

After eight years living in Singapore and Phuket, with no sign that our Asian adventure was coming to any kind of end, our son, back home in England, finally said,

"Mum, dad, you need to come and sort your stuff out. We're moving and we won't have room to store it anymore."

Oh bugger!

We made a pilgrimage of it. Back we went to the cold country. Time to sort out all that we'd left behind when we'd left for Singapore in a hurry, with just one suit case each.

It was a task and a half seeing the mountain of stuff. Had we really accumulated all that over the years? Daunting it was, but strangely like Christmas, opening boxes of long forgotten things taking us on many a trip down memory lane. Tired out and frozen stupid on that first August evening I went in to warm up with a nice cup of hot chocolate.

Yummy! You don't often drink hot chocolate in the tropics.

Ten minutes later Mick came in and handed me a small box. The same blue colour as his ring box, and I had a big grin as I said, "Oh brilliant you've found your rings," as I knew he'd left them behind when we'd done a flit, just didn't know exactly where. I will never forget the incredulity and shock when I opened it and found they were my rings not his.

The reality dawned.

They had never gone to Singapore.

They had stayed in the home country. I just burst into tears. I wish, really wish I wasn't quite so sentimentally teary.

Sometimes I feel like I'm on an emotional rollercoaster. So hard and unfeeling one minute then in a flash turn all soppy. No wonder people find me difficult to deal with. I feel maybe I'm just a bit too much to bear as I get older and grumpier. Wouldn't surprise me if people didn't start calling me Vicky Meldrew!

In keeping with my self-analysed early morning grumpiness trait, which I'd declared a couple of weeks previously that I would overcome, I just had to spout and grump and grouse today.

Lots of years ago as part of a birthday present, I was given a pair of lovely sapphire earrings set in a delicate filigree of gold that went with the necklace and ring and bracelet I also received. I never wore wear them much because the butterfly clip that goes on the end of an earring post was not very stable and I didn't want to lose them.

When our shipment of personal effects from England finally arrived in Thailand, I was re-acquainted with my 'cabinet jewelry box'. I opened it fully expecting my sapphire earrings to be there as they always were. But they weren't. I looked everywhere. I looked in places I knew they wouldn't, couldn't even be. Then had to accept they were gone. No-where else to look. It didn't stop me looking time and time again in my cabinet, pulling out the drawers one by one wondering if by some chance, some miracle, there was something I'd missed and actually they really were there. But no, they weren't.

Then came one night when I needed to get Thailand retirement visa papers together. In the 'visa paper' drawer all the papers from last year's visa stuff seemed to be somewhat lacking. I opened the next drawer in case some how they had ended up there. We are not always very tidy or methodical or at least it looks that way, though we do try. I picked up a small dark blue velvet box. In it were Mick's wedding and engagement rings. A rush of nostalgia enveloped me. Yeah nice he still has them, here now not in England, but it's sad he doesn't wear them. Not my choice. That's his to have and he prefers the matching ones we wear that were bought for our silver wedding. He says it wouldn't be the same wearing it on the other hand.

It also reminded me that at one point he lost that silver wedding ring that matches mine. When we were in Spain and so short of money, to the extent that we could hardly pay the bills, he once took on a heavy labouring job. It involved taking down some brick gate posts, which we later reused to build a fancy bar on our roof terrace. During that job his ring flew off and, in the dusk, he couldn't find it. He was devastated. We both were.

So, the next day I went with him. Whilst he took down the post at the other end of the sweeping drive, I set to shifting about a ton of bricks and rubble from the day before, convinced I would find it in there somewhere. Just as we were finishing for the day and I had to admit defeat, there being no rubble left to move and no ring, a glint of something in the grass reflecting from the setting sun caught my eye. I went over to see what it was and yes there it was, just lying there not two feet from where I'd been working all day.

We went out to celebrate with that day's earnings. It was the thing to do. Besides we could always earn the money back another day. Sometimes money is not that important, but how and when to spend it certainly is.

Back in the drawer, still looking for my visa papers, I noted too a number of watches that Mick has collected over the years and opened the box where I know the 'half hearts' live, the ones where I have the other matching half. At the very back I noted a gold stick poking out of a glass. I was immediately excited. Our son's wedding was planned for a couple of months later and Mick had just had a new suit made with a new tie to set it all off. I'd remarked at the tailors about the tie pin I'd had custom made for him one Christmas, long ago now. A time when we earned enough for me to be able to commission

304

someone to make a custom piece of jewellery for my husband. It was in the shape of a pair of skis with a tiny diamond at the tips to depict the sparkle of snow. I was so glad to have found it.

Alas, I hadn't. It was one in the shape of a golf club - yes still given by me but not the one I was looking for.

I picked up the glass, wondering what else was there. There seemed to be a key. I wondered what it was for. I remembered the day when Mick gave me a key as a birthday present in Greece. I had to go to the reception to open the safe where there was a package for me, for my birthday. In it was a beautiful sapphire and diamond ring – square saphs no less – which someone told me later were not only the in thing, but quite expensive. There was a lovely necklace in such an intricate and complicated pattern that the maker had said he would do no more as it wasn't financially viable for him to make and he needed to earn a living.

Because of that craftsman's decision, there was no matching bracelet. Instead there was an unusual one known as a graduated Albert, where each link at either end increases in size until reaching the middle, with every link having a hallmark stamp to authenticate the gold it was made from. That too I lost somewhere along the way, was distraught about but later reunited with.

I guess I'm not very good with looking after possessions no matter how much they cost. Maybe, because in my head they are beautiful gifts, given and received as tokens of love regardless of money exchanges. That is the value. Even in the loss of the actual article the giving and receiving can never change. It is still there in the memory box, to re-live and remember whenever I want.

I tipped out that shot glass to see what I thought was the tie pin I sought. What I found was so totally unexpected there were no words, just tears. Tears that my sapphire earrings were not lost. They were here and found.

I could not immediately express the emotions of that as I sat alone in the early hours compelled to write this. As a writer with a vivid imagination for many plots or turns I could make much of it with many scenarios about this discovery. As an emotional masochist I could make many more.

But emotional masochism does not logically resolve why a shot glass that is 'new' contains earrings from a time that precedes it, it just fuels that imagination. Those earrings got in there somehow. But in my heart, I knew if the whereabouts of those earrings had been known, it would not have been kept secret. It would have been shared again with the joy that they had been found and were not lost, just like all the other rings and things which have been lost and found over the years.

That includes the one which started this trip down memory lane.

That ring I thought I'd lost a couple of weeks ago I espied when I went for a shower later that day. It was much the same as when I once also found an emerald that chose at some point to lose itself from its setting, that is now firmly reset and gives me joy every time I look down at my finger and see it.

There, on the floor of the shower room was my ring: not lost but broken and in such a way that unlike the emerald ring it cannot be repaired. Looking at it and remembering the eternal significance it represented in the joy of having our son, I took it to an old small case where I keep broken rings and things that I just cannot bear to part with.

And there in the midst of them I also found the ring I thought I'd lost earlier that same week. The one, which reminded me of the joy of having our daughter too. I have no idea how it got there but refuse to dwell on it.

All these rings and things I will keep in my little case and in my heart. None of them have much monetary worth. But that is not the point because money is completely different from what is valuable. And what is valuable is often beyond price.

True Value Lies Only in Survival

By

C. I. Ripples

Jack arrived in his apartment and closed the door, bolting it from the inside, thankful he was finally home.

He'd waited for hours in the freezing cold until an old timer had found a jackhammer and manually overridden the system, plugging into the electricity still stored in the emergency fossil fuelled generator and forcing everyone's door open. It was only thanks to the Biologic leggings and undershirt he'd had the foresight to put on that morning that he'd escaped hypothermia. The expansion and contraction of the Biologic's natto cells relative to atmospheric moisture, kept him warm in the cold and cool on the way up. It was a further saving grace that they lived on the 7th floor. Imagine having to take the staircase all the way up to the more elevated 22nd!

This was one, the only time, his less privileged position had an advantage.

Status, however, was the least of his worries. He was hungry and thirsty, but unable to open his smart fridge, connected to the delivery tubes that automatically stocked it. He was no longer able to open it or the food cupboards. They opened only when the Tesco smart evaluator in partnership with the NHS software embedded in him, deduced he was validly hungry. When his body was in need of sustenance, they delivered only the food the system decided he required, carefully nutritionally balanced. That system had been introduced when the percentage of overweight people in the country had exceeded 69%. Health costs were out of control and no amount of taxation seemed to reduce the public demand for sugar and fat, despite the monetary penalties. The final straw had been the covid-19 and then 20 virus known as covid-NT, which affected mostly those suffering from excess weight and associated chronic conditions - about half the population at the time.

The ensuing near two-year global lockdown, which applied to not only the sick, but also the healthy required to drive the economy, had resulted in serious food shortages. Farmers were unable to bring in their harvest or effectively work the land. Food processing and distribution came to a halt. This was further compounded by increasing temperatures, droughts and rising sea levels due to the ongoing climate crisis. It had led to a grave threat of global starvation, a threat met by governments by issuing resources to fuel the body only when the body had run out of it.

It was all controlled by a hyper personalised ecosystem, driven by Amazon's artificial intelligence which predicted individual needs, checked affordability and engineered money-saving prompts.

Not that money existed any more. That had been abolished long ago, both the physical form and concept. After all, no one had a need for it in a system where any consumption, be it rent, utilities, food or luxury goods were automatically paid for from the allowance received every month via the Huawei powered system Alipay.

Jack's uncle remembered the days when what was known as ATMs existed, when there were shops where you paid with something called 'cash'. This consisted of either pieces of paper, known as 'notes', or pieces of metal, known as 'coins', issued by institutions known as 'banks'. He'd been to a museum of 'high street banks' on a school trip once, as part of a history of economics lesson. After these had been phased out in 2025, you could only buy things with something called a 'debit' or 'credit' card, which could be contactless or online. Uncle kept such card antiques in his home, carefully protecting their magnetic strips in glass cased boxes, conveying, recounted Jack, their significant resale value.

"Mind you," uncle would tell young Jack, "there was a time when people using paper notes, instead of metal coins to buy a chicken had seemed ridiculous. It also took a long time before people accepted electronic money transfers over wires and computer networks, or contactless transactions."

The cards too had gone out of circulation by the 2030s. Credit in itself became an unheard-of term, replaced with E-Values in contract currencies when the 5G-71 antennas, next to his and every other citizen's buildings were connected to the BTchip injected into the temple, to monitor his every need, like and feeling.

The precursor of this BTchip had been the vidbit, which was basically a rehash of something known as the 'Apple Watch' and Fitbit, introduced when Apple and Google, who bought Fitbit in 2019, realised they could make a killing from a contact tracing app. They convinced governments that this would 'protect people and get society back up and running'. It was so successful that governments around the world realised it could be used for surveillance and monitoring in general as well as behaviour modification. As such it would fit in nicely with the UN's Agenda 21. There was one snag: vidbits were worn on the wrist, which meant citizens could easily evade the mandatory system. That was when some smart ass remembered that as animals were already implanted with RFID chips, why not inject them into humans as part of the covid-NT vaccine!

As a result, the British government ditched vidbits and instead went into cahoots with Biotech, which had a proven record and improved productivity by injecting RFID chips into the hands of now redundant factory workers.

Today, children received their first limited access BTchip at the age of ten, beyond which no one learnt to read or write. After all, such skills were only required in the event of a national cyber security breach. Young brains automatically knew everything deemed age appropriate to know and could communicate via their chips. There was just no need for written script, which was now considered antiquated. With the advent of BTchips, fewer and fewer children were sent to the Gramsci or Gramart schools, where computer coding could be taken as a third language. In fact, Jack hadn't heard of any being sent there since he'd retired from Tendale on his full disability allowance, apart from those children from the ruling elite perhaps. For the remaining masses, secondary Physschool was firstly about physical education required to get a job and then, perhaps even more importantly, about learning how to navigate the BTchip. More recently BTchips also modified behaviour with 'downtime drill' lessons, when they were switched off to ensure that in the event of chip failure, children wouldn't deviate from chip instilled protocol. After all, for this unequal digitalized universal income society to function properly, contented citizens were desired.

The 'Implant BTchip Knowhow and Guidance' curriculum was upgraded remotely every year from the age of twelve after the yearend user assessment exam. Once the final BTchip navigating exam was successfully completed at the age of sixteen, students were given access to the BTchips full capabilities. It was in many ways part of the rites into adulthood, to live a balanced life.

Jack felt the now redundant BTchip and wondered how long it would be before it was reactivated, feeling strangely free, even if helpless as he realised that his Tesco currency contract would also no longer be operating, that it wasn't possible for him to buy, or them to deliver. More than that, how could the government, or Alipay, now attest to his identity and trust rating. And without an active BTchip, how could he prove that he was indeed a citizen of the country with a good financial standing?

Perhaps doing away with everything physical, such as a passport or paper money, had not been such a good idea after all.

Or it had been a good idea, but only for governments and a few large digital corporations, who'd used the covid-NT crisis to increasingly assert digitalized social control. Data was the new form of currency now, which only had a value because the central authorities decided that it had such a value and built the current system around it. Yes, Jack reflected, for the ruling human and RoboSapien elite it had been a great idea, until the unthinkable happened.

He remembered an old childhood joke which they'd found hilarious at the time, not understanding the implications … not then:

> Alphabet: I know everything!
> Huawei: I know everybody!
> Amazon: I have everything!
> BTchip: Without me you are nothing!
> Electricity: Keep talking bitches!

He still found it quite funny. How true it had turned out to be, he chuckled, as he went to the window and observed the many RS officials that stood stock still in the street below, deactivated with the power outage, most of them anyway, their reliance on solar power being reserved for all but the most advanced.

At least he was home. The last time he'd struggled to get into his smart locked apartment had been more than a decade ago when his rent had been a few seconds late. That was before the accident, before he married Felicity and before the government introduced laws which ensured what they called a 'digital living wage' and controlled individual spending so that nobody could live above their means. Based on your financial standing, it was decided which type of housing you could afford, which area, which building, which floor. That was when the government did away with debt or even the possibility of late payments, seconds or not, and made it illegal for citizens to exchange value with each other without government intervention or license. Any contravention meant eighteen months in the Woodhill social economic rehabilitation facility in Milton Keynes.

It had been at that point that his aunt, one of the few remaining trained human nurses who always lived on the fringe of society, on the fringe of E-value margins, had sought asylum on the continent. There the EU charter of fundamental human rights was still in force. This included the right to privacy and data protection, rights which had been gradually eroded in Britain after Brexit, when it finally went ahead in 2021. Of course, RSs played a major role in the EU economy too, but where the UK focused on science, EU RSs were programmed to be more artistic and compassionate, mainly because the EU ruling elite was more accepting of alternative lifestyles. Over the pond it was rumoured they ridiculed what they termed 'RS controlled autocratic Little Britain'.

Anyway, aunt had joined a community in the Eifel, which ensured that certain levels of individualism continued to be respected, where it was still possible to live off the grid as long as you remained self-sufficient. The family had owned a farm there for decades and she took full advantage of the five-year transition period the German government had allowed for proof of sustainability. Whole communities had sprung up in rural areas, relying on horse-power for transport, on wind and solar power for electricity, growing their own food and using its own bartering or old-fashioned coin-based system. From the occasional hand-written letters, he received via the off grid underground, it seemed she was quite happy.

Jack looked towards the Woodoo augmented pine sideboard by the door. He'd made a secret compartment at the back when he was stuck at home on disability leave. It contained the letter aunt had slipped into his pocket a few days before she left the country, mouthing silently, "Do not open this until the time requires it," without any further explanation apart from placing her finger on her lips.

The lights in his apartment flickered and then went out.

The generator must have run out of oil. Fossil fuels having been generally banned way back in 2030, licenses were only being issued for private non-government use in case of emergency and for only very small amounts.

He checked the plastic red round clock on the wall, an antique from the early twenty-first century inherited from his great grandmother. He'd only recently replaced the A4 batteries – they'd cost almost a week's allowance, but he could now see their value. It was only 4 p.m. but it being November, it would soon be dark. He wished he'd taken heed and listened to his aunt rather than his wife, that he'd invested in some candles or a battery powered torch. He wished he'd followed his sister's advice and kept some essentials on the shelves instead of the now unopenable cupboards. All they had was a packet of crackers and some left-over butter in the float. He wished he'd had the presence of mind to fill a few bottles of water, for just such an emergency. The smart taps no longer worked and there was now no way to flush the toilets.

Until the power was back, be it solar or other, all they had to drink was the half full jug on the counter and a few bottles of red Spätburgunder, a present from grandmother when he turned eighteen. Uncle told him at the time that it was not for drinking as 2023 was considered a 'good year' according the 10th edition of the World Wine Atlas, a copy of which uncle had had on his coffee table. Jack had never cared about the monetary value and never attempted to obtain a license for sale. He preferred to keep them for a special occasion, as this one might surely be, although he wasn't at all sure they were still drinkable.

He now saw Felicity round the corner of Worple road. She was looking rather worn out from her walk back from Tendale – it must be at least ten miles and without electric smart buses, it would have taken her considerable time to return. He was about to call out to her, when he realised the windows could no longer open at his thought, remembered that there was a lever for manual override at the top left-hand side.

He had to yank it hard several times before it released and opened the window so abruptly, he almost fell out onto Felicity, who was staring up nonplussed from below. As he veered back and caught the smart-frame and his balance he yelled at her:

"You have to push the door! Don't just stand there. It won't open until you lean against the doorknob."

He unbolted the front door just as she arrived on their landing, slightly out of breath, but otherwise happy enough:

"I passed a fossil fuel powered armoured vehicle on the way here, with loudspeakers informing residents that all systems are down due a coordinated cyber-attack simultaneously on power generation, transmission and distribution."

He'd voiced his concerns about a cyber-attack once and only once to Felicity, who was a product of what she termed 'modern' society. She, who believed in her government, her safety and had placed her complete trust in the RS dominated system, had told him he was being 'quite ridiculous'.

"This isn't South America you know," she'd snapped contemptuously.

He would've loved to tell her, 'I told you so', as she'd obviously conveniently forgotten his warning, but she was in full flow as she slumped onto the ergonomic sofa, which for once didn't change form to surround her shape, rubbing her feet:

"But we're not to worry. They've announced that a food distribution centre will be established first thing tomorrow at the old SJF Church."

It seemed the country was in for a lengthy power outage, but that the government had a well-rehearsed contingency plan. He assumed the army had access to the food warehouses of the likes of Tesco and wondered whether water too would need to be collected. His right shoulder had never been the same since the accident with the hacked roboskin and he certainly didn't fancy a thirty-minute walk back to their place lugging litres and litres of water. He wondered how they would pay for it all. Would they issue paper notes to keep track of the value of consumption, to be deducted from the digital living wage once the systems were back up?

Jack decided it didn't really matter. He knew the true value of life - they had a roof over their heads, wouldn't starve or die of thirst or cold. As he went in search of the old rusty corkscrew to open his Spätburgunder, he reflected that when all was said and done, the only true value of life lay in survival.

Uncle Willy

By

Stephanie Thornton

"Everybody has one."

"What are you muttering about now Geoffrey?" Kathleen was making breakfast toast and she could see her husband was more than a bit annoyed, "what's happened now?"

"My *favourite* relative," he replied sarcastically.

"Oh, you're talking about *that* relative."

"Yes, the doctor's said Uncle Willy has had some sort of turn. I've just been speaking to him."

"Is it serious?"

"Well, only a very bad dose of 'flu'. He's refusing to get help and won't take care of himself. Perhaps you'd better go?"

"Must I, it's such a horrible place. It's like a cross between Alcatraz and some ghastly, fusty, stately home."

"Yes, but just think of all that money. He has to leave it to someone, and it might just as well be us."

"We've already got pots of it."

"Well some more won't go amiss. Why should it go to waste? He's as rich as Croesus."

How this would work out Kathleen couldn't tell. It would certainly be a challenge.

"Why not," she consented, thinking wads of bank notes in her head.

So, Kathleen went to stay at Willy's mansion on the hill.

The disagreeable old man was sitting in a filthy bed, grumbling about everything between hideous coughing bouts. He looked just about to die, yet he still found the breath to complain.

"Why have you come?" he gasped, peering at her with rheumy eyes.

"Come on Uncle Willy. You know you are my favourite and someone has to take care of you."

"Well you can bugger off. All you want is my money and you're not getting any of it."

"Come, come, dear Willy," she said, plumping up the dirty pillows.

Willy loved playing money games. She had heard it all before.

"Well this place is filthy; we'll just have to get you clean. Why won't you get some staff or a nurse."

"Hate the buggers," came the objectionable reply.

Kathleen was a large lady and found it hard to climb the vast staircase. She managed to get him up to change the sheets, finding a new pair, which someone must have darned years ago and a pair of new pillowcases, clean but yellowed with age. She changed his nightshirt which looked like something worn by Scrooge and cleaned and shaved him. And she gave him a little bell she had found in a downstairs drawer. He must have had it since he was a child, as it had pixies painted all around the handle which was made of hideous gold scroll work. She soon wished she had never seen the pixies.

"I'm sure you're feeling better now – at least fresher," she told him, when he could hear her between coughing fits.

Her reward was a little glare, but at least he hadn't moaned about it.

The bell rang day and night whilst she climbed up and down the stairs. She didn't seem to be losing any weight so there was no compensation for her efforts. At least he paid for home delivery, so she didn't have to go out shopping. In fact, to do so would have been of great relief to get out of the place with the constantly ringing bell, the bad odours of unwashed bodies and those cheesy stinking feet which made her gag.

Whilst he was upstairs, she had ample time to look in all the drawers, to see if there was evidence of bank accounts or other treasure hidden there. But she found nothing. Just lots of hoarded clutter.

The gloomy mansion was encased in layers of dirt. Willy said there was nothing wrong with it at all. Not even with his glasses on could he see anything amiss.

The doctor gave a sideways look at Kathleen standing beside the bed advising Willy his home must be improved otherwise he would not get well. He should also stop drinking from his ancient mug with its heavy cracks and chips as he may get food poisoning from it.

Willy decided he was much too young to die. He was only ninety-seven so he would compromise – a little. He would pay for cleaners to come in and throw away his ancient mug.

A vast team of Polish workers arrived and tackled the layers of dirt. This included Kathleen's bedroom where she had resorted to sleeping on top of new sheets brought from home. Willy paid for the cleaners and shouted at them cursing his inability to understand their Polish accents. He counted out the money from a vast array of coins within a large box underneath the bed. As Kathleen dragged out the heavy box for him, a mouse ran out and underneath her skirts.

She stifled a scream. "You must get a cat, I think."

"Rubbish. Filthy beasts."

"It would be good company for you too."

"I hate all domestic beasts. Climbing on the furniture and shedding fur. I had a puppy when I was a lad, but it bit me......... then it died," he added.

She didn't ask him how, but gave a little grimace wondering if Willy's blood had poisoned it. She was thinking of the money and would put up with these annoyances. At night, she dreamed of bank balances and trips on super yachts in France.

It seemed providence stepped in and leant a hand, when a ginger tom appeared on the back doorstep trying to get the top off the milk bottle standing there. They had just started doing milk rounds once again in an attempt to reduce the use of plastic. The cat shot off round her startled legs and fled up the massive staircase before she could get hold of it.

Panting up the stairs, she found the cat had got into Willy's room.

He was red with rage.

"Get that filthy animal out of here," he yelled.

The tom had other thoughts and hid under the massive bed. All attempts to catch it failed.

A little later, Kathleen heard the frantic ringing of his pixie bell.

There was a smug smile on Willy's face. The tom had caught the mouse and eaten it. There was a savage primeval look on Willy's face. He seemed to have had some sort of sadistic pleasure seeing this.

"The cat can stay, it's more useful than a bank manager and at least it isn't after my money," he announced.

Kathleen didn't know who she loathed more. Willy or the cat. He had christened it Mr. Tibbs from a book he said he'd read. She found the dreaded Mr. Tibbs was now sharing the bed with Willy where it purred happily in the crook of his arm. But the animal only hissed at her if she approached the bed.

"See, he is looking after me," he said with glee.

He wasn't looking after Willy when he infected Willy and the bed with fleas. It was a fumigation job and Willy moaned about the bites.

Still at least Willy continued to improve. He had decided it was not yet time to meet his maker.

Kathleen was totally worn out serving meals on trays to the endless tinkling bell.

"I know you want my money," Willy said one day, "perhaps I should leave you some of it." He had a sly look on his face.

"I'm OK," she replied. "You know we only want to care for you, dear Uncle Willy, and we have plenty of money ourselves. Rest easy and just get better."

Better soon, she hoped as she took the heavy tray downstairs.

Willy began to get up and before long, he could walk downstairs. He took the pixie bell with him which he rang from the far rooms on the ground floor of the mansion. She felt she heard the dreaded bell in her sleep. She was not sure which she hated most, the bell or Mr. Tibbs following his master and winding himself around his legs. She had tried to stroke the wretched animal and the result was a long scratch all along her arm. Then she had tried to shut him out by closing all the doors and windows, but Willy went berserk when his furry friend went missing and only calmed when the postman let the cat back in during a delivery at the door.

Willy was overjoyed to see Mr. Tibbs again. He smiled at Kathleen – it was so unusual she felt she had been struck by lightning.

"I have decided to see my lawyers," he declared. "I am worried about my money so I have decided I must make things right." He smiled at her again.

It was somewhat of a surprise when five gentlemen turned up to see Willy in the study. Once they left, he announced everything was very satisfactory, but said it was time for her to leave.

"You've been so kind to me, I'm going to take you to my favourite place for lunch in a week or so to say thank you. You can wear your best dress," he declared.

What a relief to get home. Away from Willy, away from Mr. Tibbs and away from the wretched bell.

Two weeks later, Willy made the rare phone call. He didn't like spending money on the phone – it had such little value and besides the phone bill lost him interest on his savings.

"Lunch at 12 noon next week and I'll come to get you in the car, dear Kathleen."

Kathleen dressed her best. A gorgeous hat with a saucy veil and her lovely mink coat in sapphire grey and lots of diamond jewellery. She was expecting him to arrive in the Rolls, the best of the five cars parked in the massive garage, but he turned up in the staff car which was a very ancient Austin Somerset with rusty paintwork and tyres that were almost bald. They headed off to town. She was anticipating a glorious meal and almost salivating at the thought of it which would make up for sitting in the dreadful car.

"Here we are," announced Willy, as he pulled into the market car park.

She peered out from the dirty windows of the car. "Where?"

"It's over there," he said, pointing to the van parked at the end. "You'll love it, the best pie and pea place in the world. And you can have an extra portion if you like. After all, you've been so good to me!"

Two weeks later the pie and peas seemed to have been the end of Willy. He had had a dose of food poisoning and this time she did not go to make him well. At last a letter arrived from his solicitors asking her to come to their offices the next day or so.

"There you are," said Geoffrey. "I knew he would look after you in the end."

A long, delightful conversation followed as to how they'd spend the money whilst they drank a bottle of the best champagne.

The solicitor said she was now a beneficiary of Willy's will. He steepled his hands and looked at her in all seriousness.

"Just before you left, he had had a meeting with myself and my colleague and three doctors who declared he was quite sane at the time he changed his will. Originally, he had left everything to you. You are still mentioned in the new will now, as he told me how much you had cared for him and how he thought so much about you. He has left you this," he said, pushing a small box towards her.

She opened it with trembling fingers.

Within it was the bell - the horrible pixie handled bell from hell.

"What has he done with all his money?" she was outraged.

"Oh, that's all going to the league of cats. It's just a little over eleven million pounds. But he also left you something else as well."

"What?" Kathleen asked, almost too shocked to speak.

"His beloved cat, Mr. Tibbs. He's waiting for you in a basket in my secretary's room next door. And he's left you the bonus of some cat food too. What a thoughtful man!"

Author Biographies

Sacha Quinn

Now in my 60th year I've finally given up the day job to concentrate on full time writing – for the 3rd time! Yes, I kept being given opportunities to help deliver healthcare systems in around the world which I just could not refuse. I looked on it as research time and gain knowledge for my writings. Living in Singapore, India, Bangkok and now Phuket have furnished me with a myriad of colourful images, depicting lifestyles and culture so different from Western world, whilst people everywhere are just people and not so very different. Without these experiences throughout life my tapestry would be quite threadbare!

I grew up in West Yorkshire in the north of England, an only child with a Polish father and English mother. I was and still am an avid reader. Early success in a writing competition at nine and writing my first 'book' at ten spurred me on to publish my first book in 2015. After publishing my father's biography recounting his experiences under the Nazi regime in WWII, I'm now writing the spicy books I've always dreamed of in erotic romantic genre.

Contact Sacha at Sacha.Quinn@hotmail.com
Sacha has five books published on Amazon and can be found by following the links below:

Taste of Spice
http://www.amazon.co.uk/dp/B01LVVMXKB

Vanilla Spice
http://www.amazon.co.uk/dp/B01HQD1JYE

Red Spice
http://www.amazon.co.uk/dp/B01N6UJCK4
Roman's War – A Childhood Lost (biography of Sacha's
Polish father aged just 13 at the start of WWII)
http://www.amazon.co.uk/dp/B00U4ILBCY

That Big Red Book (short stories)
http://www.amazon.co.uk/dp/B00QCDHCXM

Stephanie Thornton

Now in her early seventies, Stephanie looks back on a
massive life which has helped her inspiration for the
stories. Her father showed her how to run a business from
when she was a teenager. She worked in the German steel
industry then as a dentist for children with special needs.
A business career then followed, building four companies
from scratch including one in France. She is now a
residential landlord. Hobbies include ecclesiastical
embroidery and fine art as well as writing. She lives in
four countries, the United Kingdom, Europe, Thailand
and Australia and writes for several hours each
day. Subjects include humorous looks at life and several
fantasy adventures.

Stephanie can be contacted at sth1000@hotmail.com

C.I. Ripples

Having started her writing career as a blogger and editor, C.I. Ripples loves to confront her readers with currently trending and often controversial issues. A global citizen, she has lived all over the world and has not only absorbed many cultural experiences, but also studied their languages, history and customs. After graduating from Oxford University, where she read Modern History, she delved deeper into the subjects of psychology, business, law and even the sciences. Einstein is right: the more she learns, the less she knows. As such, her thirst for the unattainable - understanding - is never ending.

C.I. Ripples blog can be found at ripplesincontext.com.

Renata Kelly

After a life of globe-trotting, Renata and her husband now live in Phuket and Greece. Though a prolific writer during her undergraduate studies in the U.S., Renata did not pursue creative writing whilst continuing with graduate studies (at Oxford University and later at the University of Essex where she earned a Ph.D. in Theoretical Linguistics). Following her husband, whose career took the family to a total of 10 countries on four continents, Renata was able to teach at various Universities in the U.S.A., Hong Kong, Singapore and England. Now retired, she has once again found the fulfillment and fun of "taking up the pen" (or more correctly, typing away on her computer.

Marion McNally

Having spent most of my working life in International Schools in Asia and Europe - as a classroom teacher, Literacy Co-ordinator, ESL Co-ordinator - as well as, finally, a Vice Principal, I decided to leave full time education for good in 2007. With a Master's Degree in Primary Education under my belt the time was ripe for me do what I had been yearning to do for years – set up my own business. Since starting my Masters in 1995 I had been developing writing workshop materials for my students - I loved seeing young people becoming enthusiastic, confident - and in many cases, prolific writers and knew that I wanted to develop my courses further in order take my workshops to the next level.

Leaving full time education gave me the opportunity to focus much more deeply on how children develop as writers and in 2102 I had the great fortune to attend the world - renowned Teachers College in Columbia University, New York where I was able to hear my guru, Lucy Calkins, speak. The Reading and Writing Project at Columbia is renowned for a very good reason – the project consistently produces materials that are at the cutting edge of what's possible in the world of teaching reading and writing. Returning from two weeks immersed in the pedagogy of my 'gurus' I was inspired to create the best courses possible for my students.

My business, Primary Matters, went from strength to strength and eventually I had nine teachers working with me teaching after school classes throughout Hong Kong. During this period, I too developed an interest in becoming a writer – I regularly wrote for the students producing 'model' pieces of writing - simply written I hasten to add and only just at the level above the best writers we taught! However, I did find as I wrote these pieces that my creative juices began to flow and I would become absorbed in the process of writing.

Fast - forward ten years and I am now living in Phuket where I discovered the Spilt Ink writers' group. With encouragement from all involved I am fining my true writer's voice and looking forward to learning and growing as a writer of short stories.

FYI after being dormant for a few years Primary Matters is back and we are teaching online lessons to students aged 9-11.

For more information contact me at
marion.mcnally@gmail.com

Follow us on www.facebook.com/PrimaryMattersHK

Look out for our WordPress website which is coming soon:
primary-matters@wordpress.com

Authors' Notes, Dedications and Acknowledgements

All the stories in this anthology are inspired by the various categories that the title 'Layers of Life' conjured up. Each of the authors wrote the stories on the categories which spoke to them. Some are based on true stories, others are wholly within a vivid and imaginative fictional world, and some may be a mixture of the two, just like life itself often is.

Where there are words, abbreviations or acronyms which may not be understood, there are annotations in brackets with a number (1 like this) which is then explained at the end of the story.

A book like this cannot be produced and published without those who contribute, not just from the authors writing the stories but from those who also give up their valuable time to edit and proof read, design book covers, collate and standardize the manuscripts and of course publish the book itself in accordance with the distributor's requirements.

Thanks therefore go to everyone who has been involved in this book.

It is dedicated to everyone and everything in a world where the Layers of Life is peopled by those who live, have lived or are yet to live in it.

This is the first book in the 'Looking at Life' series.

Printed in Great Britain
by Amazon